BECK BROWNING

Vial Darkness

The Monstrous Cost of Eternal Life

To my Dad,
For your constant encouragement to pursue my creative efforts,
for being the first to read this book, and for teaching me to always
make the best of any situation. Thank you.

"Love is always harder.
Love means weathering blows for another's sake and not counting them.
Love is loss of self, loss of other, and
faith in the death of loss."

— CHRISTOPHER BUEHLMAN

Contents

Preface

Global Regenerative Medicine Summit – Notre Dame of Jerusalem Center

"The Role of XN-34 in Cellular Signaling Pathways: Implications for Regenerative Medicine"

Dr. James Armstrong

Thank you. Okay—thank you all for being here. It is an honor to address a room full of the brightest minds in history, a portion of whom intend to put their minds to work solving the riddles of regenerative medicine.

XN-34, a protein that emerged from our work in partnership with the North Carolina Biotechnology Center, under the stewardship of Doctor Harold Faust, represents a fundamental shift in our approach to cellular regeneration.

In 2012, our research began with a simple question:

Could we accelerate tissue repair by enhancing cellular signaling within the wound microenvironment?

At the time, our hypothesis assumed that increasing growth factor production in damaged cells would be the key to stimulating faster repair.

The basic idea was: if we could get cells to overproduce

fibroblast growth factor and vascular endothelial growth factor, they would, in theory, heal faster by enhancing angiogenesis and collagen deposition. That turned out to be true only in theory.

For years, we pursued this model; however, the results were inconsistent at best and, in some cases, entirely counterproductive. We had hoped to amplify the natural healing response, but in reality, we were triggering excessive fibrosis, uncontrolled cell division, and, in some cases, pre-cancerous tissue formations.

The breakthrough came in 2018, when we shifted our focus to single-cell analysis. Partnering with Xytech Biosciences and their miraculous next-gen flow cytometer, the FC-9600—with high-throughput proteomics, spectral detection, and high-resolution single-cell sorting—we were able to analyze post-degenerative fibroblast populations at an unprecedented level of detail.

What we found overturned our previous assumptions: instead of growth factors driving regeneration, certain cell populations were responding to an unknown intracellular signal—one that hadn't been accounted for in our original model. The unknown signal wasn't a cytokine or a traditional regenerative factor—it was a small regulatory protein—you guessed it: XN-34.

Unlike FGF and VEGF stimulation, which led to dysregulated repair and unexpected growths, XN-34 acted as a central coordinator, enhancing cellular resilience, extracellular matrix remodeling, and apoptosis suppression in a controlled manner.

XN-34's most remarkable property is its ability to coordinate the repair process at the cellular level—not simply by accelerating wound healing, but by guiding damaged cells back to a functional state, restoring them to the condition of their healthiest counterparts.

Through controlled proteomic and transcriptomic profiling, we have demonstrated that XN-34 can reprogram senescent or degenerating cells, repairing structural and functional integrity to a previously impossible degree in post-mitotic tissues. This has profound implications for regenerative medicine, shifting the paradigm from passive intervention to active cellular reprogramming.

But let me be clear—this is not a fountain of youth.

What XN-34 does not do is reset a cell to its pre-degenerative state. While we have observed functional restoration, we have yet to identify a mechanism that allows for a complete reversal of epigenetic aging markers or restores a cell to its earliest, most optimal state.

This tells us one thing: we are missing a critical piece of the puzzle.

The ability to halt degenerative decline and prevent cellular failure—that remains elusive. XN-34 has taken us closer than ever, but the full blueprint of cellular resilience is still out of reach.

For now.

We stand on the edge of one of the most significant discoveries in regenerative biology, with a protein that defies conventional understanding of cellular repair. The implications extend beyond wound healing and disease mitigation. If we can uncover what XN-34 is activating—what latent instructions in the genome that dictate cellular survival—we may be looking at the foundation of a new class of biological intervention, one that doesn't simply slow the inevitable, but fundamentally redefines the limits of human longevity and resilience.

That is what lies ahead.

Thank you.

I

Part One

1

The Marketplace

Jerusalem, Present Day

The marketplace was alive with movement, sounds, and smells—a vibrant chaos that pressed in from every direction. Narrow streets wound between stalls overflowing with wares: baskets of vibrant spices, colorful fabrics fluttering in the breeze, and racks of intricate trinkets that glittered in the late afternoon sun. The air was thick with roasting meat, fresh herbs, and something sweet I couldn't quite place.

With a few hours to kill before my flight, I had already made my way through most of it, weaving between the surging crowd and dodging a particularly aggressive woman wielding a broom who seemed determined to keep the walkway clear. I was on the hunt for "treasures" to bring home to my family.

For Ethan, I had stopped at a stall that looked more like an experiment gone awry than a marketplace stand. Jars of brightly colored liquids were stacked three high, their labels bearing a mix of indecipherable symbols and faded script. The vendor, built like a Greek statue, stood behind the counter with his arms crossed, looking as though he could bench-press the entire stall.

Since he left for NYU last fall, Ethan tells me he's been trying his best to put on muscle. I think it has more to do with getting noticed by the ladies in his dorm than anything else. Not that there's anything wrong with that. I'm just glad he's not spending his college days holed up in his dorm either studying or playing *World of Warcraft*, like I did.

"Strength and honor!" the man boomed, thumping his chest, sending the jars quivering. "You look like a man of great intellect. A thinker, no? But even the sharpest minds need strong bodies."

I forgave the fact that we were standing in the streets of the Old City Bazaar in Jerusalem, not anywhere near the Roman Colosseum—*Gladiator* quotes are always a way to a forty-something American tourist's heart—and decided to entertain him with a conversation.

"A strong body, huh?" I asked, raising an eyebrow. "Because I've made it through three days of lectures and five panels purely on caffeine and spite. My sharp mind seems to be working just fine."

The vendor let out a laugh so hearty it startled a nearby customer. "Caffeine is the fuel of the weak! What you need," he said, pulling a jar from the precarious tower, "is this. It's an elderberry and turmeric tonic. The secret of strength, endurance, and vitality!"

I tilted my head, examining the jar with the skepticism of a man who had spent years questioning data sets. "And this miracle brew… has it been peer-reviewed?"

"Peer-reviewed?" The vendor tilted his head, confused for

a moment, before recovering with a grin. "No need! My own strength is all the proof you require."

He extended his arm, placing the jar inches from my face while he flexed his other bicep for a nice touch of flair, the muscles straining against his tunic.

"Well," I said, raising my right eyebrow, "correlation doesn't equal causation. But I can't say I'm not impressed."

I wasn't sure if he caught my sarcasm.

The vendor grinned wider, clearly enjoying the banter. "You are a scientist, yes? Then you will appreciate this: elderberries for immune strength, turmeric for anti-inflammation, with a touch of honey for sweetness and energy. This is no experiment—it is a formula perfected by my family through generations!"

"Generations?" I echoed, leaning on the counter. "Interesting, considering elderberries and turmeric don't exactly grow in the same regions. Unless your ancestors had access to some ancient global trade routes."

He barked a laugh and set the jar on the counter with a flourish. "Your mind is clearly making up for your lack of muscles. Perhaps this would make a good gift for a growing boy. This tonic will make your son strong as a lion, sharp as an eagle, swift as the wind!"

"I do, in fact, have a son. And… he is trying to bulk up for the ladies." While I hated to admit it, his enthusiasm was winning me over.

"Then this is perfect!" the vendor declared, unfazed. "It will transform him, I promise you."

"Transform?" I repeated, holding up the jar to inspect the murky golden liquid inside. "Because right now, it looks like a salad dressing recipe gone wrong."

"Ah, but tasting is believing!" he countered, producing a tiny wooden cup and pouring a sample into a paper cup with a dramatic flourish.

I held up my hand. "No sample for me, thank you. My curiosity doesn't extend to ingesting unverified concoctions, but I've enjoyed our conversation." And to be honest, I was ready to end it. "I'll take the smallest one you have."

He roared with laughter, slapping the counter so hard the jars rattled dangerously. "The smallest, he says! You are cautious, like all great minds! But wise to trust me. This tonic will be perfect for your son. I'll give you a special price."

"How kind," I said dryly, handing over a few bills. "Fine. One jar of transformation soup."

He grinned as he passed the jar into my hands, slapping my shoulder with enough force to make me stumble. "Strength and honor!" he bellowed, his enthusiasm drawing stares from passersby.

"Right," I muttered, tucking the jar into my bag. "Now all I need is a tonic for patience."

"Ah," he said, winking. "For that, you must look within."

"Figures," I said under my breath, stepping back into the chaos of the marketplace.

A few stalls down, I stopped at a jeweler's table draped in dark velvet, the trinkets glinting against the cloth like tiny stars. The merchant, a wiry woman with sharp eyes that seemed to miss nothing, leaned forward as though she were sizing me up. "Something for a wife, perhaps? Or a sweetheart?" she asked, her voice smooth as silk and laced with practiced charm.

"Wife," I said, my gaze falling on a delicate necklace displayed near the center. An emerald stone nestled in an ornate gold setting, its soft green glow cutting through the noise and clutter of the market. It looked like something Sara would wear to a dinner party, understated yet striking—exactly her style. "How much for this one?"

"Ah, an excellent choice," the merchant said, her face lighting up with the enthusiasm of a woman who smelled a sale. She picked up the necklace with deliberate care, holding it out as though it were a relic from a lost kingdom. "This emerald is flawless, cut to perfection, and the gold—most definitely real."

"'Most definitely,' huh?" I asked, crossing my arms. "That's a glowing endorsement if I've ever heard one."

The merchant's lips quirked into a sly smile. "I assure you, sir, you won't find finer craftsmanship anywhere in the market. A gift worthy of love as enduring as an emerald's brilliance." She leaned in slightly, as though revealing a secret. "And for true love, a special price—"

I held up my hands, stopping her pitch in its tracks. "Alright, alright. What's true love going to cost me today?"

The merchant chuckled, a sound as smooth as her sales pitch. "This piece is priced modestly for a man of distinction like yourself—only fifty American dollars."

I sighed, pulling out my wallet. "All right, fine. You win. But if this 'most definitely real gold' turns my wife's neck green, I'm coming back for a refund."

"Ah, but you won't need to, sir," she said, her grin widening. "Your wife will look radiant, I guarantee it. This is a piece made to last—just like true love."

"Right, true love," I muttered, handing over a fifty and accepting the necklace, now tucked into a small velvet pouch.

The woman gave a theatrical bow as she pocketed the cash

with the grace of a magician, her sharp eyes gleaming with triumph. "A wise purchase, sir. May your travels be safe, and your love eternal."

* * *

After being away most of the past two years, I knew a necklace wouldn't make up for my absence. A gold necklace and emerald couldn't rewind missed dinners, late-night conversations, or Sara's quiet sighs when I packed another suitcase.

The calls started after my keynote speech at the "International Symposium on Cellular Innovations" (ISCI) in Boston. Something in my talk, titled *"The Role of XN-34 in Cellular Signaling Pathways: Implications for Regenerative Medicine,"* got me six-figure offers to speak worldwide. When she read my notes, Sara never got past the title—I don't blame her.

The work that led to XN-34 consumed years of my life. My team had been studying protein interactions within cellular pathways, particularly those involved in tissue repair and regeneration. I hypothesized that activating the right combination of proteins within a damaged cell would enable it to transmit a code to other damaged cells once it identified a blueprint for repairing itself, significantly accelerating the rate at which all affected cells could be restored.

After twenty months of hitting dead ends, with funding beginning to run dry, we identified XN-34. Well, a research assistant named Neil did—accidentally. This protein, when activated, acted as a sort of molecular switchboard, sending out repair signals to other cells—just as I had hypothesized.

The results were staggering. XN-34 (or, as Neil jokingly

called it, *Transformative Neil Thirty-Four*) sped up cellular repair by 250–300%. In early trials on mice, we observed reduced scar tissue formation and even partial reversal of spinal cord injuries.

The real game-changer—and the reason pharmaceutical companies hound me—is that we discovered the protein could be synthesized in a lab, meaning production wouldn't be limited by stem cell harvesting. For the first time in history, we have the opportunity to make affordable regenerative therapies accessible to the masses.

The discovery appeared on the front page of *The New England Journal of Medicine*. They called it "revolutionary." And though my headshot was flattering, Neil's name was unfortunately left out of the article.

We obtained a provisional patent almost immediately, and while we wait for the official patent, the North Carolina Biotechnology Center, my research sponsor, gave me the go-ahead to take on speaking engagements. Everyone wanted me on their stage. The invites came fast and furious: symposiums, research conferences, investor events—you name it. They all wanted to hear about the protein that could potentially rewrite the rules of healing.

At first, the invitations felt like validation for years of work hunched over a microscope, praying that my latest grant application would be approved so that my team could still be paid. I became an "in-demand" name on programs in cities I'd once only read about: Geneva, Vienna, Stockholm, Sydney, Tokyo, Singapore—it was a whirlwind. I thought I'd just do a few, but each one led to another offer, and the money was… hard to turn down.

This stop in Jerusalem was meant to be the last for a while. I was the keynote speaker at the Global Regenerative Medicine Summit, held at the Notre Dame of Jerusalem Center—just north of the Jaffa Gate. The symbolism wasn't lost on me—or anyone, judging by how the event organizers kept mentioning it. Jerusalem, a city layered with centuries of healing and conflict, renewal and ruin, felt like the perfect backdrop for a conference centered on repairing what was broken.

The summit had drawn biotech innovators from across the globe, all eager to learn from their peers and to brag about their latest accomplishments. Standing in front of the mega-sized wall of LED displays—with my face ten times larger than reality—and looking out over hundreds of the world's brightest minds, the gravity of the history of this place rested heavy on my shoulders. Yet while I delivered my well-polished and practiced TED-talk-style speech, I longed for home.

Somewhere between the business-class flights and the five-star hotels, the balance shifted. I was no longer educating and inspiring those seeking new discoveries—I was drowning in minutiae. Amongst the regimented conference schedule, boorish investor dinners, and small talk with attendees, Sara and Ethan remained my anchor.

Each time I'd land back at RDU, I could feel the energy radiating from our home, even in the smallest moments. Without fail, Sara would greet me at the door with a welcoming smile, and Ethan would be close behind with a goofy grin and a goofier story. Our time together over the past few years has been fleeting, but we've made the most of it. I've made the mundane aspects of home my sanctuary. The late-night family debates, spontaneous games of chess with Ethan, and holding Sara's hand while we binge-watch the new season of whatever—those moments have given me purpose and reminded me what I'm working for.

I've missed some big moments too, like driving Ethan to college and moving him into his dorm for the first time. He never doubted that I was proud of him, and Sara—she never stopped asking how soon I'd be home, no matter how unpredictable the answer.

* * *

I nodded at the jeweler, slipping the pouch into my bag alongside the tonic. The constant noise and shouting of the market were starting to wear on me, the relentless energy draining what little patience I had left after three days of lectures and networking.

Yet, as I wandered through the final stretch of stalls in the Old Bazaar, something caught my eye. Not something, really. Someone. An old man stood by his stall, his hands clasped in front of him, resting on his heavy-looking, elegantly embroidered tunic. His gaze locked on me as I passed by, but the rest of his body didn't move. At all. Like an old, leathery Mona Lisa.

I slowed as I passed, pretending to glance at his assortment of wares to be polite—a collection of strange, dusty relics that belonged in a museum or an attic, not in the middle of a busy street market. Old coins, amulets, tarnished jewelry, and bottles. Glass bottles with intricate etchings that made them seem like they had once held something important, but nothing that would say *I love you. I'm sorry I've been away from you* more than the necklace.

About five paces beyond his canopy-covered stall, I peeked

over my shoulder to make sure he didn't have plans to pick my pocket. Though I was pretty sure my slacks were tight enough to keep my wallet securely in my back pocket—travel works miracles at maintaining this dad bod. He still hadn't moved, and his eyes were on mine before mine met his.

"You okay, friend?" I shouted, loud enough to be heard over the cacophony of the market. "Hell-ooo?" He still didn't move. I started to think he was waiting for something—or someone—and that maybe I was a target. I looked over both shoulders quickly to be sure there wasn't a hit squad sneaking up on me. With the coast clear, I looked back at the old man to see the corners of his lips raise into a genuinely friendly smile.

Didn't see that coming.

"Masaa' al-khayr! Good afternoon, friend. Searching for a treasure for the wife, perhaps?" he said, holding up a silver amulet with a faded inscription. "It is ancient. Said to bring protection to whoever wears it."

I took a deep breath to slow my heart rate. Hassan, as I inferred from the crooked "Hassan's Things" sign hanging above him in English, wasn't a threat. His teeth were yellowed with age, but his smile showed me his kind soul.

I stepped a few feet in his direction and smiled politely. "Thanks, but I've already picked up a few things."

His grin didn't falter, and he leaned in, lowering his voice. "For the young one at home, then? I have coins that have traveled across centuries. Perfect for a boy."

I glanced at the coins—small, darkened pieces that could've come from any number of places. Considering Ethan had lost interest in coin collecting long ago, I shook my head, starting to back away. "Yeah, I think I'm done looking for anything today."

Hassan's eyes flickered and narrowed ever so slightly. For a second, I thought he was going to let me leave. But instead, his smile widened like the Cheshire Cat, as though he'd been waiting for this moment for a long time.

"Perhaps," he said slowly, "something is looking for you." His hand disappeared behind the counter, and when it returned, it cradled something small, wrapped in a delicate cloth. He unfolded it carefully, revealing a vial no larger than the palm of his hand.

It was beautiful, in a strange way. Old, definitely. The glass had fine etchings that glinted in the sunlight, with symbols I couldn't quite decipher. It seemed to be filled with a deep red fluid—almost black.

"This," he said, his voice dropping low, "is unlike anything else in this market. It has passed through many hands, over many generations, each one bound by its power."

I raised an eyebrow, unimpressed. "A magical vial?" I said sarcastically.

He met my gaze, holding it for a long, unblinking moment before speaking again.

"The contents of this vial," he said, his voice barely above a whisper, "grant eternal life."

I blinked, the words hitting me like a cold draft. I stared at the vial, then back at him, waiting for the punchline.

"Eternal life?" I echoed, my voice flat, disbelieving.

"That's correct." He didn't smile this time. The seriousness he wore on his face made my skin crawl.

I opened my mouth to respond—probably with a dismissive quip to break the tension, like *when is the expiration date on that stuff?*—but nothing came out. Instead, I found myself standing frozen, staring at the vial with a nagging curiosity creeping in. Eternal life? I had been to church enough times and conducted enough clinical studies to know drinking unidentified contents from a glass vial wouldn't do the trick. That I was sure of. And yet, I couldn't will my legs to turn and leave.

Hassan must have sensed me desperately brewing up a good response. He broke the stalemate by gesturing toward a nearby bench and sending a kind smile in my direction. "Sit with me, and I'll tell you how I came to hold the key to life and death. Won't you, Mister—?" his words cut as a question.

"James." I helped him out, but wasn't sure I wanted to listen to nonsense from an oddball today. And yet, I felt an inexplicable pull to stay.

I glanced at my watch, then at the marketplace around me. The thought of sitting down in the middle of all this felt ridiculous. I had a flight to catch. A flight that I definitely didn't want to miss. But somehow, the urgency I'd felt minutes earlier evaporated. The sounds of the market seemed distant, muffled, as if the world around me was holding its breath.

My face scrunched with hesitation. "Just a quick story?" I muttered to myself. Surely, it would make a good story for Ethan and Sara.

Hassan gestured once again to the bench, a bit more insistently this time, as though he was losing his patience with me.

With a nod of my head and a sigh of resignation, I gave in.

As I entered his cluttered stall, I couldn't help but bump a table holding glass bottles, knocking one to the ground, shattering it. Hassan didn't seem to notice or care, while he continued to pull down the canvas around his shop. With my eyes adjusting to the fresh darkness, I hardly noticed him motioning for me to sit next to him. The bench creaked under my weight, and as I settled in, Hassan leaned closer, holding the vial with both hands as if it were more precious than anything else in the world. I began to feel a bit uneasy, unsure if the nausea I now felt was caused by his breath or the heat, with the breeze now blocked by the thick canvas.

"Let me tell you where it all began," he whispered.

As he began, the drone of the market faded. The darkened stall became illuminated by candles behind Hassan that I hadn't previously noticed—neat trick.

"This story begins not with kings or warriors, but with a boy," Hassan said, his voice still soft but commanding. "A boy who sought to save that which was dearest to him, to save the only thing he still cared about. In the hills of ancient Judea, not too far from here, long before the vial was passed into my hands, long before it changed the course of so many lives…"

He paused, looking up from his hands directly into my eyes. Caught in his stare, my skepticism waned. His words began to paint an ancient world in my mind.

"…we find a village, ravaged by sickness, where hope was more scarce than a cool breeze. And in that village, there lived a boy named Asher, whose story begins at the end of so many other lives."

2

Ar-Rawda

Jordan, 33 C.E.

The air inside the small Judean home was thick with the scent of boiling herbs, but it did little to mask the oppressive stench of sickness. A single narrow window let in slivers of the fading evening light, casting long shadows across the earthen walls. The space was modest, its walls made of sun-baked mudbrick, and the thatched roof above did little to keep out the chill of the encroaching night. The dried herbs and onions dangling from the low beams offered a fleeting hint of warmth, but the odor of illness clung to everything.

The room was sparsely furnished—a simple wooden table with uneven legs stood in one corner, its surface worn smooth from years of use. A few clay pots lined a shelf on the far wall, alongside a solitary oil lamp casting the space in dim, flickering light. In the center of the room, a hearth smoldered, the embers struggling to keep the pot of boiling herbs alive. It wasn't much, but it was home—a place Asher had shared with his family for as long as he could remember.

He knelt beside his younger sister, Miriam, her small frame trembling beneath the sweat-soaked blanket that covered her. Her skin, once flushed with youthful energy, was pale and clammy to the touch. Tzavár Fever had taken hold of her, the same illness that had already claimed so many lives in the village. The weak sound of her labored breathing filled the room, a cruel metronome marking the passing of precious time.

The fever moved quickly, spreading through the village like a rising tide of death. The symptoms began innocently enough, slight tremors in the hands, a light cough, fatigue, but soon worsened, leaving its victims pale and weak, their bodies shaking uncontrollably as the fever burned them from the inside. Two weeks. That was all they had once the fever set in. Just two weeks until a rash appeared on the chest, creeping upward to engulf the throat and face, signaling the end. Miriam's hands had begun twitching just three days ago, but already she was so frail, her breathing shallow and strained.

The rough wool blanket seemed to do little to keep her warm, and every time she began shaking, Asher feared her body might just break apart. Their family's entire existence had dwindled to mere echoes. The table in the corner was where their father had repaired tools after long days in the olive groves. The hearth had been where their mother simmered stews, singing softly to herself as the enticing fragrance filled the air. Even the threadbare mat beneath him carried the ghost of better days, when he and Miriam had played on it, rolling clay marbles and laughing until their sides hurt.

But now, laughter felt like a distant memory. The home that had once been Asher's sanctuary now felt like a tomb. The silence of the evening was broken only by the pop of burning olive wood or the cries of jackals beyond the edge of the village known as Ar-Rawda. The streets had grown quiet over the past few weeks, all the usual chatter of bartering and children playing replaced by hushed whispers of fear and grief.

Asher reached out to clear Miriam's hair from her face, the back of his hand pausing on her forehead. She was burning up.

"Stay with me, sister," he whispered. "We'll figure something out."

Miriam had always been strong, full of energy and mischief, a spark of life that seemed inexhaustible. She had a knack for finding adventure in the most ordinary places—a patch of wildflowers became a secret kingdom, a pile of stones a fortress, a stream winding through the hills a far-off land full of adventure. She was only ten years old and still retained her strong spirit. Her laughter had the uncanny ability to ease the burden of even the hardest days in the olive grove. The sound always brought a smile to Asher's face as he debated whether to chase her or ignore her and continue working. It was a sound he never imagined he could miss so much until it was gone.

Flashes of her eyes, full of mischief, filled his mind. Her hair, the dark curls bouncing as she ran between the trees, plotting her next "attack."

"You'd better keep one eye on your basket, Ash!" she'd call out, her voice tinged with the confidence only a younger sister could have. "You never know what dangers lurk in the shadows," she'd recite, mimicking a line from their father's favorite bedtime story.

It wasn't fair. Miriam wasn't meant to fade like this, not in a bleak room, bound by sickness.

* * *

Their parents had been given charge of a small grove near their home. Ever since Asher was old enough to climb a ladder, he had helped his father and mother diligently pluck olives from their branches. Miriam was never much help, but she always made the day interesting. He remembered a time when Miriam was eight years old, and the air had just started to cool—a nice change from the oppressive heat of the summer months.

Mother and Father had already headed back to the storeroom, their cart full of baskets of green olives. As soon as Asher reached the top rung of the ladder, Miriam snatched the basket from the branch he had set it on and started running off. "If you can catch me, you can have it back!" she shouted. Father had just promised him ten shekels if he returned with a full load of olives.

"Come on, Miriam! Just come back so we can finish and go home," he replied.

Not wanting to do anything productive, Miriam put the basket upside down over her head, covering herself down to her waist. She started running in place and yelled, "Bet you can't catch a basket with legs!" She took off, running full speed down the row of trees, veering slightly to the right.

After about ten brisk but wobbly paces, she went basket-first into the thick trunk of an olive tree, bouncing back onto her backside and sending olives raining down on her. She let out a loud scream, followed by a deep, high-pitched belly laugh. Asher couldn't help but give in to laughter. He descended the ladder and ran to her side. When he pulled the basket off her head, her hair looked like a destroyed sparrow's nest.

"Gotcha!" Asher laughed. The smile on her face filled him with love that lasted for years.

* * *

Now, her face was gaunt, her skin pale and slick with sweat. Asher reached out to gently touch her forehead, his hand trembling with emotion. He couldn't lose her, not like this. Not after everything they'd already been through.

The pot of boiling herbs hissed and bubbled over the fire. Hyssop, frankincense, myrrh—an herbalist's concoction that was supposed to draw out the sickness. Asher had spent nearly everything he had left after their parents died on these herbs, clinging to the hope that it might somehow break the fever.

It had worked for some. Asher's neighbors had an elderly woman staying with them—his friend's grandmother. Last month, his friend told him she had been in bed for two days, barely breathing. They had also given her the herbalist's tea, and a few days later, he saw his friend in the market buying figs with a hunched-over, cane-carrying woman. He was fairly certain it was her, but it was hard to tell with the head covering obscuring most of her face.

He ladled the bitter brew into a small cup, gently lifting it to Miriam's lips. Her eyes fluttered open, glazed with fever.

"Just a little more," Asher whispered, trying to keep his voice steady. "It'll help."

Miriam took a small sip, wincing at the taste before slowly lowering her head back onto the lumpy pillow. Her breath was still shallow, her skin still burning. Asher set the cup aside, his heart sinking. Shadows on the walls danced in the flickering candlelight as Asher returned to his own bed.

Miriam's strained, rhythmic breathing gnawed at his ears for hours. Frustration welled up inside him. He couldn't bear the thought of losing her too.

* * *

Last winter, he left Miriam to tend the still-simmering goat and lentil stew while he went to check if his parents needed help bringing in the last load of olives destined for the press. He expected them back by dinner, but they still hadn't returned.

As he approached the border of the orchard, he knew something wasn't right. It was silent—only the sound of cicadas permeated the cool evening air. On a normal day, his parents never seemed to stop talking about what was new at the market or whether the odor wafting from Martha's window was lovely or foul. Making his way through the trees, he came upon their family's overturned cart.

"Asher…" a soft voice carried through the cold air, barely audible over the droning of the cicadas.

His heart pounded as he ran toward the sound, stumbling through the branches until he found her—his mother, lying on the ground. Her body was marked with deep gashes, and her eyes were wide with fear. His father lay motionless nearby, his clothes torn, blood seeping into the soil.

"Mother!" Asher dropped to his knees beside her, his hands trembling as he reached for her. "What happened?"

Her hand, cold and weak, found his, gripping with the little strength she had left.

"Wolves… they came so fast…" she whispered, her voice barely more than a breath. "Your father… tried to fight them off."

Asher's throat tightened, his eyes filling with tears.

"Stay with me," he pleaded, brushing the hair from her face. "I'll get help. Just keep breathing." Her grip tightened slightly, a weak smile tugging at the corners of her mouth despite the searing pain.

"No… there's no time, Asher," she said, her voice fading. "Listen to me… you have to… take care of Miriam. Protect her, promise me."

"I will," he choked, nodding furiously. "I swear, I will."

Her gaze softened, her breathing becoming more labored. "We love you both so much…" she whispered, her voice trailing off as her hand slipped from his.

Asher sat there in the cold, holding her hand as her breath stilled, the wind carrying away the last remnants of her voice.

* * *

The sun peeked through the corner of his window after a night that felt like an eternity of listening and waiting. Miriam's breathing continued, and he could still feel a weak pulse as he pressed his fingers to her neck.

"I'll be right back. Just stay with me."

Asher grabbed his cloak, wrapping it tightly around his face, and stepped out from under the canopy covering their front door into the harsh sun. The streets felt dangerous in the morning. So much activity, so many people desperate to find remedies for their suffering or someone to bless their dying child—all of them filled with fear. Most covered their faces not only to protect themselves from the illness but also to remain anonymous, lest they be recognized as relatives of the sick or, worse, spotted with a rash on their neck. Last week, he had seen a man dragged outside the village and tied to a post. Asher didn't stick around to find out what became of him.

Asher made his way through the marketplace, scanning the stalls for anything—anything—that might help. The herbalist had been his best option, but with his sister still showing no signs of improvement, he knew he had to turn to more desperate measures.

That's when he saw the peddler.

The man stood behind a rickety stall, not unlike the one we're in now, his face hidden beneath a hood. His wares hung from hooks and lay in piles on the table—talismans, charms, and amulets that swayed lightly in the morning breeze. Most of them looked like junk, the kind of trinket that fools bought for luck or to ward off bad dreams. It was all rubbish, Asher knew. But desperation has a way of loosening the grip of reason, and he was already too desperate to dismiss any possible cure.

As Asher approached, the man looked up from rearranging the goods on the table, immediately locking eyes with him.

"You seek protection..." the man said, his voice laced with the timbre of a sales pitch delivered a thousand times before.

Asher held his gaze for a moment before looking around at the polished stones, leather bracelets, and coins with strange markings from lands far away. An unassuming silver amulet with faded etchings of spirals and foreign text captured his attention.

"…for your sister?" the peddler said, his voice deepening as he sensed the potential sale. The deep hood covered most of his face with shadows, but through the darkness, the man's yellowed teeth stood out as he spoke.

"Tzavár… an unfortunate curse… it takes the weak first. But this, young man," he tapped the amulet with a bony finger, "this can cure her."

Asher's stomach sank. "How so?" he asked, his whispered voice barely loud enough for the peddler to hear.

The man tilted his head and looked up at the sky as though considering whether the truth or a lie was better suited for this occasion.

"This is no ordinary piece of metal, boy. This amulet was blessed by the sages at Qumran. It has been imbued with protection against all kinds of curses, even ones as vile as Tzavár."

"Can it make her well again?"

"Your sister—I presume—will be dancing by the time the stars come out this evening," he said enthusiastically, reaching his hands upward and spreading them as though to reveal the stars above them. As he looked back down at Asher, he saw the skepticism still covering the boy's face.

"You know, I just came from Zarqa, and while I was there a man bought that very amulet from me. His boy was struck with a fever too, far worse than your sister, I'm sure. The boy was covered in rashes, he could hardly breathe, and he was sweating like a camel." He paused, looking for recognition in Asher's face, then continued. "I sold that man this amulet, and when he returned in the morning with the good news that his boy was cured, he gave it back to me so that I could share its power with someone else who needed it."

Asher's pulse quickened. He wanted badly to dismiss the story as yet another tactic to prey on the desperate, but the sincerity in the peddler's voice clawed at the fragile hope still inside him.

"How much?" Asher asked, his voice unsteady.

A crooked smile spread across the peddler's face. "Not too much, for something so powerful."

"Well," Asher started, peering into his pouch, "I only have two shekels," the words spilling out before he could think.

The man scoffed, shaking his head as he continued arranging his goods.

"Two shekels, he says. Two shekels wouldn't even buy the thread that holds it—" He stopped as his gaze landed on Asher's hand, where a bronze ring caught his eye. "But that ring will."

Asher instinctively covered the bronze band on his finger with his other hand, his heart pounding now. It had been his father's, passed down to him from his father. It was more than a piece of bronze—it was the last reminder of the man who had taught him everything he knew about this world.

"That's not an option," Asher said, his voice hardening.

The peddler leaned back, slightly nodding his head as his fingers traced the edge of the amulet.

"Desperation is a cruel master, my boy," he said, his voice almost pitying. "But the fever is crueler. It doesn't care who you are or what tragedies you've seen. Do you really think that ring will save her, or will the memories of your father cure the girl?"

Confusion flooded Asher's mind. *How does he know all of this?*

"This will work," the peddler said, his voice shifting from pity to certainty. "This will save her." He raised the amulet from the table, moving it toward Asher's face. "Tzavár takes no favorites. It burns savagely through the weak ones, like your sister. But this," he pinched the metal trinket between his fingers, his hands now trembling, "this has the power to hold the fever back. If there's even a chance, boy, you have to take it."

Asher clenched his fist, pressing his thumb over the ring on his finger. He thought of Miriam, lying pale and motionless under the sweat-soaked blanket. The silence in the home was a stark contrast to the joyful squeals she would let out as they wrestled on the floor. The spark of life was fading with every shallow breath she took.

"This is foolish," Asher muttered. "You speak lies, meant to take advantage of desperate fools."

"Maybe," the peddler replied with a sharp smile. "Or maybe this is your last chance to save her. Does that ring mean more to you than her life?"

The words landed like a blow across Asher's face. His hands shook as he worked to slide the ring from his finger. It felt as though he were tearing away the last connection to a life that was slipping through his grasp.

Don't be foolish. It's just a piece of metal. What would your father say about throwing away the last piece of the family legacy?

But his father wasn't there. His father wasn't there to tell him what to do or to guide him through this. He was alone.

What would your mother say? He thought.

He had made a promise to his dying mother to protect

Miriam, and that was all that mattered now.

Asher held the ring in his palm for a moment longer, staring at its dull shine. *This isn't about me. It's about saving her.* With a final, shaky breath, he placed the ring on the table next to the amulet.

"You're sick," he muttered, his voice hollow.

The peddler's fingers closed around the ring, his smile growing as he placed the amulet in Asher's hand. "May it bring you the protection you seek."

Asher turned away, the burden of the trade pressing down on him like a curse. As he disappeared into the crowd, the peddler's voice followed him, low and haunting.

"May the light of the morning sun shine brightly upon her."

* * *

Not unexpectedly, Miriam's condition had only worsened in Asher's absence. Her breaths still came in shallow gasps, and her fever burned hotter than ever. He shuffled quietly through the darkened space and knelt beside his sister. He bowed his head and whispered a prayer as he pulled the amulet from his pocket. The metal was cool against his skin as he squeezed it, leaving an indentation of the amulet in his palm when he opened his hand. He set the small metal trinket on her chest and tied the string around her neck, her sweat-laden hair sticking to his hands as he worked to tie the knot.

"Do you remember when we used to race through the olive groves?" he asked softly, his voice cracking under his growing emotions. "You always made the work take longer than it needed to." A smile rose to his face. "Any chance you got, you'd steal my basket and run off," he chuckled to himself.

"You'd laugh so hard when I caught you. You never cared if the work got done." He stopped, looking at Miriam's face. He wished she would open her eyes and say something to him, so he could hear her voice again.

Her chest rose and fell with effort, her breaths thin and rasping. She didn't respond, her once bright, mischievous eyes now glazed and distant. Yet, Asher kept talking, as if his words could somehow tether her to this life a little longer.

"I used to get so annoyed with you back then," he admitted, brushing his sleeve across his face to catch the tears he couldn't hold back. "I've given up everything to hear you laugh again, Mir. You have to get better, please."

The rays of light traveled across the floor and climbed up the wall. Asher couldn't escape the sound of her breathing—slow, shallow, inconsistent, and horribly fragile. It was a cadence that gnawed at his mind. Each uneven inhale was a desperate plea for a little more time.

His gaze fell to the amulet rhythmically rising and falling. He could swear it was more tarnished than when he had traded his family ring for it just this morning. Rage began to fill his body, starting in his fists, a side effect of the despair warring within him. It was just another empty promise. Another failed cure. Just like the herbs. Just like everything else.

The day wore on, and the amulet did nothing. Tzavár Fever continued its merciless work, and Asher's hope continued to fade.

He sat beside Miriam's bed, watching her sleep. Her small frame seemed even smaller now, her skin stretched thin over her delicate bones. He reached out, taking her limp hand in his. It was cold, her fingers unmoving in his grasp.

"I promised to protect you," he whispered, his voice barely audible. "But I… I don't know what else to do." He lowered his head, his tears falling freely onto her hand.

At that moment, every memory of her—her laughter, her mischief, her fearless spirit—rushed through his mind like a flood. He couldn't lose her. He wouldn't lose her. Sickness and despair lingered in the room, and the flickering candlelight seemed to mock him with its fragile, wavering aura. The shadows danced on the walls, indifferent to his pain, as though the world was determined to carry on without her.

3

Rumors

The final light of the evening sun cast long shadows across the walls, stretching like fingers desperate to hold onto the day. Asher sat motionless beside Miriam's bed, elbows on his knees, his hands clasped tightly together. The sound of her breathing, shallow and uneven, filled the room like the ticking of a clock counting down to something inevitable. The herbs still simmered on the hearth, their aroma mingling with the bitterness of sweat and sickness—a smell that had become all too familiar. The amulet still lay dormant on her sternum. He hadn't left the house in two days, too fearful of what might await him outside, or what might happen to Miriam while he was gone.

Through the silence of the evening, the muffled voices of two men approached. Normally, Asher would tune out their chatter, but tonight, something about their tone cut through the haze of his exhaustion.

"He cured Jethro's boy, I swear it. That boy was on death's door. I figured I had seen the last of him when they rolled his body away on a cart. But they came back, with the boy—still alive, and better than ever."

Asher's heart skipped a beat. He rose and moved closer to the window. The wooden shutters creaked as he nudged them apart just enough to poke his head outside. Two men sat on the stone wall across the street from Asher's home.

"We also thought that Martha's mother got better," the man on the left said, his voice hushed, "but she's dead. They buried her with that forsaken amulet still around her neck. I can hardly afford barley for bread, and you expect me to spend what little I have left on another 'miracle cure'?"

"This one is different, Titus. I swear," the other replied, his tone sharp with conviction. "A true healer. He doesn't even ask for payment. Only faith."

A skeptical grunt followed. "Faith won't keep my family safe."

"It's getting late, and Shoshana wants me back before it's dark." The men's voices faded as they disappeared into the night, their words lingering in Asher's mind.

Asher had heard the stories of so-called miracle workers before, traveling from town to town claiming to heal all sorts of maladies. They were nothing more than con artists preying on the desperate. But the way the men spoke, their words tinged with both awe and doubt, made this feel... different. What's the con if you're not asking for shekels or gold, only faith? Asher asked himself.

While he considered the likelihood of the men's words being true, he closed the shutters and quietly returned to Miriam. She stirred in her bed, her hand continuing to twitch beneath the woolen blanket. For her sake, if there was even a sliver of truth to their words, he couldn't ignore it.

* * *

The next morning, Asher woke before dawn, the possibility of a cure refusing to let him stay asleep. He moved about their home quietly and with a new purpose as he gathered the barley flour, added water and salt, and began kneading the dough. His hands worked mechanically, the motions soothing in their familiarity even as his mind churned with anxious thoughts. The healer, if he was real, might not save her, but perhaps he could ease her suffering. If there was any chance at all, Asher had to take it.

The oven hissed softly, the lovely bouquet of baking flatbread filling the room. Asher glanced toward Miriam's bed, her pale face barely visible in the light creeping through the shutters. A pang of guilt gripped him as he thought about leaving her, even for a moment. But he had no choice. The bread was ready now, its crust golden and warm to the touch as he wrapped it in a cloth. With a final glance at Miriam, he pressed the bundle against his body, the heat seeping through the fabric, and stepped out into the cold morning air.

Asher hesitated at the door to Jethro's home, the warmth of the bread cradled in his hands. Samuel, Jethro's youngest son, had been a sort of informal apprentice to Asher for a season—more of a shadow, really. Constantly trailing Asher, asking endless questions about the trees, the harvest, life beyond the village—some of them making sense, all without waiting for a response before the next question spilled from his lips.

"Why do trees grow up and not down? Do olives only grow in Ar-Rawda, or do they grow in other villages too? How does water go through the wood and get to the olives?"

Samuel had been six years old when he decided he would

be *the best olive tree climber in the whole world.* While Asher worked, carefully plucking the fruit from the higher branches, Samuel would scramble up the trunks like a squirrel, shouting triumphantly whenever he reached a particularly high perch. "See, Asher? I told you I could do it!"

"You're supposed to pick them, not just climb," Asher would shout back, trying to sound stern but failing to hide his grin.

Samuel had been a blur of motion back then, too wild to be contained, but too endearing to truly scold. When Samuel inevitably lost his footing—again—Asher was always— usually—there to catch him, or at least to cushion the fall a bit. The two of them were scolded frequently by Jethro for returning Samuel in sub-par condition. The torn clothing and scraped hands were evidence of the bond they'd built out in the grove.

That was years ago, of course. Samuel was older now, still spirited but with a heavier step, a boy on the cusp of manhood. They'd grown apart over time, and with Asher's parents gone, his life became consumed with work in the grove. Samuel still made an effort to visit, offering to help Asher with errands— really just looking for an opportunity to consult his shadow once again. But Asher's focus had narrowed. He needed to stay focused to ensure tasks got done. And so, Samuel faded into the background of Asher's life, another thread in the tapestry of his village.

Asher didn't even realize Samuel had fallen ill, or that he'd been cured, for that matter. Tzavár Fever came for everyone eventually, whether or not you were paying attention. A guilt he couldn't name had built up in him since hearing about Samuel's recovery—guilt that he hadn't been there for the boy who once idolized him.

Hope threatened to replace the guilt. Words heard through the window last night still churned inside of Asher. A healer had saved Samuel. Asher couldn't deny the small flicker of relief he'd felt, even as his thoughts returned to Miriam. If the healer had saved Samuel, he might be able to save her too. It was the first sliver of light Asher had felt in weeks, and it had grown into a desperate, burning need to confirm the rumors for himself.

The three timid taps on the door were loud enough to catch the attention of Jethro's wife, Leah. She flung the door open with an uncovered face and a wide smile, her joy radiating into the early morning air.

"Asher! You must come in and say hello to Samuel."

Her voice was so bright, so filled with relief, that Asher's resolve nearly faltered. He hadn't seen Leah smile like this in months. For a brief moment, her expression filled him with a fleeting comfort, as though the impossible might actually be true.

The energy briefly disoriented Asher. Through the weeks of fear and disappointment, it had become uncommon to hear anything other than whispers.

"Samuel, your friend is here!" she shouted, her voice reverberating off the walls.

Hope began to boil inside of him, simmering alongside disbelief and worry. As he stepped through the foyer, Asher's hands fidgeted with the cloth wrapping his own rounds of bread, his eyes scanning the room for Samuel.

When the boy appeared from the back room, Asher froze. Samuel looked thinner than before, but alive, his skin no longer ashen and sunken. There was color in his cheeks, and his step, though slow, was steady. Samuel's face lit up when he saw Asher, and he offered a hesitant smile.

"Samuel," Asher breathed. The tension he had long held in his face eased a bit. He stepped closer, scanning the boy for any sign of lingering sickness. "You look… you're better."

"It was the healer," Samuel nodded, his voice soft but with conviction. "He touched my shoulder, and… he saved me."

Leah had snuck behind Asher, placing a comforting hand on his shoulder. "He is truly a miracle worker. I don't know how he did it, but I also don't know what we would've done without him."

Asher had seen all he needed, but the relief was fleeting, overtaken by urgency. He turned and gripped Leah's hand tightly, his words escaping faster than his mind could process. "Ma'am, I'm so sorry, but this is urgent. Where did you find him? Who is he? How do I get to him?"

Samuel opened his mouth to respond, but Leah spoke for him. "Jericho. We just got back last night."

Jericho. Asher's mind raced. Jericho was only a half-day's walk from Ar-Rawda. Pulling Miriam in their cart, maybe a day. She can hold on that long. She has to.

"I'm glad you're well, Samuel!" Asher shouted over his shoulder as his feet slid in the dirt rounding the corner. The boy's voice called after him, confused, but Asher didn't stop. There wasn't time. Not anymore.

He had seen it with his own eyes. Hope was real, and it was within reach. He just had to get to Jericho—before it was too late.

4

Glimmer of Hope

The clatter of Asher bursting into their home evoked a groan from Miriam, her fragile form shifting beneath the thick blanket.

"Sister! It's time to go," Asher said, his voice sharp with urgency as he rushed to her bedside. He knelt down, taking her hands in his. "You'll never believe what I just saw. There's no time now, but I'll tell you about it on the way. We have to get going."

Miriam turned her head, her glassy eyes narrowing slightly as if to focus on his face.

"Ash…" she rasped, her voice so frail it could barely reach him. "It's too late. I'm not going anywhere."

"No," he said, shaking his head, his voice suddenly softer. "No, it's not too late. I've seen it, Miriam. He's healed Samuel. He saved him. He can save you too," Asher cried, pleading with her to believe him.

"No one can save me now, Ash."

Her gaze dropped to her clammy hands as she moved them to adjust her blanket.

"Look," she whispered, pulling the fabric down to reveal the creeping rash across her collarbone. The red patches spread like vines, angry and raw against her ashen skin.

A cold wind howled through the cracks in the walls. He filled her cup with water and held it to her lips, guiding her as she took a few slow, labored sips. Each moment an eternity, her shallow breaths counting down time he didn't have.

"Miriam," he said quietly, forcing steadiness into his voice, "if I can get you to the cart, you can rest while I take you there. You just have to hold on a little longer."

He slipped an arm under her knees and the other behind her neck, gently lifting her frail body. But the moment he tried to stand, a pained moan escaped her lips, low and gravelly, like the sound of something breaking deep within.

"Stop, Ash!" Those were the loudest and most convincing words she had said in days. "Please, just stop."

Her eyes looked into his and said more. *You need to go. Get far from here. Find somewhere safe.*

He stared back at her, his heart shattering as he felt the truth behind her eyes. Leaving her here to die felt impossible. She was the only family he had left, the only person who kept the memory of their parents alive. But staying here would mean they both died, and they both knew it.

"I promised I'd protect you, Mir," he said as tears spilled freely down his face. "I can't leave you."

"You've done enough." Miriam sighed, her voice sounding wise beyond her years. "Now, go."

Her words weren't a question; they were a command. The last words the dying girl would ever say, spoken with the strength of someone who had already accepted what her brother couldn't.

Asher took a deep, stuttering breath, fighting off the hopelessness that worked to claw its way out.

But then, the edges of an idea began to form. A desperate, reckless idea that surely would fail—but it was all he had left. He couldn't take her to Jericho, but he could still save her by bringing the healer here.

"Miriam," he said in a steadier voice, though his hands still trembled. "I'll come back for you. I'm going to find the healer and bring him here. I'll make him come. Whatever it takes, he will come here and save you."

Her face winced slightly, but she didn't utter a word. Exhaustion had already claimed her again; the few spoken words were enough for the day.

Asher leaned in and wiped a strand of hair from her forehead, his jaw tightening with determination.

He couldn't waste another moment. Grabbing his water skin and the remaining flatbread from the table, he paused at the door. Looking over his shoulder at his sister, lying motionless on the bed, her small form rising and falling, he smiled at her.

"You have to hold on," he whispered, the words more for himself than for her.

And with that, he entered the darkness, the cold wind biting at his skin as he made his way through the town of Ar-Rawda and took his first steps on the path to Jericho. It was a desperate plan, but it was all he had. If he could reach the healer, if he could convince him to come back with him, there might still be time. For Miriam. For the promise he'd made. For the hope he couldn't let go of.

5

Road to Jericho

The sun loomed overhead as Jericho first came into view, a shifting and undefined outline against the endless horizon. Asher had made faster progress than he had expected; leaving the cart behind had been a wise decision. The healer could walk back with him, or perhaps he had a horse with a cart of his own.

His legs burned as he pressed on, the relentless heat wringing the energy from his core. But still, he continued.

The vastness of the desert stretched around him, the dried ground supporting only sparse tufts of dying grass, edges browned by the unforgiving sun. Large, round stones lined the path toward the city, their shadows sharp and short in the midday light. The distance between them was uneven, as though some giant had been mindlessly kicking the stones along as he walked. The occasional acacia tree stood twisted and solitary, offering neither shade nor solace.

Asher's cloak flapped against his back in the hot breeze, its edges coarse and stiff with dust. It offered little relief from the sun's merciless glare, which seemed to burn straight through the fabric. His water skin, nearly empty, dangled at his side, its contents tepid and unappealing—yet all he had left. The bread he'd packed, now hard and dry, weighed in his bag but promised no satisfaction.

The horizon, always just beyond reach, mocked his progress. No matter how far he walked, Jericho seemed stubbornly distant, its outlines distorted by waves of heat rising from the ground. The vast emptiness pressed in, endless and oppressive, the silence of the desert broken only by the rustle of wind across the stones.

Even so, it wasn't the heat that threatened to break him—it was the memory of Miriam, frail and fevered beneath sweat-soaked blankets, consuming his thoughts with every step that might have ended this journey. Her laughter and bright face had been swallowed by sickness. Through the cracks in his mind, he could still see her as she had been, before Tzavár tore through their village.

But now, she was alone, lying in bed, her breaths shallow and strained, her voice barely more than a whisper—or perhaps, already dead.

Had he made the right choice? He had told her he was leaving to find a cure, but did she really believe that? It didn't matter—but he hoped she did. He hoped Miriam was in bed, counting the moments since he left, eagerly awaiting his return. But what if she wasn't? What if she called out, and he wasn't there?

Surely, he had no other choice. Staying would have meant death for both of them. Staying would have meant that he had given up. Leaving was the right decision. The plan was simple enough: find the healer and bring him back. He cures Miriam, and their life continues on. It had to work. It was too simple not to.

But as the sun beat down on his shoulders and his knees screamed for rest, doubt crept in—insidious and unwelcome.

What if I'm too late?

Why didn't I leave sooner?

Where will I bury her?

Why didn't I stay and die with her?

Asher forced himself to look forward, his gaze fixing on the distant outline of Jericho. He wasn't sure how much further he had to go, but the city would come into focus eventually. It had to. It was the only thread of hope left to him.

He paused his progress for a moment, took a slow, measured breath through his nostrils, drawing in the fine dust of the desert air, and began counting with his eyes closed.

One, two...

* * *

"Three!"

Their arms swung forward, propelling their bodies off the cliff. Miriam screamed, but Asher held his breath, waiting for the impact.

When their heads broke through the surface of the Wadi al-Kafrein waters, still holding hands, he shouted, "You did it, Mir! I'm so proud of you!"

On her seventh birthday, Asher had dared Miriam to jump from the cliffs into the water when it was high enough to be safe. He dared her again on her eighth birthday, but it wasn't until her ninth that she finally mustered the courage to leap.

Miriam pushed both her hands toward him, sending a wall of water splashing into his open eyes. "I told you I'd do it!

You can't call me chicken anymore," she laughed.

That spring, she begged him almost every day to take her back to the cliffs. And more often than not, he did.

****

...three.

The memory faded, giving way to the present. The hot wind blew at his face, as though mocking him for the hope he carried. Every step now felt like a battle against the elements. The dust clung to his skin. The heat clawed at his will. If there was a healer, he needed to find him soon.

He slowly released the air from his lungs and continued toward Jericho.

The heat shimmered on the horizon, distorting the edges of the desert. It was then that Asher saw the outline of palm trees swaying lazily, their long shadows barely moving in the still heat. A well. The distant sight of it filled him with the smallest glimmer of hope. Water. Rest. Perhaps even news.

As he approached the oasis, two men reclined in the shade of the trees beside the well, their voices carrying a buoyant energy that cut through the stillness.

"...made a crippled man walk again," one of them said, his tone laced with awe. "Just like that." The man reached out his arm and snapped his fingers directly in front of the other man's eyes. "No herbs, no ointments—nothing but words."

The second man let out a scoffing laugh, his disbelief as sharp as the crunch of dried mud beneath Asher's feet.

"With just a word, you say? And I suppose he turned water into wine right after? You can't expect me to believe such nonsense, Eliezer. We've seen enough charlatans to fill the market square twice over."

Eliezer shook his head fervently, leaning forward as though trying to drag the truth closer to his companion.

"I saw it, Caleb, with my own eyes! This poor man, bent and frail, sitting by the gates in Capernaum, begging for shekels like he had done for years. I've seen him there every time I pass through! But this Yeshua—he walks up to him, says something about his sins being forgiven, and then tells him to stand."

"And he just… stood?" Caleb's thick brows furrowed as he imagined the scene. The only thing thicker was the tone of skepticism in his voice. "No stumbles, no cries of pain, just up and about like nothing happened?"

"He didn't just stand, my friend," Eliezer said, rising from the ground with cheerful enthusiasm. "He danced!" Eliezer threw his arms wide as he began shuffling in circles. "He danced like a boy at a wedding." Pausing, Eliezer looked upward. "And the man raised his cane over his head, took it in both hands, and brought it down on his knee like this!" He mimicked the breaking of the cane over his knee, kicking up dust with his fervent acting.

Caleb leaned his head back against the roots of the palm tree, looking up at the thinning clouds as he envisioned the scene.

"If this really happened," he said, pausing to consider the implications, "then why isn't the whole of Galilee chasing after him?"

Asher strained his ears and quieted his steps as he continued his approach to the oasis.

Eliezer gave a knowing smile and dropped his voice to a near whisper.

"They are," he said, looking around for dramatic effect. "Everywhere he goes, the crowds follow. I had to elbow my way through just to get close enough for a glimpse of his face. And let me tell you, Caleb, when he speaks, oh…" His face lit up as he closed his eyes, slowly turning his head side to side. "…it's as though the air itself listens to his words…"

Caleb crossed his arms impatiently. "Eliezer!" He snapped his fingers to wake his friend from the dream. "What exactly did he say that had you, and the air, so enraptured?"

Eliezer kept his eyes closed, as if weighing whether to share the words or keep them to himself. Finally, he squatted down next to his friend, his voice hushed.

"He spoke of eternal life. He said something strange too—'Whoever eats my flesh and drinks my blood will live forever.' It sounded absurd at first, but Caleb… there was power in his voice. If you heard it—"

"Eats his flesh?" Caleb interrupted. "Drinks his blood? That is absurd."

"Maybe," Eliezer admitted, shrugging his shoulders as he stood back up. "But what if it's true, and Yeshua truly has the power of God? Would you risk dismissing him so easily?"

The power of God. Asher stopped, considering the possibilities. Yeshua. The healer's name was Yeshua?

In Asher's early childhood, there had been a boy named Yeshua—a mischievous little nuisance who used to knock things out of Asher's hands whenever he passed him on the street. Yeshua's family had left Ar-Rawda last year, moving east to who knows where. It couldn't be the same person. The boy Asher knew hadn't a shred of reverence in him, much less the power to heal. And yet, the name hung in his mind, a tantalizing thread that demanded to be followed.

Asher cleared his throat, both to prepare to speak and to get the men's attention.

"Excuse me," Asher said, his voice desperate for a drink of water. "Yeshua—did you see which way he went?"

Eliezer's face filled with I-told-you-so as he looked down at his friend before looking back up at Asher.

"I'm sorry, young man, but you just missed him. He passed through a few hours ago. His companions mentioned heading toward Jericho, or maybe Jerusalem. One of the two, I'm not sure, but they're both that way."

Asher's eyes followed the man's hand as he pointed toward the horizon, in the direction he was already heading.

Leah had been right—Yeshua was real, and he was close.

"Are you sure he was heading to Jericho?" he repeated, needing to hear confirmation aloud, as though the words could solidify the hope rising inside of him like evaporating moisture.

Eliezer nodded patiently. "Yes, that's what I said. *Or maybe* Jerusalem. That's what they told me. He has quite a large group of followers walking with him. You can't miss 'em."

Caleb folded his arms, regarding Asher with a mix of curiosity and suspicion. "What do you want with him, boy?"

Asher hesitated, squinting as he looked off toward Jericho.

"My sister, she's... sick," he said finally. "I heard he can heal people, and it sounds like you heard the same. I need to find him."

Caleb glanced up at Eliezer, a flicker of understanding passing between them. Eliezer's expression softened as he stepped toward Asher.

"If it's healing you're after, you've got the right man. He made a crippled man walk again, just like that—" Again,

Eliezer reached his arm out and snapped, but this time, right in front of Asher's eyes.

Asher let out a small laugh. "Thank you," he interrupted. "Thank you, both."

He turned toward the well, filling his water skin with excited hands. The cool splash of water against his fingers steadied him, though his heart still raced. Yeshua was close—close enough that the hope Asher had kept buried for so long began to stir, fragile but undeniable.

"You'll need to hurry," Caleb called after him, a warning laced in his voice. "Jericho's not far, but if he's heading to Jerusalem after, you might lose him. He doesn't stay in one place for long."

Asher nodded, clutching the water skin firmly in his grasp as he straightened.

"I'll find him," he said, bowing his head slightly toward the man still reclining in the shade of the palm tree.

As he turned, his legs moved forward as though spurred on by the urgency in his mind. Each step away from the oasis brought him one step closer to the promise of a miracle. The doubts that had haunted him since leaving Miriam began to fade. He didn't know how it worked, but he had no choice but to believe the healer could save her—and that it wouldn't be too late.

* * *

As the walls rose before him, the sun dipped behind Jericho, casting long golden rays through the stone parapets. The city glowed in the evening light, and the formidable walls told stories of battles, sieges, and the resilience of ages.

He had never seen anything like it. The history, the grandeur—Jericho felt almost ethereal, as if it were suspended between worlds. For a moment, the weariness in his legs eased, replaced by awe.

The gates were propped open, allowing a steady flow of people to pass in and out. The chatter of merchants and would-be buyers spilled over the walls and through the gates, mingling with the tantalizing aromas of roasted meat and freshly baked bread.

These walls had once crumbled under the impact of a divine command, falling to ruin as the city was laid bare. Asher had heard the stories—how the power of faith reduced the indestructible walls to rubble. Yet here the city stood, resurrected against all odds.

Asher paused at the main road leading through the gates, his cloak shifting in the warm breeze that carried the welcome aromas. He felt the same tug of hope now for Miriam. Her body, like those ancient walls, had crumbled under the relentless assault of Tzavár Fever. She was a shell of the girl she once was, weakened in its grip. But just as Jericho's walls had fallen, and the city had risen again, perhaps there was still hope for Miriam—fragile as it was.

Asher worked his way through the vibrant chaos of color and sound. The stalls held a variety of pleasantly banal wares: bolts of colorful fabric, copper trinkets, and jars filled with familiar spices. A young boy darted through the crowd carrying a basket of dates, kicking up swirls of dust as he wove through the gates. A group of camels loaded with lumber marched ahead of Asher, their drivers shouting commands in a language he couldn't place.

He took it all in—every sight, smell, and sound brimming

with energy and promise. Every detail felt louder and larger than he could have imagined, the world expanding around him in a way that made Ar-Rawda feel like a distant memory.

Adjusting his cloak and tunic, Asher stepped through the open gate, entering the flow of people. Each step was a mix of anticipation and trepidation. He didn't have time to marvel at the carved details etched into the stones holding the gate upright. Miriam was waiting, and he needed to find Yeshua—now.

His heart pounded as he asked after Yeshua. He spoke to a woman selling bread, a man repairing his cart, and a child carrying water from the well, and every person had a version of the same response.

"Yes, he's here."

"I just saw him by the well."

"He just greeted me as I came in through the gates. There's something *different* about him."

The healer was here in Jericho.

Asher's heart raced. He could feel it—he was close now, closer than he had ever been.

Looking for some specific direction, he asked one more person, a young woman carrying a basket of flowers. She smiled kindly as she formed her response.

"He was here," she said with a soft, apologetic voice.

Asher winced, waiting for her to finish.

"But he left."

Her words both crushed and confused him.

How could he be gone? He was just here. They saw him.

Asher's legs felt weak, his head spinning.

"What?!" he cried. He gestured with his hand, pointing behind him. "They said he…"

The woman nodded, noting the pain in his eyes.

"He's heading to Jerusalem... something about a festival or a prophecy, maybe?" she said, shifting the basket in her arms. "I couldn't hear everything, but it seemed important."

Jerusalem was another half-day's journey, maybe longer. His legs threatened to give out from exhaustion, but worse than the physical toll of the journey was the sudden, crushing weight of disappointment.

Without so much as a glimpse of him, Yeshua was once again out of reach. Asher stood frozen in the street, the tide of people swirling around him in every direction. His mind raced with a thousand thoughts, all leading to the same question: Would there be enough time?

He blinked, the woman's words echoing in his mind—*"He's heading to Jerusalem."*

It felt as distant as the horizon itself. His legs wobbled beneath him, and for the first time, the exhaustion he had been ignoring for days slammed into him. His body trembled, but it wasn't just from the strain of the journey.

His chest tightened, a subtle twinge that had been creeping up on him since leaving Ar-Rawda. He brought his hand to his mouth, stifling a dry cough, but it tore through his lungs. As his head heaved forward to brace against the pain, cool drops of sweat dripped from his brow into his palm.

Was that a tremor?

His stomach churned with the sick realization that he had been ignoring the symptoms for too long.

It can't be.

6

Arrival in Jerusalem

Asher continued westward toward Jerusalem, his legs burning with every step. The wind had continued blowing on his left side, bringing the smell of the sea and the sting of the sand. The barren expanses of desert had begun to give way to the Judean Mountains. The well-traveled trade routes and the hills now on his left and right made walking easier. His footsteps carried the sound of despair as they fell unevenly on the packed, dry dirt.

Up ahead, he noticed three men reclining under a rocky overhang, nearly out of sight from the path. As he passed, they didn't look at him, but he heard the small one demanding to get the share that he deserved.

He continued on, shifting his gaze from his feet to the path ahead. A creaking sound from behind broke the silence of the narrow valley. Asher turned to see a merchant's cart full of goods being pulled by a donkey at a speed he didn't know donkeys were capable of. The man driving the cart was portly, with a thick beard, and he slowed the pack animal as he approached Asher.

"You look like you've been wrestling the desert itself, my friend," the merchant said with a raised eyebrow. "Would you like to rest your feet a bit? I could take you into the city if you'd like."

Asher said nothing in return, but noticed the kindness beneath his gruff voice.

"You'll collapse if you walk much further. And those bandits aren't far behind me. I think you might want to get a move on," the merchant said, looking over his shoulder back in the direction he had come.

Asher knew he was right and could feel his body betraying him. "Yes," he croaked, his voice hoarse. "I need to get to Jerusalem."

The merchant chuckled. "Don't we all. As it happens, I'm headed that way myself. Climb in back, and we'll be there in no time," he said, motioning toward the rear of the cart.

Asher hoisted himself aboard and lay flat on his back to avoid falling off as the ass resumed its steady run. The merchant began whispering a cheerful tune that sounded familiar, but Asher couldn't quite place it.

He sat back up, leaning heavily against the sacks of grain and bundles of cloth to steady himself. The road behind him blurred as exhaustion washed over him, but he could see the three men raising their fists in the air and shouting toward the cart.

For a while, he sat in silence, trying not to breathe too deeply, aware of every tremor in his body, praying the fever wouldn't overtake him before he found Yeshua.

The merchant glanced over his shoulder. "You alright, friend? Lookin' a bit pale back there, aren't you?"

Asher nodded. "Just… tired," he murmured.

The man gave a sympathetic grunt and turned his attention back toward the road. "Well, lean off the back if you need to empty your stomach, okay? I'm Ezra. Got a particular reason for making this death march into Jerusalem?" He trailed off, probing for a name to call the boy.

"Asher."

"So, Asher, what's waiting in Jerusalem for you?"

"A healer. Yeshua. Have you heard of him?"

Ezra's brow furrowed. "Yes, I've heard the name. People say he's doing miracles. Now, as for me, I don't believe in that sort of thing. I've lost too many people to believe in miracles," he said. "Looks like you've gone through a lot to find him, though. You must be hoping for a miracle yourself."

"Something like that," Asher said in a low voice the merchant could hardly hear.

"Well, for your sake, I hope what they're saying is true. Looks like you need it."

As the cart crested a small hill, Ezra looked over his shoulder and shouted, "Just up ahead now!"

Asher turned hesitantly and took in his first glimpse of the city. Its ancient walls came into view, majestic and formidable, bathed in the golden light of the setting sun, the layered imprint of centuries stacked atop each other—history, prophecy, dust.

"Asher, I think there's something happening," Ezra said.

A crowd of people, moving in unison, had gathered just outside the city walls. Their movement was purposeful, heading outward from the gates toward the hill north of them. A shiver of unease trickled down Asher's spine.

He nodded to the merchant and slipped out of the cart, his legs still shaky but driven by the gnawing need to understand what was happening.

"You sure you want to get off here?"

"Thank you," Asher shouted as loud as his body would allow.

"Well, good luck, Asher," the merchant said. His voice was tinged with sympathy. Asher could see the sadness in the man's eyes, as if he knew what fate awaited in the city ahead.

Asher's legs were wobbly and tingled as he began to walk. But his pace quickened as he merged in with the back of the crowd. Dust swirled in the air, kicked up by the throng of people. Eager to learn what had gathered them, and sensing it had something to do with Yeshua, Asher grabbed the arm of the first person he encountered. It felt mostly of bone.

"What's happening?" he asked breathlessly.

The woman who turned to him was old, the wrinkles on her face showing years of hardship. She gazed at him with a bewildered expression.

"They're going to kill the king of the Jews," she said, her voice flat, as if the words themselves didn't make sense to her.

"What?" Asher's face contorted slightly. "There's no king here."

The idea seemed absurd. He had known for as long as he could remember that Judea had been under Roman rule, its people taxed by an empire that had no king of their own among the Jews.

The woman shrugged, pulling her arm free from his grasp. "I'm not sure what's happening, but I saw a man, covered in blood, carrying a cross." She paused, shaking her head. "Poor man, they haven't done this sort of thing here in ages."

The woman continued along with the crowd while Asher stood still, his stomach churning with dread.

Finding the healer—his last hope for his sister—was slipping away.

With everyone so focused on, *whatever this was,* it would be impossible to find him in time.

He pushed on through the crowd, trying to make sense of the situation. Shouts of anger, desperation, and pleas for mercy stumbled over each other. The whirlwind of bodies and emotions clashed in a deafening uproar that echoed through the dusty streets.

Ahead, he spotted a small child stumbling to keep pace with the mob. The girl's eyes were wide with fear as she fell to her knees. Asher pushed aside two men who were about to walk right over her. Kneeling beside the girl, he brought her back to her feet.

"You're okay. I've got you," he said as she brushed the dirt from her knees.

"Thank you. I thought I was dead," she replied.

He looked her in the eyes and saw the fear fade away. "Do you know who that man is? The one with the cross?" Asher asked.

The girl bent down and picked a small rock out of her knee. A trail of blood ran down her shin as she looked toward the throng of onlookers.

"Yeshua."

The girl was swallowed once again by the crowd, but Asher remained in place, their bodies parting around him like a river flowing around a stone.

The thunderous noise faded as he fixed his eyes on the scene unfolding ahead.

Up on the hill, the man, the healer—Yeshua—was being nailed to a cross, each strike of the hammer echoing in Asher's mind like a death knell.

Everything around him blurred, except for the image of Yeshua's body on the cross.

Asher's heart sank. This was the end—he had come all this way, *for what?*

There was no hope left for Miriam.

As he stood there, numb and defeated, his thumb began to twitch, followed by the rest of his hand. Asher's time was running short as well.

Yeshua's cry pierced the air, but Asher couldn't make out his words over the shouts of the crowd. His eyes locked on the spear thrust into Yeshua's side, where blood began to flow.

It was finished.

Asher dropped to his knees and buried his face in his hands, tears falling through the cracks between his fingers into the dirt below.

The mob began to disperse now that the spectacle was over. Asher remained rooted in place, his heart and mind void of any plan. His world had collapsed, and the air closed in around him.

Behind his puffy red eyes, a light sparked in the center of his mind.

The words from the man at the well came back to him: *Whoever eats my flesh and drinks my blood has eternal life.*

The spark became a desperate idea that surely wouldn't work.

It was irrational, almost certainly blasphemous.

Asher opened his eyes and looked back up at Yeshua, to the blood trickling from his pierced side. It flowed down his leg, past his knee, and dripped off his foot into the dirt below. The crimson pool was stark against the dry, cracked ground, pooling briefly before being swallowed into the thirsty earth.

Asher's pulse quickened—not with hope, but with the frantic energy of a young man grasping at a thin thread of a plan.

He wiped the tears from his eyes as he scanned the ground, searching. Among the discarded food and other waste left behind by the crowd, his eyes landed on a small vial. Half-buried in the dirt, a corner of its glass caught the light of the fading sun. *That might actually work.* The thought gripped him like a vice, irrational yet undeniable.

Asher scurried on his hands and knees toward the vial and snatched it from its resting place. The fine grooves in the glass were caked with dirt. Its interior held a meager residue of brownish liquid, but it appeared otherwise clean. His breath came in gasps as he held the vial to the light, his hand shaking. A tiny crack ran along the neck, but it would hold. It had to hold.

He flicked the metal latch holding the cap in place, the metallic snap ringing out louder than expected. He upended the vial, shaking out the remnants of whatever it had once held. A tiny amount clung stubbornly to the crevassed point, but it didn't matter.

As he rose from his knees, his heart pounded harder. The weight of what he was about to do pressed on his bones. What remained of his rational mind screamed at him to stop—that this was wrong, that it didn't have a chance of working anyway. But there was no time for thought. No time for doubt.

Miriam's face manifested in his mind—the way her smile used to light up their little home, the way she would dart through the olive groves, daring him to catch her. That life, that spirit, could not end like this.

He walked up the rest of the hill to the cross and knelt, his knees pressing into the hard dirt. His hand steadied as he extended the vial toward the slow, steady drip of blood falling off the end of Yeshua's big toe.

The first drop struck the edge of the glass and ran down the side, trailing over his finger. It was still warm. He adjusted to the left, and the next drop landed in the vial with a soft *plink*, then another, and another, the crimson liquid beginning to pool at the bottom.

The air surrounding him felt heavier, and his posture began to sag, though his skin prickled with energy. The crowd had mostly dispersed, but a few still lingered. Their murmured sobs of disbelief filled the space. Asher didn't dare meet their eyes, let alone look in their general direction.

His actions felt unspeakable. Profane. Yet, he couldn't stop.

When the vial was full, he pulled it from the slow stream. His fingers fumbled with the latch, securing it in place with a sharp click. He once again held the vial up to the sun. This time, the blood within cast a reddish hue across his face, and his stomach churned with regret.

A quiet voice spoke to him from behind, in a tone simultaneously comforting and terrifying.

"No absolution will ever be found."

He abruptly turned and looked over his shoulder, but no one was there. Rising to his feet, he slipped the vial into the safety of his cloak and took a deep breath through his nostrils.

Returning the vial to Miriam was his plan now—the last chance he had to bring her back from the brink. Whether this blood carried miracles or madness, Asher didn't care.

All that mattered was that it was more than he had moments ago.

It was something.

It was a chance.

7

Returning Home

The road stretched out before him once again. Asher watched his shadow grow longer with every wobbly step. His throat ached, his lungs burned, and his body cried out for rest, but there would be none—not until he reached Miriam.

Upon leaving the city, he fell in with a group of travelers who had come to Jerusalem with Yeshua. Now, as they walked with the sun at their backs, none said a word. In the long walk through the desert, there would be safety in their numbers, but he couldn't keep their pace. The reality that he would be walking alone through the night struck him with dread as a cool breeze nipped at his ankles.

The whispers of wind were constant, broken only by his dull footsteps and the calls of jackals in the distance. Shivers rippled through his body, brought on by the wind but driven by the fever. Just as his vision began to blur, and his steps faltered, a familiar creaking sound crept up from behind.

"Did you find him?" the merchant shouted.

Asher looked back and saw the stout donkey and cart piled

high with goods, Ezra at the reins. Reaching Asher, Ezra slowed the cart and looked down at him with a frown, shaking his head.

"Guess not. Get in." The merchant motioned toward the back of the cart. "You're headed home, right? Ar-Rawda? It's on my way."

Asher didn't argue. He didn't have the strength to. Without a word, he climbed into the cart, collapsing against the sacks of grain and fabric bundles as the merchant flicked the reins.

"Yhep," Ezra muttered, and the donkey trotted forward.

The road rolled beneath them. Each bump of a wheel over a rock jostled Asher's exhausted frame, but his mind was elsewhere. Stuck in the hollow silence of his thoughts, he pulled the vial from his pocket and cradled it in his lap. It felt heavier now, the presence of it the only thing tethering him to reality.

He stared up at the sky, watching the stars begin to appear. The cool wind licked his neck. His hand moved to warm his skin, and that's when he felt it. The rash. His fingers brushed against the telltale roughness of Tzavár Fever, the raised skin now visible in the fading daylight. The rash was spreading, slowly but surely making its way up toward his face.

It's happening, he thought. The sickness was consuming him. Time was running out.

The cart rumbled on, but Asher's focus narrowed to the burning sensation on his neck. He could feel it crawling up his skin, a final reminder of the fate that awaited him if the blood in the vial didn't work. Asher gripped the vial tighter.

When the cart came to a stop near the edge of his village, stars filled the sky. Asher staggered out, nodding his thanks to the merchant before making his way toward the house.

The home stood silent, dark, and lifeless. Miriam hadn't lit a candle—she hadn't been able to for days now—but the absolute stillness weighed heavy on his heart. His hand, trembling, reached toward the small table just inside the entryway. He struck the flint, bringing the candle's flame to life. It was barely enough to see by, but it was all that was left.

There was no sound. No wheezing breath, no rasp of life struggling against the fever. The air was thick with the stench of sickness and death. Asher's heart sank deeper with every step. He dropped to his knees beside the bed where Miriam lay. She was still, her small frame draped beneath the blanket, her face gaunt and pale. His fingers refused to stay still as he placed them on her cheek—it was cold.

She was gone.

Tears flowed freely from his eyes, his heart drained of every ounce of hope.

"I'm so sorry," he whispered, his voice breaking, choking on his words. "I tried… I tried so hard, Miriam."

He rested his forehead against the side of the bed, his body convulsing with silent sobs. The weight of his failure pressed down on him, crushing him under the enormity of his loss. He had promised their mother, he had sworn to protect his sister—and now, he had nothing left.

His throat tightened, and for a moment, he couldn't breathe. The raspy sound of his own labored inhalations filled the silence that Miriam had once occupied. Asher fell toward the ground, his tears pooling on the dirt floor.

But then, his gaze caught the shape of the vial in the corner of his eye. It rested on the same entryway table where he had lit the candle, the small glass bottle holding and scattering the light. The dark liquid inside cast an ominous shadow on the wall. It had been Miriam's last hope. Was it truly too late?

He retrieved it and crawled back up to her side, fumbling to release the cap. As it came loose, the tang of iron rose from the dark liquid within. His fevered mind clung desperately to the stories he had heard, to the miracles whispered on the road to Jericho.

Could it be possible? Was there still a chance?

His hands trembled as he cradled her lifeless face. Her pale skin was cold. "Come back," he whispered. "Please, come back."

He tilted her head back gently, prying her lips apart, crust breaking as they separated. Carefully, he poured a few drops into her mouth, watching as it slid over her tongue and down her throat. For a moment, hope rose—an impossible, fragile hope that perhaps this might work, that the blood would perform the miracle he so desperately needed.

He waited. The silence pressed in around him, broken only by the spitting of the candle's wick. His eyes searched her face for any sign of change, any movement, any breath.

Nothing.

"Miriam," he choked out, his voice raw and desperate. He gripped her shoulders, shaking her lightly. Her arms moved freely as he shook them, but her body remained still, and the room remained silent.

The vial slipped off the blanket, clinking against the floor— half of the blood spilling out. Asher sat back, his ragged breaths permeating the silence. Tears continued streaming down his face as reality crushed him.

She was gone. Truly gone.

His head fell into his hands, his body shaking with sobs. As his fevered mind swam with exhaustion and grief, the vial seemed to call to him—a whisper, a pull he couldn't ignore.

Slowly, Asher lifted his head, his bloodshot eyes settling on the small glass bottle. The liquid inside swirled sluggishly, thick, almost alive. It was her last hope, and it had failed her. But now, as the fever clawed at his own body, it was all that was left for him.

He reached for the vial. The rash crept toward his jawline. His muscles spasmed in short, painful bursts, and his breath came in shallow gasps.

With a final act, he raised the vial to his lips and took a small sip. The liquid bitter on his tongue, warm as it slid down his throat. He coughed, gagging on the taste, but forced himself to swallow. The vial still held some blood—but he couldn't drink more. His body sagged, the last of his strength draining as he fell back against the floor, his hand releasing the vial beside him.

Asher's pulse weakened, and darkness closed in. The silence returned, enveloping the room like a thick fog as his entire body lay flat against the earth.

And then, just like that—

His breathing stopped. His pulse did as well.

Asher was no longer a boy, no longer a brother, no longer anything but organic matter.

The candle burned out, and the room blackened.

Yet in the cold blackness, something stirred.

II

Part Two

8

Interlude

Hassan looked up at me from the vial, one corner of his mouth bent into a wry smile. I leaned back, blinking to break his stare. The rankness of the story hung in the air with the foul must of the marketplace. I shifted uncomfortably, rubbing the back of my neck, stuck somewhere between disbelief and intrigue.

Reentering reality, I leaned forward and pressed my finger onto the wooden table next to the vial.

"Hang on, Hassan, do you mean to tell me that this thing contains… Jesus' blood?" I said, shaking my head and raising my eyebrows. "You expect me to believe that over two thousand years later, you've got the actual blood of Jesus Christ in that little glass vial?"

My words came out sharp, almost incredulous, but I couldn't deny the trace of discomfort in my tone. The sheer absurdity of it all clashed with the unsettling certainty in Hassan's eyes.

He smiled, his gaze calm and steady. It wasn't mocking, but it wasn't exactly reassuring either. There was something ancient in the way he held himself, like he carried secrets too heavy for words.

"So," he said softly, "you think this isn't just a story?" Hassan chuckled.

"That's not what I said."

"But I can see it in your eyes. They're looking for the truth."

I let out an awkward laugh, looking up at the cloth shifting in the wind overhead.

"Hassan, I'm a scientist. I spend my days unraveling cellular mysteries, not chasing fairytales. You tell me this thing has survived over two thousand years—intact—and it came from Jesus. *The* Jesus. So of course I'm looking for any truth in this myth. But you said there was a crack in the vial when that boy found it." I leaned forward and met Hassan with a wide-eyed stare. "Where's the crack, Hassan? The damn glass is in perfect condition." I raised my arm and pointed to my right. "You bought it from one of these guys, and you're just screwing with me, like you probably do with dumb-looking tourists like me every day. Is that what you're doing here?"

The words tumbled out fast, trying to drown the small, irrational part of me that wanted to hear more. Logic told me this was ridiculous. But curiosity, stubborn as it was, had walked in like an unwelcome guest.

Hassan kept smiling, patiently gauging if I had finished. "You find all this difficult to believe," he said slowly, as though trying to comfort a confused child. "But belief is not necessary for truth to exist."

I blinked and looked away from him. "No offense, friend, but that's a convenient way to dodge my questions."

"Is it?" Hassan reached out and tapped the vial lightly with his finger. The *plink* of his dry skin on the glass was sharp, cutting through the steady hum of the marketplace. "Many things you call 'myths' today are just truths long forgotten. The details fade, the stories blur, but the truth remains. This vial has passed through many hands, and very few know of its true origins. But I know. And now, so do you."

I exhaled through my nose, the air whistling as it came out. Scientific doubt and something uncomfortably close to curiosity wrestled inside of me. My eyes drifted down to the vial again, spotting the shadowy gleam of its contents swirling sluggishly as Hassan removed his finger.

"Okay, amigo," I said finally. "But let's just pretend for a second that this story is true. Even if Asher did all of that, how do you explain this?" I gestured toward the vial, the disbelief practically dripping from my words. "Two thousand years, Hassan. Liquids don't stay liquid forever—they evaporate, degrade, and solidify. Yet here it is, defying every law of science."

Hassan's smile didn't waver. "Ah," he said, "and therein lies your dilemma. You want an explanation that fits your science, your rules. But some things exist just beyond those boundaries, James."

I shook my head. "Well, that's convenient. 'Beyond boundaries.' Right. You're telling me this vial has endured wars, plagues, weather, and time itself—untouched—and the blood inside hasn't even dried up? Forgive me if that's a tough pill to swallow."

Hassan leaned forward, resting his elbows on the table as he interlaced his calloused fingers. There was something magnetic about his posture. He was drawing me into a story I didn't want to hear but couldn't walk away from.

"You find it hard to believe because you're looking for what's missing. A crack in the glass, a trace of decay. You'll never find fault in that which has been restored."

"What the hell is that supposed to mean, Hassan?" The words leapt from my mouth, full of anger and confusion.

The scientist in me screamed for evidence, facts—anything tangible. My mind churned with questions, doubts crashing into one another.

"Sorry. Sorry, let me try that again." I paused, feeling embarrassed that my emotions got the best of me, and a little ashamed that I had raised my voice at this kind, yet eccentric man. "You would like me to ignore thousands of years of observable science for... for a story—"

"No," Hassan said, cutting me off. "I'm asking you to open your mind to the possibility that some truths defy explanation."

I pressed my middle fingers into the corners of my closed eyes, wiping away the accumulated dust, my thoughts entangled in a mess of disbelief and reluctant fascination. "Okay, okay. So, what happened to Asher?"

Hassan leaned back, pleased with himself. "Ah, there you go." He gestured again at the vial with the same air of mystery that had gripped me from the start. "That dark home, rich with the smell of death, was just the beginning..."

What's this guy's deal?

"...you see, the vial traveled far, and one day, it found its way into the hands of a woman."

His voice deepened, and the shadows in the stall darkened with it.

9

Lucien's Childhood

Denmark, 1000 C.E.

L ucien's existence had been marked by shadows long before she ever drank from the vial. She first thought that perhaps life would be miserable the night her mother made them leave everything behind.

She awoke to a tapping on her shoulder and felt her favorite stuffed hare being pulled from her arms. She watched her mother throw it to the floor, whispering, "Wake up, we have to leave." The urgency in her mother's voice sent a chill through the young girl. "We can't let them find us," her mother added under her breath, as though the words themselves might invite danger.

"Now, Sweet Angel. Time to go."

As she rubbed the sleep from her eyes, her mother was already at the door, gripping the hand of her brother, Cassius. He, too, was still suspended in the fog of slumber—swaying unsteadily as though he might fall flat on his face. They disappeared into the night, leaving Lucien sitting upright

69

in her bed of hay, the cold seeping into her bones, her heart racing. The memory dissolved there, as if swallowed by the dark itself, leaving only the echo of fear behind.

It was always like that—the darkness, the hurried footsteps, the whisper of urgency in her mother's voice. In the days that followed each escape, Lucien would ask questions that never found answers.

"Where are we going, Mama?" she would whisper, her small fingers clutching at the hem of her mother's skirt as the fields of Brunvik stretched before them.

"Somewhere safe," was always the reply, curt and distant.

And so, she learned to stop asking. The world became a blur of muddy roads and fleeting shelters: the hayloft of a kind farmer in one village, the cellar of an abandoned tavern in another. The names never stuck in her mind for long; only fragments of memory remained—the smoky perfume of a fire, the murmur of unfamiliar accents, the way her mother's voice grew quieter the farther they traveled.

On the night when the setting sun cast a long shadow off a rotting sign reading *Vindheim*, Lucien experienced her first taste of excitement. The village sat on a high plain, and the wind at their backs had pushed them up the winding trail. As they entered the marketplace, the air was alive with the mingling fragrance of roasted chestnuts, freshly baked bread, and the occasional tinge of vinegar wafting from a stall where a woman with wrinkled hands loaded jars with pickled fish. The village was loud, merchants calling out their wares in booming voices as Lucien's family walked past them.

The torches had just been lit when Lucien wandered off from her mother to a man selling hand-carved toys—wooden animals painted in vibrant colors, their tiny faces smiling despite their stillness. Her hand hovered across the line of charming beasts, her fingers coming to rest on a fox with a red coat. The paint had started to show wear from the touch of many curious hands before hers.

The craftsman, a gruff man with a thick beard and kind eyes, leaned over.

"When the snow gets deep, the fox waits and listens. The mouse, believing she's safe beneath the snow, picks at some straw to build a little bed. But the fox hears the movement. He leaps high into the air, and diving deep into the snow, his teeth head straight for the poor mouse. The fox pops back up and brings the bloody creature back to its den, sleeping soundly with a full belly. Do you know why the fox eats while other creatures hibernate?"

This was the first time anyone besides her mother or brother had spoken directly to her. While he told the story, she hadn't made eye contact.

"Because he's quick and *clever*. Just like little girls should be," he said, probing for a response. "Do you want it?"

She glanced over her shoulder at her mother, who was bartering for bread and cheese at a nearby stall. Cassius stood next to her, a basket in hand, his watchful eyes scanning the crowd.

"I don't have any coins," she admitted softly, drawing her hand back.

He chuckled, reaching into his pocket and pulling out a small piece of twine.

"I'll make you a deal," he said while carefully tying the fox onto the string. "You can have it *if* you promise me something."

Lucien tilted her head as she looked him in the eyes. "What

kind of promise?"

"Never let anyone tell you that you're not clever enough to figure things out on your own," he said, looping the string over her head so that the fox rested against her belly. "Even when it's cold and scary, you'll find a way. Just like the fox."

She nodded solemnly, her small fingers wrapping around the wooden figure. "I promise."

The craftsman gave her a smile and a kind wink as she turned to find her mother.

That night, they slept on beds of hay, and a small hearth held enough fire to keep them warm.

Lucien awoke to a beam of light piercing a crack in the mud-and-stone wall. The smell of smoke from the embers and the damp chill of dawn brought a smile to her face. She rubbed her thumb over the belly of the fox while staring at the thatched roof. A soft, familiar tune reached her ears—her mother's voice, low and haunting, rising and falling in the melodic lilt of an ancient song.

"Undar måna's vigil thur
Jhalan dansar, sufi mur."

The melody wrapped around Lucien, drawing her forward. She didn't understand the words; her mother had always refused to teach her their meaning. But their cadence spoke of things long past, of stories whispered in forgotten tongues.

Lucien pushed the thin blanket aside and stepped softly across the packed dirt floor, the chill biting at her bare feet.

Her mother sat by the fire, her back to Lucien, silhouetted against the pale light creeping in through the narrow window. The fire smoldered, its orange glow landing on the edges of the small wooden box balanced on her lap. Her fingers traced the carvings, lingering on symbols that seemed older than the room itself.

"I'll keep it safe," her mother murmured, her voice soft and distant.

Lucien froze, unsure if the words were meant for her or the shadows beyond.

> *"Håmran fayad, 'vur narra dyr,*
> *Sirr'an fi layl, thura myr,"*

Her mother continued singing. The tune faltered when Lucien's foot slid over a twig, producing a barely audible sound. Her mother's fingers paused, hovering over the carvings.

Lucien thought for just a moment that she should return to her bed, close her eyes and wait for morning. But as her mother resumed the tune, Lucien stepped closer, drawn by both the song and the sight of the box.

> *"Ay, warda min, threnn an'mir,*
> *Riyah'sa håmla, ard tajir..."*

Her mother's voice wavered, as if caught in a distant memory. The last verse hung unfinished in the air.

> *"Lakin qalb harib, khafa ghana,*
> *Jeldi firar, a'nan fa'ine–"*

Lucien reached out and placed a gentle hand on her mother's shoulder. "Mama."

Her mother spun around, eyes wide with something that looked almost like panic. Lucien took an instinctive step back when she saw her mother's face, and the moment shattered.

Blood, dry and cracked, clung to her mother's skin in streaks, matting the hair at her temples. It was smeared across her cheekbones and ran from her mouth down her neck, like war paint from some unseen battle.

"M-Mama, what's in there?" Lucien's voice quavered as she tried to be brave. The room seemed to close in, the heat of the fire becoming suffocating. The box in her mother's lap slipped and thudded onto the floor. Her mother's frightened expression eased, the panic melting into something unreadable, and she reached out with a cautious hand to touch Lucien's face.

The blood on her fingers was wet and cold. Lucien flinched as it slid across her skin. Her eyes drifted from her mother's face to the box on the floor. For a heartbeat, there was silence—save for the crackle of the fire and their ragged breathing—before her mother spoke, her voice rasping and weary.

"You don't want to know, Lucien. I promise you."

* * *

Those words clung to her long after they were spoken. The wooden box was always there. Its presence, and the way her mother held it when she thought Lucien and Cassius were asleep, was both comforting and unnerving.

The surface was dark and polished, the wood grain so fine and pronounced it seemed unnatural. Carved into its exterior were symbols—spirals that interlocked, forming shapes that told a story just out of reach of her understanding.

When the firelight hit just right, the carvings shimmered, their edges illuminating as if alive. The symbols reminded her of the ones she had seen etched into the stones of forgotten ruins on the outskirts of a village they had fled—symbols her mother had warned her never to touch.

Somewhere in the depths of her childhood memories, she recalled sitting by her grandmother's feet as the old woman spoke in hushed tones about "the sacred vessel" that must always remain hidden.

"It holds the weight of life and death," she had said, her bony fingers weaving the edges of a shawl. *"There are things that men would burn the world to possess. Your mother keeps it safe. One day, she'll tell you why—but pray that day never comes."*

Lucien had asked what was inside, but her grandmother only smiled, a flicker of sadness in her eyes, and kissed her forehead. *"What's inside isn't meant for little girls to know."*

At the time, Lucien thought it was nothing more than a bedtime story meant to frighten children into obedience. But now, the story lingered in her thoughts, filling her with trepidation.

The aura of the box was impossible to ignore. The air around it felt heavier, charged with an energy that made Lucien's skin prickle. It was as if the box recognized her—or waited for her.

When it wasn't clutched tightly in her mother's arms, it rested under her bed, hidden but never truly out of sight. A sentinel of secrets, it exuded a silent significance that pressed down on the room like a storm about to break.

* * *

One afternoon, when her mother was away at the market and Cassius was busy tending the fire, Lucien's gaze settled on the corner of the box, just visible beneath the folds of her mother's blanket. The flames seemed to dance across the carvings, pulling her forward.

She had been warned time and again to leave the box alone, but the urge to know what lay within was overwhelming. Lucien held her breath as she stepped lightly across the room. The wooden floorboards protested under her foot.

Her hand trembled as she reached for the box. The carvings felt warm, and she noticed her pulse in her fingertips as she touched the metal latch.

"Lucien. Stop!"

Her brother's voice cut through the air. She froze and lifted her hands slightly, hovering just over the closed lid before turning to see him standing behind her. His figure was partially cloaked in shadow, but his eyes burned with an intensity that sent a shiver racing down her spine.

There was something unfamiliar about him, something unsettling.

"Don't," he said again, his tone both commanding and hollow, as if channeling the rumblings of a storm. His gaze locked onto her hands with an unnatural stillness that seized her stomach. "You don't understand what you're doing."

Her heart hammered against her ribs, but curiosity burned too brightly. Something beneath the carvings called to her, a whisper she couldn't ignore.

"What are you so afraid of?" she said, her voice uneasy but defiant.

Cassius's jaw tightened. "It's not for you," he said, his voice dipping lower and softer. "Not yet."

Lucien turned her attention back to the box. Her fingers tapped open the latch, and it gave way with a quiet click. She raised the lid a crack while her brother looked on.

A glow emanated from within.

The light was soft, golden, and pulsed with the quick tempo of her breath. A chill swept over her, seeping into her skin. It was unlike anything she had ever felt—beautiful, yet unnervingly alive.

She began to raise the lid further, but before she could tell what was inside, the door to their house flew open and slammed against the wall like thunder.

Lucien scrambled backward as her mother stormed into the room. Her mother's face was ashen, her eyes blazing with a fury that bordered on terror.

"Get away from it!" she shouted, her voice sharp and cracking.

Lucien froze, her heart pounding as her mother crossed the room in two quick strides and snatched the box from the floor. Clutching it to her breast, her mother's breathing was ragged, her gaze darting between Lucien and Cassius.

Lucien opened her mouth to speak but couldn't find words to justify her actions.

Her mother's eyes filled with fear and grief as she looked at her daughter.

"Oh, Lucien," she said, her quiet tone a stark contrast to her entrance. "The time may come for you to know the truth, but that time is not today, young one."

Cassius avoided the confrontation, clenching his jaw as he walked back to his bed. His silence deepened the knot of unease inside Lucien.

Their mother's hands cradled the box with care, mindlessly

tracing the carvings as though seeking strength from the ancient symbols. She didn't say anything else—she wrapped it in a thick wool blanket and tucked it back beneath her bed. Out of sight but never out of reach.

Lucien sat on her knees, watching her mother move, questions burning in her mind but lacking the courage to voice them.

Her hesitancy told her that perhaps some truths were too heavy to bear.

* * *

Years passed, and Lucien became familiar with the cycle of fear and fleeing.

She learned to read the silent language foretelling their next move—days spent in quiet vigilance, fleeting glances between her mother and Cassius, nights blanketed in whispered songs and restless sleep, waking to her mother's absence and her quiet return before dawn.

By the time Lucien had reached the edge of adolescence, she knew how to blend into the background, to keep her curiosity at bay even as it gnawed at her. On sleepless nights, she would watch her mother sit by the fire, fingers tracing the carvings on the box with an expression that was half reverence, half sorrow. In those moments, Lucien felt the legacy of a story she was not part of—a history older than their current reality, older even than the whispered songs in her mother's breath.

10

England

When they finally arrived in England in 1010, Lucien was no longer a child but a young woman of seventeen—her beauty quiet and sharp, her eyes full of questions she had long since learned not to ask.

This land was warmer but carried the same darkness she had always known. The roads bore deep ruts, remnants of old war paths that snaked toward weathered fortresses. The horizon was jagged with the ruins of once-great walls, standing like the bones of a long-dead giant. Stories of raiders and kings buzzed around them, the echoes of Norsemen who had pillaged the coasts not long ago still fresh in the minds of the villagers.

The forests held their breath, ancient oaks and yews standing watch, their gnarled branches reaching out like crooked fingers. Lucien could hear whispers in the wind—stories of druids, pagan rites, and battles long past. The air felt charged with an energy that watched them, judged them, and demanded they go back to where they came from.

London, however, held a promise unlike the other places

they had fled—a hope that here, in the crowded streets, they might find anonymity and a chance to stop running. Her mother had promised as much when they crossed the Channel, silently hiding among the boxes in the thick wooden hull of a merchant vessel.

While Lucien and her brother gathered food in the market, their mother found them a new home in the back of a narrow cobblestone alley. She whispered something into the ear of a woman who opened the wooden door, then left quietly.

Her mother's absences at night carried an unspoken burden, and when Cassius began to join her, the silence between them grew thick. They would return at dawn, their faces pale and their pockets heavy with foreign coins stamped with strange sigils. Lucien wanted to ask where they had been, why they always seemed a step ahead of some invisible danger. But the look in her mother's eyes—haunted and tired—kept her questions silent.

London was new, but the watch of the villagers' eyes felt the same as it always had. Travelers were not unheard of here, but her family carried an air of otherness that even the busy streets couldn't smother.

As months passed, the glances in the market lingered longer. Lucien began hearing whispered stories as she gathered goods from vendors—murmurs about those who had disappeared. A drunk who regularly leered and shouted at passersby hadn't been seen in days. A shepherd's dog returned home without its owner. An old couple vanished, their home painted with sprays of fresh blood.

The disappearances cast a shadow over the bustling city that even the sun peeking through the fog couldn't dispel. Fear grew slowly, weaving through conversations like smoke, leaving the air heavy with apprehension.

Lucien could feel it pressing in on her whenever she walked through the market—a prickle of unease that clung to her like a second skin. When she dared to look at the villagers' faces, their eyes flicked to her, their expressions unreadable, yet she could sense their silent accusations.

You brought this upon us. Leave, or we'll all die.

"Will we really stay this time?" Lucien dared to ask her mother one night as the wind howled outside, rattling the shutters.

"We'll see," her mother said after a long pause, the promise she'd once made now sounding fragile.

Lucien's frustration simmered beneath the surface, like a flame carefully hidden but never extinguished. The whispers of secrecy that surrounded her life grew suffocating, and with each unanswered question, her resolve to break free strengthened.

Yet, amidst the cold familiarity of survival, Lucien finally discovered something she had never known before—friendship.

11

Friendship

Crooked Root Bridge sat at the threshold to the marketplace, its gray, weathered stones spotted with water sprayed from the stream below. The bridge marked the end of the market and the beginning of a path that led up a grassy hill to the ancient yew tree.

Lucien had first noticed two of the girls—about her age—perched on the ledge of the bridge when a third danced up to the others, singing a song about a knight who saved a girl and seemingly wedded her. The words of the tune didn't sit well with Lucien, but the joy in the girl's voice brought a smile to her face. The three of them laughed as the song concluded and walked arm in arm up the hill.

For weeks, Lucien had observed their brief, friendly gathering from a distance before they headed off, and she went for bread. One day, as she passed by the bridge, the sing-song voice of the girl with the chestnut hair called out to her.

"You there," the girl shouted in a tone as bright as the morning. "We see you watching us."

Lucien held her breath and looked away, her eyes wandering

among the stalls of food, hoping the girl wasn't talking to her.

"I like your necklace," the girl called again, stepping toward her. "Is that a fox?"

There was no denying her greeting any longer. Lucien turned toward the girl and feigned a smile, masking her discomfort at the kindness being shown to her.

"Ellyn."

Lucien looked in her direction, then awkwardly glanced up toward the distant tree.

"And you are?"

"Lucien," she said after a long pause.

Ellyn smiled and stepped within arm's reach of Lucien. She reached out and grasped the small fox charm between her fingertips, pulling it forward for a better look.

"It's cute. I used to have one like this, but it was a hare," Ellyn said, her light-brown eyes locking with Lucien's. "You should come with us."

Lucien looked down at her feet as Ellyn released the fox charm.

"Don't worry, you'll be back before your mother realizes you're gone," Ellyn said in a teasing tone. She reached down and took Lucien's hand. Ellyn's skin was soft, unlike anything Lucien had ever felt.

Before Lucien could protest, Ellyn was pulling her toward the bridge where the other girls stood, each holding a basket. As they pranced up the hill, the girls began singing.

> *"Sir John so brave with sword in hand,*
> *Rode back and forth across the land.*
> *A young maid locked in a tower high,*
> *He swore to save her or to die."*

Ellyn glanced over at Lucien and nodded, encouraging her to join in, but Lucien didn't know the words.

> *"The dragon fell at his mighty blade,*
> *The knight set free the grateful maid.*
> *You're mine now girl, no need to plead,*
> *And took her off upon his steed."*

Lucien's face scrunched at the last line, but Ellyn didn't seem to notice. As the girls spread their blankets on the ground beneath the tree and began pulling items from the baskets, Lucien looked up at its ancient branches. The trunk must have been twenty paces around. By the time Lucien had counted five, she noticed a grouping of headstones on the other side. She hunched as she stepped closer to inspect them further.

> **Thomas Wright** *Forever in the Grace of God*
> 951–979
> **Margaret Wright** *Her Love Lit the Darkest Days*
> 959–979

The larger markers sat side by side, with two smaller ones behind. Lucien stepped gently around them to read the epitaphs.

> **Farris Wright** *A Boy of Laughter and Light* 977–979
> **Beatrice "Betsy" Wright** *In the Embrace of the Lord*
> 979

Lucien's eyes began to tear as she read the last engraving.

Her grief didn't have time to surface as Ellyn's call broke the stillness of the moment.

"Over here, Lucien," she called. "Come join us."

Lucien sat down next to the girls and looked around at them to figure out what to do with her hands. They seemed so at ease, their movements unhurried, their voices weaving together in conversation like a song she didn't know. Their accents all held clipped vowels and lilting tones, and she knew her own voice must sound strange to them. It carried the traces of many lands, shaped by constant travel, but it was her mother's cadence that came through the strongest—a soft, deliberate tone that seemed so out of place here. She tried to hide it and emulate the tone of her new friends.

"It's quite beautiful here, no?"

All three girls looked at her, their heads turning in sequence toward Lucien. They laughed and carried on.

"Ellyn," Margery, the shepherd's daughter, said, her freckled, rosy cheeks dimpling as she grinned. "Did you hear what Tommy said about Becca and the miller's boy? Tommy said they were holding hands yesterday."

"Not this again," Becca groaned, though her lips twitched with amusement. She sat cross-legged, plucking at a blade of grass, her golden hair dancing with the light.

"It's true!" Margery insisted in a bright voice. "Apparently Gareth tripped over his own boot and Becca helped him up."

Becca shook her head as a smile crossed her face and her cheeks turned red.

"But after he had gotten back on his feet, he kept hold of her hand," Margery said, each word coming out quicker than the last. "Tommy said Gareth wanted to kiss her, but he chickened out—"

"No!" Becca broke in. "That's not what happened," she said, tossing the tuft of grass aside. "If he trips that much, he should keep his eyes on the ground instead of on me."

"Maybe he just likes the view," Ellyn teased, her hair sparkling as she tilted her head back and laughed.

Lucien's gaze held on Ellyn's smile, marveling at her confidence and easy grace. All three girls seemed so certain of themselves, so tied to this land and to one another.

"What about you, Lucien?" Margery asked, drawing Lucien into their circle of trust. Her green eyes sparkled with mischief. "Any boys tripping over their own feet for you?"

Lucien straightened her posture, unsure how to respond. "No," she said quickly, her cheeks warming despite the shade of the tree. "I mean, I've been too busy helping my mother to notice."

"You're always on a mission, head down, beneath that hood of yours," Ellyn said, shaking her head with a teasing sigh. "It's no wonder the boys are afraid to approach you—they probably think you'll run them right over."

Lucien's lips twitched into a smile, and she shrugged off the remark.

"Well, what if it wasn't a boy?" Becca said, leaning in conspiratorially. "What if it was Sir John? Tall, dark, and brooding, with a sword so sharp it could cut your heart in two?"

The other girls giggled, their voices rising with delight at the thought of being rescued by the predatory knight. Lucien laughed along with them.

"And you, Ellyn?" Margery asked, nudging her with a pointed elbow. "Have you met Sir John yet?"

Ellyn jokingly buried her face in her palms while Becca and

Margery leaned back in laughter. Lucien didn't get the joke, but she found herself relaxing nonetheless. She wrapped her knees in her arms as she continued listening to their stories, their teasing, their dreams. For the first time, she felt like she belonged.

On days dry enough for pleasantries, Lucien joined the girls under the tree for as long as possible. Its sprawling branches offered a reprieve from the prying eyes of townsfolk. On one especially delightful afternoon, when the scent of blooming wildflowers surrounded them, Lucien sat on a blanket with Becca and Margery, who were bantering about which flower was the best. Lucien had grown comfortable enough with them—and the sound of her own voice—to jump in freely.

"Obviously bluebells," she said. "Violet is my favorite color, so that makes it a clear choice."

"*Ew, Lucy,*" Becca replied. "They're so droopy and sad-looking." She raised her arm and dropped her hand at the wrist as a demonstration. Lucien hated being called 'Lucy,' but Becca was the only one who called her that, and she hadn't worked up the courage to correct her.

"Flowers only look sad when they die—" Margery stopped mid-sentence and looked past Lucien. "She *didn't.*"

Lucien and Becca turned to see what Margery was on about and saw Ellyn coming up the hill with a tall man behind her. Not quite a man, but certainly not a boy.

"Ellyn," Becca called, squinting against the sun as Ellyn approached with the handsome lad. "You brought your brother?"

Margery's grin widened as she sat up straighter, smoothing her skirt. "Thomas! You're back already?"

Thomas chuckled. His voice, low and warm, made Lucien's

face flush with color. "Don't sound so disappointed, Marge. I thought you'd be happy to see me."

"We'd be happier if you brought us something from *Spain*," Becca teased.

Following Margery's lead, Lucien straightened as well, brushing a lock of stray hair behind her ear as she eyed the newcomer. He was older—perhaps four or five years older than Ellyn—and his tanned skin and dark eyes complemented his easy confidence.

"Lucien, this is my brother, Thomas," Ellyn said as she gestured toward her brother. "He got back yesterday from Córdoba. That's in Spain," she added. "*This* is Lucien. She's new—came here with her mother a few months back. We like her." Ellyn smiled as she shifted her shoulders from side to side.

Lucien managed a polite smile, unsure of how to respond.

"Well, in that case, our new friend deserves a gift," Thomas said as he knelt on the damp grass, drawing their attention to the small pouch in his hand. From it, he drew a pinch of vivid crimson threads and extended his arm toward Lucien's face.

"This is for you," Thomas said, his voice low and inviting. "Smell it." She looked down her nose at his strong hand and raised her arm, her pale fingers hovering near his before taking the gift and bringing it to her nose. The fragrance was sweet yet sharp, rich yet fleeting—unlike anything she had ever known. She looked up at Thomas, who watched her with an amused smile.

"It's saffron," he explained, his voice carrying hints of pride. "It's worth more than gold. Smells like sunlight, doesn't it?"

Lucien nodded. Her lips parted as she touched the threads to the tip of her tongue. "It's bitter," she said as they all watched her. "Oh, and sweet too."

"Beautiful, isn't it," Thomas said, watching her enjoy the experience.

Becca and Margery giggled in delight, and Ellyn rolled her eyes.

Thomas gestured for them all to take a seat and removed a bag from his shoulders. Lucien watched his movements as he did so. He retrieved a large sheet of cloth, about the size of the blanket they had picnicked on. His eyes beamed with the thrill of his journey as he unfurled it. The girls all gasped at the deep indigos, rich crimsons, and gold-embroidered edges as they reached out to feel its magnificence.

"This is the finest cloth in all of Córdoba. It's woven with threads spun by silkworms and dyed with pigments so rare you can only find them in that region—"

"What's it like there?" Becca chimed in.

"Córdoba is the kind of place where radiance fills every corner, sun by day, and lanterns line the streets at night. The streets are paved with stones, set by craftsmen so skilled that you don't even feel the bumps as you ride across them." He paused, letting the awe settle over them before continuing. "The mosques rise high with domes that touch the sky, and libraries so large you can get lost in them. There's lush green everywhere..."

Lucien's heart pounded strongly enough that it affected her breath, each word awakening a longing so fierce it bordered on pain. She could see it all—the ivory towers, the vibrant gardens where fountains sang, the streets alive with people who had truly lived. It felt like freedom. She glanced at Thomas again. He was still recounting the city's beauty while she wondered what those streets must have felt like beneath his boots and how the sunlight might have illuminated his dark hair as he walked the streets.

"Do they really have libraries as large as cathedrals?" Margery whispered, her voice full of wonder.

Thomas nodded, a smile playing on his lips. "Filled with more books than you can imagine, with writing so elegant that each page is a work of art. Not just books though—scrolls, ancient maps, and poems that sing of love and loss."

The girls continued prodding him with questions that tumbled over one another. Lucien carefully placed the threads in her pocket and brought her fingers to her nose, smelling the earthy aroma clinging to her skin.

That night, as she lay on her bed, the cool draft seeping through the gaps in the wall, her mind drifted far from London. She walked sunlit streets. Her sandals glided across smooth cobblestones, heat from the sun rising through her toes. The air was alive with the sounds of a bustling bazaar— vendors calling out in rich, lyrical voices, the jangling of coins exchanged for spices and silks. A bright perfume of orange blossoms and honeyed dates filled her soul. She tilted her face toward the sun, a smile touching her lips as a salty breeze, carried on an imaginary wind, kissed her skin.

She stepped through a tiled doorway. Flittering hues of turquoise and gold danced over her. Inside, the light spilled across the space through carved wooden screens, casting intricate patterns on the brownish-red tile floor and dancing on the walls. Shelves on the far wall overflowed with books. Flowers lined the halls—vivid reds, yellows, and blues—set in elegant vases. Each object felt familiar. The flowers had come from the market—*no*—from her garden—that morning.

A fountain murmured in the courtyard, its water sparkling as it flowed over smooth marble. The stone cool beneath her fingers. Her silk robe brushed her ankles as she walked, and music from town reached her ears. She looked up at the streaks of wispy clouds above, and white flower petals blew across her view.

But reality returned with the sound of a door creaking and the rumblings of her mother's voice. The draft in the room grew colder, slicing through her dream. The cold whisper of fear crept back into her mind. The stories of Córdoba and its wonders were nothing more than a cruel taunt, a world out of reach behind the iron bars of her life's invisible cage. Lucien glared at the wooden beams above her bed.

"You're still awake," her mother said, her eyes darting to the window as though expecting a shadowed figure to crawl through. Her voice was steady, though Lucien could feel the bite to it, a tightness wound by years of vigilance. Lucien nodded but said nothing, swallowing the words that burned on her tongue.

* * *

The next morning dawned clear, the golden light of sunrise spilling across the town in soft, warm hues. Lucien sat on a low wooden stool just outside their home, her shawl wrapped around her shoulders. For once, the air wasn't heavy with fog, and the sky above was a pale, endless blue. It was a rare kind of morning, one that felt fragile and fleeting, like something too perfect to last.

The village began to stir around her, the muffled clang

of hammers ringing out in the distance, mingling with the bleating of sheep and a tangle of voices as people emerged to begin their day. The simplicity of it all filled Lucien with a bittersweet longing—an ache for a life unburdened by fear or secrecy.

A delicate buzz of dragonfly wings captured her attention. They flitted above the dewy grass with quick yet graceful movements. She watched one land, mesmerized as the morning light filtered through the translucent patterns of its wings, turning them into tiny, living mosaics.

For a moment, Lucien let herself imagine being as free as those dragonflies—untethered and unafraid, her life her own to shape. The thought of it all filled her with equal parts hope and sorrow. She knew it was nothing more than a fantasy, but today, it almost felt within reach.

The creak of the door behind her pulled her from her ruminations. She turned to see her mother stepping out of their home, her tired expression softening when she saw her daughter.

"You're up early," her mother remarked. She tied her apron around her waist as she glanced at the sky. "It's a beautiful morning, no?"

Lucien nodded, her gaze returning to the dragonflies. "I've made friends, Mother," she said quietly as she pointed toward the insects.

Her mother smiled, but there was a heaviness in her eyes that fogged the peaceful clarity of the moment. "Well, come inside," she said, gesturing toward the door. "The porridge will be ready soon."

Lucien hesitated, glancing once more at the dragonflies before rising to follow her mother. The serenity of the morning clung to her as she stepped inside. Her mother was already stirring the barley porridge, her steady movements filling the home with a comforting rhythm.

Lucien perched herself on the side of her bed, her fingers twisting as she watched her mother work. The moment felt lighter than most. Perhaps it was the sunrise, or the scent of saffron still lingering in her nose, but something emboldened her to finally speak.

"Mother," she began, her voice tentative yet determined.

Her mother paused her stirring, glancing over her shoulder. A smile rose on her face, and Lucien thought that maybe this time, things would be different.

"Yes, my love?" her mother asked, her tone cautious yet kind.

Lucien drew a deep breath, her heart beating faster as she began the conversation she had been turning over in her mind.

"I spoke with Thomas yesterday," Lucien began.

"A boy, huh?" her mother rhetorically questioned as she turned back to the porridge.

"He brought saffron and cloth from Córdoba. He said the city is beautiful—full of light and music." She paused, waiting for her mother's response, but the tightening of her mother's jaw worried her.

"Córdoba," her mother repeated quietly. She stirred the porridge with slow, deliberate motions. "What else did he tell you?"

Lucien pressed on, her words spilling out with the fervor of longing. "He spoke of libraries as large as cathedrals, gardens where fountains sing, and markets filled with silks and spices from faraway lands." Her voice softened, almost pleading. "I want to see it, Mother. I want to live somewhere warm, somewhere alive, where life isn't just survival." She paused, knowing her next words would cut her mother deep. Her mother had raised the spoon from the porridge and stood silently, waiting for her daughter to finish. "Maybe it's time I experience the world on my own."

At those words, her mother abruptly slammed the spoon onto the counter. Brown spots flung from it and stuck to the walls. She turned and looked at Lucien with fire in her eyes. "You don't know what you're saying, Lucien," she said, her voice trembling with a mixture of anger and sorrow. "You speak of dreams that cannot be."

"Why not?" Lucien challenged. She stood, her voice rising with each word. "Why must we live like this? Always looking over our shoulders, never staying in one place long enough to feel real. You said we could stay here, but we both know we won't. We never do."

Her mother's hands gripped the edge of the table, her knuckles whitening. "You don't understand what's out there. There are things—truths—you're not ready to know. I've kept you safe, Lucien. I've kept your brother safe. That is what matters, and that is why we live like this."

"What truths?" Lucien's voice cracked, frustration pouring out of her. "Why can't you tell me what we're running from? And what's in that box that you guard like it's life itself?"

Her mother's shoulders sagged; Lucien had hit a nerve. "It's not just what's inside the box," she said, her voice quieter now. "It's what it represents, Lucien. The choices I've been forced to make. Choices I've made to protect you."

Lucien adjusted her tone, hearing the pain in her mother's voice. "Why can't I decide my own fate?"

Her mother stepped closer to her and rested her hands on

Lucien's shoulders. "Because it's not your time. You're still young, Lucien. So, not yet."

Lucien stood still under the presence of her mother's hands and looked into her eyes. She watched them turn cold and narrow as she opened her mouth to speak again.

"Promise me you'll stay away from Córdoba," she said, not so much a request, but a command. "And promise me you won't speak to that boy again, Lucien."

Lucien's gaze dropped to the table in defeat. "I can't promise that," she whispered, her voice barely audible yet weighted with a resolve she'd never dared show before.

Her mother silently turned her back to Lucien, retrieved the wooden spoon, and resumed stirring. Lucien waited for a retort, a plea, or even anger, but none came.

The morning light streamed through the gaps in the shutters as she crossed the room, the warmth on her skin at odds with the chill that lingered inside. Her bed sat waiting in the corner, and though the day had barely begun, the effort of confronting her mother had drained her entirely.

She sank onto the worn fabric, her body curling instinctively as she lay down. Her eyes traced the beams overhead, their sturdy lines blurring as her mind wandered. She let her lids fall, and in the vague light behind them, the streets of Córdoba unfolded in vivid hues. She saw herself walking beneath the shade of fruit-laden trees, her fingers trailing across vibrant tiles and her hair glowing in the sunlight. The air was sweet with jasmine and citrus, and the comfort of the imagined world wrapped around her like a long-forgotten embrace.

As the daydream deepened, Lucien thought she heard her mother's voice, soft and distant, barely above a whisper.

"Perhaps, it's time…"

Lucien didn't open her eyes, unsure if the words had been real or just another fragment of her restless imagination. Either way, they lingered—sparking a glimmer of hope—as her breathing slowed, and the morning light stretched across the room.

12

Decision

While Lucien slept, her mother sat alone in the room, the wooden box resting on the table before her. The carvings glinted in the midday light breaking through the cracks in their thatched roof, their intricate patterns whispering of a power she had carried in silence for far too long. Her hands trembled as she traced the familiar lines, the magnitude of this decision pressing against her like a physical force.

The creak of the door startled her, but she relaxed, seeing Cassius standing in the doorway. He gave pause, examining the expression on his mother's face before stepping forward.

"Are you troubled, Mother?" he said softly, his voice still thick with the uncertainty of a young man trying to understand his life's purpose. He gestured toward the box. "Did you tell her?"

She closed her eyes and inhaled slowly through her nose, as if seeking guidance from somewhere beyond this space in time. "I had hoped there was another way," she admitted quietly. "You should understand that."

Cassius noticed Lucien on the far side of the room, her face buried under the thick blanket. He walked to his mother's side cautiously to avoid making a sound and waking Lucien. "You think she's ready?"

Her hand stilled, hovering over the lid of the box. "She'll never be ready," she said, her voice heavy. "No one ever truly is. But she wants to leave, Cassius. I can't let her. We need her with us. I had hoped to wait just a while longer." Her eyes lowered to the box in front of her as Cassius took a seat across from her.

"She's still a child," he said, his tone uncertain. "She hasn't experienced the world as it truly is. She's still—" He hesitated, searching for the word. "—wild. What if she refuses?"

"She can't," she whispered. "But if she does, then I'll lose her. Maybe forever," the admission threatened to shatter her resolve. "And if I don't do this, I might lose her anyway. This—" She gestured to the box. "This is ours, Cassius. It's not just a gift, not just a curse—" her eyes became glossy with tears as she inhaled a shuddering breath. "It's our family's responsibility. It always has been. It always must be."

Cassius shifted uncomfortably, his hands curling into fists. "You have me, Mother. We can protect it. Why not just let her go? Let her see the world, and someday she'll find us again."

Her head snapped up, her eyes narrowing. "Because the world will destroy her." Her voice softened, but the steel in her gaze remained. "This isn't just about her, Cassius. If she leaves, if she doesn't understand what we are, what we carry… she won't survive. And neither will we."

Cassius leaned back, the tension in his shoulders easing, though his expression remained conflicted. "She'll hate you if you don't let her choose," he said after a long pause. "She might hate us both."

His mother's whispers wavered, though she tried to keep them steady. "You're probably right. But I have no other choice."

The crackle of the fire filled the silence. Cassius stared at the box and rubbed his temples. Finally, he nodded. "If you're sure about this," he said, "I'll stand by you."

With his words, dread filled her stomach, realizing that it was the confirmation she needed. She reached across the table and took her son's hands in hers.

"Thank you," she whispered. "She will need you. I will need you."

"Tonight?" he asked, quietly pushing the chair back as he stood. His mother nodded up at him as he passed her. Her gaze stayed fixed on him as he stepped through the doorway. The sun silhouetted his face, its golden light spilling through the edges of his long hair. He turned back toward her with a half-smile and a subtle nod, then stepped outside.

The fire in her daughter's voice was a painful reminder of her own youth—before the curse, before the vial, before the blood. She, too, had dreamed of a life unburdened by fear. But that dream had been snuffed out long ago, buried beneath the demands of survival and the grim legacy set upon her.

She turned to examine the side of the box, scratches she was all too familiar with etched into the surface. The marks were left by her own mother's fingernails in her final moments. She had made the same choice for her daughter. The echo of that legacy now sat on the table in front of her.

Love and fear. The two emotions warred within her as she gently rubbed the scratched wood. She loved Lucien fiercely, loved her independent spirit and stubborn defiance. But fear loomed larger, whispering of the dangers that awaited her daughter outside of their fragile sanctuary. Her spirit, so bright and uncontainable, was slipping further from her grasp with each passing day. Lucien was growing restless, and that threatened to sever the bond between them.

She couldn't bear it.

Lucien was her only ray of sunshine in this endless burden. And then there was the box. The vial inside wasn't meant to be a responsibility that she alone carried forever. It was a part of them, an inheritance passed on for generations—a rite of passage tied to the blood that had kept their family alive and bound for generations.

She felt each undulating grain of wood as her finger traced the lid. Her own mother's words came to her, spoken long ago in the darkened corner of another distant home. "It's not a choice. It's inevitable. One day, you'll see." Perhaps she had felt the same turmoil speaking those words; surely she must have.

"I won't lose you," she muttered to no one. "I can't lose you."

She lifted the lid with her thumb and looked at the vial within. It was more than a promise of survival—it was the binding thread of their family. The thread that had tied her to her mother would now tie Lucien to her.

Even if Lucien hated her for it, even if it shattered the fragile trust between them, she would do what had to be done.

"I'm sorry, my love."

* * *

Lucien lay undisturbed on the bed, her breaths slow and even, her body curled into itself. The light shifted across her

100

sleeping form as the day waned, the fading sun casting long streaks of amber across the floor before retreating entirely into the cool stillness of night.

Her mother spent the day at the table, searching for answers where there were none. The fire's once steady crackle dwindled to a whisper. The air grew colder, the warm embrace of the morning hearth now only a lingering memory. Each moment brought her closer to the finality of her decision. Her hand trembled as she raised it from her lap, and with a deep breath, she reached for the vial.

Lucien would stay. Lucien would live. And the vial, as it had always been, would remain in their bloodline.

* * *

Lucien was roused from sleep by a thick, bitter taste on her tongue.

"Just a sip," her mother's voice croaked.

Gasping, she tried to push the liquid away, but her mother's hand was firm on her chin, holding her mouth closed. She sputtered, feeling some of it slip down her throat, burning as it went. She opened her eyes to find her mother leaning over her, a small glass vial in hand. Her brother watched from across the room; only his legs were visible among the shadows.

Scrambling, she pushed her mother's hand off her chin. "What are you doing?" she choked, her voice laced with fear and confusion.

Her mother's eyes were wide with desperation as she replied, "You're meant to stay—with us." She gestured toward Cassius, hidden in the corner.

Lucien's body spasmed, a wave of agony crashing through her. She screamed, her limbs thrashing uncontrollably as her skin burned, searing from the inside out. "What did you give me?" she begged, her voice splintering as the pain swelled and tightened her jaw. Her mother whispered soothing words that dissolved into the haze of torment. Lucien's heart thudded erratically, slowing as if each beat might be her last. Her vision tunneled, narrowing into blackness as she struggled to cling to the thin threads of consciousness. The last thing she saw was Cassius's worried face as he asked, "Will she be alright?"

* * *

Death, or something like it, pulled at her with a sickening silence. Time became elastic—expanding, contracting—slipping through her grasp like water. The blackest night paled in comparison to the depths of darkness around her. She felt herself being dragged by her wrist. A faraway glimmer of light pierced the abyss, illuminating the edges of the long corridor. But as Lucien reached for the light, a torrent of shadows surged forward, engulfing her in their relentless tide.

A roar filled her ears, and the world flipped violently, dropping her face-first onto the ground. The clanging of swords brought her to her knees as she looked across the grassy battlefield painted with sprays of violent red. She looked down at her hands to find them covered in the same red hue. A man in badly damaged armor ran toward her, a sword raised above his head as he shouted. Lucien saw the sword beside her and gripped its hilt as she rose to her feet. The weight of the blade felt familiar, though she had never held it before. She struck with precision, her movements seamless and brutal. His head rolled as his body collapsed to the ground.

Then, darkness once again. In a blink, she was somewhere else entirely, her surroundings impossibly vivid yet disjointed. She found herself running through a dense forest, her feet silent, her movements graceful, predatory. Ahead, a figure stumbled through the underbrush. She lunged, her vision blurring with hunger, and when the rush of blood hit her tongue, an abhorrent thrill coursed through her.

Another flash of black. She was in a grand hall adorned with gilded tapestries. A man of some importance slumped on a throne before her, his crown askew, his breaths ragged and wet, barely scraping past his lips. Lucien's hands reached out—no, someone else's hands. A final gasp, a quick crack, then silence.

The visions came faster now, each one a whirlwind of violence and vitality, despair and ecstasy. A woman's laugh rang out in a cavernous chamber, echoing like the chime of bells as she drained the life from a man crumpled at her feet. Flames licked at the sky while screams filled the air above a burning village. Pure redness on the cutting edge of a dagger and eyes deep with the rage of a feral beast, yet deeply human.

She stood in the ruins of a cathedral, its once-mighty arches crumbling, stones impacting the ground around her. A stained-glass window overhead held the figure of a boy grasping at a savior who looked out over a crowd shattered. Fragments of glass scattered like jewels across the stone floor. In her hand—their hand—the vial. It glowed with an otherworldly light, and it pulsed, each flicker illuminating the destruction around her.

Bodies lay strewn across the floor, some clutching at each other in their final moments, others frozen mid-fight, their terror etched into stone-like expressions. Among the smoke and dust, the odors of blood and lavender wrestled.

And then, movement—a hooded figure emerged from the shadows, silently moving toward Lucien. Its face remained obscured by the deep hood, but its presence was commanding, carrying an air of undeniable purpose. Without a word, a gloved hand extended, gesturing toward the vial. As if compelled by an unseen force, Lucien raised her arm and placed it into the waiting palm.

The figure produced a wooden box from beneath its robe, the surface of which was marked with symbols Lucien recognized. The carvings resonated with the same energy that pulsed from the vial. With practiced care, the figure opened the box, gently setting the vial to rest inside.

The lid closed with a click that echoed between the crumbling walls, and the symbols flared briefly before dimming into stillness. The figure paused, fingers tracing the carvings in a slow, deliberate motion, as if sealing it with an unspoken vow. Without a word, the figure passed the box back to Lucien, disappearing as swiftly as it had come.

The silence of the cathedral pressed in around her, heavy and absolute. But then, like the wind threading through broken glass, she heard the echo of her mother's song. The melody, distant and haunting, wove its way through the ruins, each note heavy with sorrow and warning.

> *"Undar måna's vigil thur,*
> *Jhalan dansar, sufi mur.*
> *Håmran fayad, 'vur narra dyr,*

Sirr'an fi layl thura myr,"

The stolen gift beckons,
Shadows dance, whispering loss.
Our cursed hands, never clean,
No absolution will ever be found.

"Ay, warda min, threnn an'mir,
Riyah'sa håmla, ard tajir
Lakin qalb harib, khafa ghana,
Jeldi firar, a'nan fa'ine"

Oh, my rose, this endless burden,
Evil seeks us, but never finds.
Through their suffering, and in ours,
We endure, this is the price.

The words floated to her, darkening her soul.

The coppery scent of blood flooded her senses, the taste lingering on her tongue, before she saw it. It covered her hands—warm and sticky—smeared across her forearms. It dripped from her fingers in slow, viscous trails, as it fell on the body crumpled beneath her.

13

Awakening

The man's vacant eyes stared at the ceiling, a gaping wound at his neck still oozing. She found a knife in her hand, still sticky with the man's blood. It slipped from her fingers and landed with a dull thud in the black pool beneath his head.

"What... what did I do?" she whispered, her voice barely audible over the screaming in her mind. Her eyes darted around the room, searching for answers, for some shred of reason to explain the horror beneath her.

This is my house, she thought, but the fragments wouldn't fit—her memories blurred and tangled with something foreign, something unreal. Cloaked figures, symbols, a vial, and a box. The same box her mother had been hiding.

The realization brought her to her feet. She stepped back from the scene beneath her, her body trembling. From the dark corner, her mother stepped forward, her face lined with a weariness that deepened the unease churning in Lucien's stomach. Her voice was low. "It's not what you think."

Lucien flinched, just realizing she wasn't alone. "Not what

106

I think? What do you think I think? There's a dead man—" Her voice cracked, her shaking hands pointing at the lifeless figure.

Her mother hesitated, her expression searching for the words to calm her daughter. "I know how you feel, Lucien. Your body—your mind—it's adjusting. It will take some time for you—" She paused, shifting her tone. "—I'm here to help you. I'll explain everything."

Lucien tried to make sense of what she was feeling. Her muscles ached with an unfamiliar strain, as though they were both weak and incredibly strong. Her entire being felt wrong, too heavy and too light all at once. The bitter taste returned to her mouth. Her hand flew to her lips as the memory resurfaced, vivid and real. Gasping awake, her mother's hand firm on her chin, forcing her to swallow. The burn as the liquid slid down her throat.

Lucien's muscles locked, her breaths coming faster. "You," she rasped, her eyes snapping to her mother, who still lingered in the shadows. "You did this."

"This…" she searched for a word that might provide her daughter comfort, "it is who we are, who we've always been, and who we will always be." Her mother's words were slow and deliberate, each one measured as though to ensure Lucien absorbed them. "The vision, the strength you feel, and yes, even the blood—it's part of it."

Lucien's stomach churned. "The vision," she whispered, her mind flashing with unreal images. Her mother's words pressed against her skull, too much and too little all at once. "What I saw—was that real?"

"I need you to trust me, Lucien. It's hard to explain," her mother admitted, her tone heavy with regret. "But yes. It's all real."

Lucien backed herself against the wall, shaking her head, trying to push away what her mother had just said.

"No. No, you don't get to do this—you don't get to control my life anymore. Just trust you? How can I trust you?" Her words came out faster, reigniting her anger. "You've never told me anything, Mother. And I've kept silent. I've always gone where you've pulled me, stuck in whatever shithole you've dragged us to!"

Her mother recoiled at the hatred boiling in her daughter. *It wasn't meant to be this way*, she thought.

"I did this because I wanted you to see the world as it truly is. And because I love you, and I couldn't let you leave without knowing."

Lucien's ferocity didn't wane, her emotions now a storm threatening to drown her. "Love and control aren't the same thing. You didn't do this because you love me—you did it to keep me here, didn't you?"

Her mother flinched, her composure cracking under the force of Lucien's accusation. "That's not true," she said, though her voice lacked conviction. "I did it because I love you. Because I couldn't bear to lose you. There are things, evil things, looking for us. And if you left before—"

"Stop! You've run from evil our entire lives," Lucien interrupted, her voice trembling with rage. "Now it's my turn."

Lucien couldn't stand in the room any longer. Her thoughts swirled with too many questions, too much anger, too much betrayal. She needed to get out. She needed air.

Her mother took a step toward her, but Lucien backed away sharply, her eyes blazing.

"Don't follow me," she warned, her voice low and trembling. "Don't try to stop me."

"Lucien, wait," her mother pleaded, her voice breaking. "Please. Just let me explain."

But Lucien had already crossed the gruesome scene, making her way to the door before her mother could say another word. The cool night air hit her skin as she stepped outside. The confusion she felt hadn't lifted, but the space around her felt less suffocating. She didn't know where she was going, only that she couldn't stay.

Behind her, her mother's voice echoed, fragile and full of sorrow. "I'm sorry."

Lucien didn't look back.

14

Withering

Lucien slammed the door with enough force to rattle the hinges as she stepped into the night, her mother's pleading words still ringing in her ears. The small street was silent, save for a dog barking in the distance. The cold night air flushed her cheeks but did little to temper the anger burning inside her. Each step away from the house felt like an act of defiance, a silent scream of betrayal.

How could she? The thought churned in her mind. Her mother's words—*"It's who we are, who we've always been"*—were chains, not a promise. Lucien's hands clenched into fists as she made her way through the narrow alleyways.

Every movement, every breath, felt strange—heightened, sharper. Her skin tingled with an intensity she couldn't understand. The undulations of the cobblestones beneath her boots seemed to shift under her weight, the uneven edges pressing through the soles as if the earth itself were trying to speak. She stopped in the middle of the road as she examined the soft edges of a speck of ash falling past her face. Looking toward the rooflines, she was struck by the clarity of each particle that emanated from the chimneys. The aromas of roasting meat, bay leaves, barley, and the skin of a chicken mixed with the fragrance of burning oak and hazelwood.

"Don't cry, sweet angel, Mama's here," a voice spoke.

Lucien turned around abruptly but saw no one. The empty street filled with the gentle cooing of an infant and the soft pats on its back. Sounds began to flood the street, threatening to drown her: two men arguing about how a plow ought to be fixed, the rough scraping of embers being spread in a hearth, a father reminding his son to rest before their journey tomorrow. Each fragment amplified and ricocheted inside her skull. A cold bead of sweat traced a path down her temple, her body trembling as it struggled to contain itself.

She stumbled forward, her fingers grazing the rough edge of a wall. The cool stone spoke beneath her passing palm. The gritty surface scraping against her skin was almost painful. Her throat tightened as the crisp air stung her lungs. The soft light of lanterns spilled across her path, so warm and golden, vibrating at the edge of her vision while shadows danced unnaturally, their shapes writhing and stretching as though mocking her unease.

Lucien stopped again, her heart pounding so loudly she was certain the whole world could hear it. And then, the melody rose from some long-forgotten place in fragments of her mother's voice and a deep, haunting hum.

"Lakin qalb harib, khafa ghana,
Jeldi firar, a'nan fa'ine."

Her mother had hummed that song for as long as Lucien could

remember, but now it carried a new meaning—a promise, a warning, or perhaps a curse.

This is the price.

She shook her head, trying to push the thought away, but the words settled in her chest like a stone. What price? Whose price? Her mother had carried the answers, but now it seemed those answers had been passed on to her only in cryptic pieces. The cloaked figure, the faces, the destruction—it was as though they belonged to her, even though she had never lived them. The head spurting bright streaks of red as it rolled along the grass, the wooden box, the shimmering vial. *You'll see the world as I do*, her mother's words surfaced. This wasn't a world Lucien wanted any part of.

A wave of dizziness rolled over her. She leaned against a rough brick wall, the realization crashing over her: her mother hadn't just betrayed her. She had changed her—turned her into something… unnatural. Lucien had always known her mother to be secretive, even controlling, but this—this was monstrous. Not just controlling her life but reshaping it, stealing away any future Lucien might have chosen for herself.

She drew a long breath through her nose and held her head between her knees. Her arms filled with a restless longing to be released, and her throat felt dry—not from lack of water, but from something deeper, something primal and wrong.

The moonlight filtered through the alleyway, bathing her in a silvery glow as Lucien worked to calm the disquiet in her heart. She couldn't go back—not to her mother, not to the house that now felt more like a prison than a home. Tonight, she would stay here, away from her mother's lies and manipulations. She pulled her knees closer to her chest, resting her head against the wall, willing the fire inside her to burn itself out.

For a time, she sat in silence, the occasional sounds of the city fading into the background. But as the hours crept by, a new sensation began to stir. It started as hunger always does, but quickly spread through her torso and coiled around her like a serpent tightening to end a life. Knowing there was no food to find at this hour, and without any money anyway, Lucien simply embraced the discomfort as she nodded off.

She opened her eyes when the pale light of dawn filtered through the cracks between the buildings and landed on her. Her limbs felt stiff, her head heavy, her senses dulled. The vibrant sharpness of the night before had faded, replaced by an aching void that made every movement a struggle.

Dragging herself to her feet, she stepped into the bustle of the city streets. London was waking, its people moving with purpose, unaware of the storm raging within her. She wandered aimlessly, her feet carrying her past shops and vendors setting up their wares. The smell of bread baking, once warm and inviting, now churned her stomach—the hunger inside her rejecting it.

Lucien scooped a handful of water from the rim of a barrel and splashed it on her face. As the water settled, she saw her reflection. Her porcelain skin and rosy cheeks were gone, replaced by a pale, gaunt face staring back at her, dark circles under her eyes, lips cracked and dry. Lucien barely recognized herself. Her hand moved to her stomach, where hunger coiled tighter, its grip unrelenting.

Her gaze flicked to a young man selling apples nearby, his face strikingly familiar. Thomas. His presence stirred something sharp and painful within. The tales of vibrant markets and wide, sunlit streets, a place that promised freedom and escape—everything she had longed for—now felt like a cruel joke. He represented everything she could never have, every dream her mother had torn from her hands.

I could go with him. Leave all of this behind, she thought, clinging to the idea like a lifeline. But even as the plan took root, her vision darkened with the shadow of reality. Ellyn's laugh echoed in her mind, the carefree ring of it now a witless taunt. She thought of her friends sitting beneath the yew tree, their conversations full of innocent dreams about love, marriage, children. Lives that would unfold naturally, untouched by the darkness now coursing through her.

She glanced back at Thomas. His tanned skin radiated in the soft light, his confident stride full of the knowledge of someone who had seen the world and belonged to it. He exchanged words with a merchant, his voice carrying across the square like a melody from a world she could never touch.

Lucien's heart ached with longing, but something darker churned beneath the surface—envy, sharp and cutting. She envied his freedom, his vitality, his unburdened existence. Rage waited like dry grass ready to ignite. She couldn't approach him. She couldn't risk him seeing her like this, couldn't bear to watch the light in his eyes turn to fear.

And yet, as the hunger clawed at her insides, the thought whispered in her mind: *What would it feel like to take his life and quiet the rage screaming within me?* A single step was all it would take to close the distance between them and bring her closer to release. Her fists clenched, her breath shallow as she fought to steady herself.

No. She turned sharply, forcing herself away from the square. She wouldn't—couldn't. The cobblestones blurred beneath her feet as she fled. The resolve carried her away from the square before her strength gave out. Her legs buckled, and she collapsed into a narrow alleyway. The world spun, her vision swimming as the hunger climbed up her throat. She pressed her back against the wall, her breaths coming in ragged gasps.

A coppery, salty taste filled her mouth. She reached up, wiping at her lips, and her fingers came away blackened and wet. Something like blood dripped from the corners of her lips, staining her chin. She swallowed and felt a rippling ache under her tongue. The serpent tightened its grip as her thoughts grew darker, more primal. The alley spun, narrowing into a tunnel of shadow and hunger.

Lucien's nails dug into her palms. The hunger whispered to her, seductive and cruel, urging her to give in, to take what her body demanded. But she refused. Even as her body betrayed her, even as the rage tore at her mind, she refused.

* * *

Lucien's senses returned slowly, each one heavier and more oppressive than the last. The pungency of hay and sweat hung heavy in the air, a suffocating mix that made her stomach churn. Her body felt as though it had been shattered and pieced back together—every muscle throbbed in protest at even the smallest twitch. The dim glow of a lantern broke through her eyelids as it swayed gently from a beam above. Its flickering light painted restless shadows across the wooden walls of the stable.

"You're awake."

The voice was close—her mother's voice, calm and soothing,

though it carried an undercurrent that worried Lucien. She scanned the dimly lit barn as she twisted her head toward the sound. Her mother knelt a few feet away, her face half-hidden in shadow.

Lucien tried to sit up, panic rising as her mind grasped for answers. Straw pricked her palms, and her arms were too weak to hold herself upright. She collapsed back into the straw, breathing in shallow gasps from the exertion.

"Where…?" she croaked. Her throat burned at the word, dry and raw. She winced at the sound of her own voice.

"You're safe," her mother said, rising slowly to her feet. The sharp angles of her face were unreadable in the lantern's glow, a mask of composure that revealed nothing. "That's all you need to know right now."

The words brought no comfort.

"How did I get…" The question broke apart, the effort of speaking too much for her fragile state.

Her mother stepped closer, her footsteps scratching the hay against the splintered wood, and placed a cool hand against Lucien's burning forehead. "You've been through a great deal, but you'll feel better soon."

Lucien's gaze shifted past her mother, drawn to the dim corner of the stable. There, upright yet unmoving against a post, was a man. His head hung low, but he was still breathing. His face sparkled with sweat, and his lips quivered as they pulled in air. The man's wide, bloodshot eyes glared at Lucien for a moment before his head sagged toward the ground.

Behind the captive, another figure stood in the shadows. "Cas—what are you doing?" she cried, Lucien's nose tingling as tears filled her eyes.

He said nothing in response.

Her mother's voice broke the silence.

"This is necessary," she said, stepping toward the man with her arms swinging gently at her side. A glint of light on metal caught Lucien's eye, and her breath hitched as she recognized the object in her mother's hand—a dagger.

Lucien had seen it before, always at her mother's side, its hilt wrapped in dark, weathered leather. The intricate etchings along the narrow blade hinted at stories far older than any Lucien knew of.

Her mother now stood beside the man, gripping his jaw with her hand to tilt his head back. The man stirred, his eyes fluttering as he tugged at the ropes binding his hands. A low, broken sound escaped his throat, barely more than a whimper.

"You need this to survive," her mother said as she pressed the point to the man's neck. The steel kissed his skin, and a thin line of blood began to trickle down his neck. "The hunger will only get worse. You've felt it already, haven't you? The ache. The need."

Lucien's nostrils flared as the scent of blood hit her. Her throat burned, and the ache beneath her tongue returned. Her hands grasped at the straw in desperation.

"No," she whispered. "I won't. I can't."

Cassius moved from the shadows, untying the man's hands before leading him forward. His movements spoke of familiarity.

Lucien's gaze darted between the man, her mother, and her brother, her heart pounding.

"Cas—" she rasped, the half-spoken word filled with equal parts disbelief and plea. But her brother didn't look at her.

Her mother stepped aside, and Cassius let the man fall to

his knees in front of Lucien.

Her mother spoke again. "If you resist, it will destroy you, slowly and painfully. Your body cannot sustain itself. You must take his life. This is the only way."

"I'd rather die," she spat, her voice raw with defiance. She tried to push herself back, to create some distance between her and the man about to die, but her body rebelled. The scent of blood wrapped around her and refused to release her.

Her mother sighed, a sound tinged with pity. "You say that. But the hunger breaks us all. It will break you too." She leaned over and pressed the edge to the man's neck again, the wound deepening as blood spilled freely in a steady stream. "Let it take you, Lucien. Only then will you understand."

"Stop!" Lucien screamed. The hunger roared in her ears, drowning out every thought. Lucien clutched her head, attempting to silence the terror that consumed her. Her limbs twitched violently, her muscles straining against her will as they dragged her forward, inch by inch.

Her mother stepped back, leaving the man slumped and bleeding. The lantern's light fell over the blood pooling on the ground, and Lucien's pupils dilated as the scent enveloped her completely. The ache beneath her tongue became unbearable, the strange openings pulsing and alive, slick with heat and pressure.

She fought against it, her nails scraping against the wooden boards beneath her, but the primal force within her was too strong. With a desperate cry, she lunged forward, her hands seizing the man's shoulders as her tongue found the wound on his neck.

The first taste of blood was electric, a jolt that shot through her body like lightning. It burned going down her throat, searing through her veins, but it also filled her with a vitality so overwhelming it drowned out everything else.

When it was over, Lucien pulled back, gasping for air. The man hung limp in her grasp, his skin pale and lifeless. Blood stained her lips and hands, dripping onto the floor in dark rivulets. She stared at his body, revulsion dawning as the crushing truth of what she had done settled over her like a shroud.

Her mother knelt beside her, placing a steadying hand on her shoulder.

"You see now, don't you?" she said softly, her voice almost kind. "This is what we are. This is what it means to survive."

Lucien tore herself away, stumbling backward until her shoulders hit the stable wall. Her breath came in ragged bursts, her hands gripping the rough boards behind her as though they could anchor her to something solid. Her tongue ran over her lips, the metallic taste still clinging to them. Her voice broke as she rasped, "What have you done to me?"

Her mother stood silently at first, her expression unreadable in the dim lantern light. Slowly, she reached inside her cloak and withdrew a small glass vial. The dark liquid within shifted as she turned it on display to her daughter. She held it up, her grip firm yet reverent, as though the object in her hand held far more than its fragile form suggested.

"This," her mother began, her voice deliberate and heavy with meaning, "is the reason for everything. The reason for what you feel, for what I've done, and for the life we've lived." She stepped closer, holding the vial between them. "The blood it contains is not like any blood you've known."

Lucien's eyes fixed on the vial, her body tense but too

drained to react further. She managed a question, her voice hoarse. "That's what you poured down my throat?"

Her mother's gaze softened as she nodded. "When you drink from it, you see visions. They're real—fragments of the past, truths tied to the vial itself. I've seen them myself, and so has Cassius." She glanced toward her son with a knowing smile. "But that's just the beginning—"

Lucien swallowed hard, the images from her vision flashing through her mind—the destruction that felt too vivid to be anything but real.

"—Then comes the rage."

Lucien quickly glanced up to meet her mother's eyes.

Her mother continued despite the pained look on her daughter's face. "As the visions fade, your body desperately seeks blood. So—"

"So I really killed him, too? The man in our home?" Lucien said, hardly believing the words coming from her own mouth.

From her earliest memories, Lucien had longed for a life without chaos, a quiet existence where the world's cruelties didn't reach her doorstep. She had never sought conflict, let alone inflicted harm. As a child, even stepping on a spider filled her with guilt, her instinct always to release it outside rather than crush it. She once nursed an injured bird for weeks, feeding it crumbs and water despite her mother's sharp admonitions that it wouldn't survive. Her brother had teased her endlessly for being "soft," but she wore the label with quiet pride.

And now—now, her hands and face were stained with the blood of two men, their lives taken by her own actions, even if she hadn't meant it.

"Yes," her mother said softly, her voice devoid of judgment.

"And you performed well."

Lucien flinched at the words, the pride in her mother's tone striking a nerve.

Her mother pressed on. "There's more. The blood transforms you. It makes you stronger, faster, and heightens your senses to a level you could never have imagined—"

The sound of ants scurrying in a line, avoiding the pool of fresh blood, briefly crawled into her ears.

"—any injury you sustain will heal faster than you'll believe. Sickness, age… they're no longer a threat to us. You've become something far beyond human, and to stay this way…" She paused, hoping the meaning of her words would sink in. "…we do what must be done to keep the vial's curse at bay."

Lucien swung her arm forward, pointing at the vial, her jaw tightening.

"And this is a good thing? I'm cursed to a living nightmare so I don't get sick? I don't want any of this!" Tears welled in her eyes, spilling over as she screamed, her voice thick with anguish and fury.

"Wait, Lucien. Please." Her mother's voice softened, almost pleading. "It's not about what you want. It's about survival—for everyone."

Lucien tilted her head in confusion, waiting for something that made sense of the situation.

"The vial gives us the means to endure, to survive, no matter what danger we face so that we can keep it safe."

"Safe?" Lucien's voice rose again, her anger breaking through her exhaustion. "You're talking about something that turns us into… monsters, or whatever the hell we are, and you're worried about keeping it safe?"

Her mother didn't flinch. "Yes," she said firmly. "For

centuries, our family has been responsible for protecting this vial. My parents entrusted it to me and gave their lives to see that it didn't fall into the wrong hands."

"Centuries…" Lucien whispered, the word heavy with implications she couldn't yet grasp.

"There are people out there, Lucien—evil people—who want this." She raised the vial to Lucien's eye line. "They desire the power it brings. They would use it to build an army, to wreak havoc on the world."

Lucien's laugh was bitter, almost hysterical. "An army? Mother. There's hardly a ladleful of liquid in there. Do you have a barrel of mysterious blood somewhere I don't know about?"

Her mother's eyes darkened. "It's never-ending." She released the clasp holding the lid in place and turned the vial over, spilling its contents onto the floor. After the last drop fell, she righted it. "Just watch, Lucien."

At the pointed bottom of the vessel, a dark red color began to appear, slowly filling the vial to the brim. Her mother re-sealed it as Lucien watched in astonishment.

"Like I said, never-ending. And that's why it must never fall into the wrong hands."

Lucien's mind reeled, the room seeming to shift off-kilter. She glanced back at the vial, watching the dark liquid within pulse with a life of its own. "Then why not just destroy it or bury it somewhere it can't be found?" she asked, her voice desperate. "If it's so dangerous, just be done with it."

Her mother's expression tightened, weariness flickering across her face. "I've tried," she said quietly. "I once felt as you do now, and came to the same conclusion; that destroying the vial would rid me and the world of this curse. So I tried, again and again. I've broken blades and hammers, even smashed boulders against it. Every time, the vial remains whole and untouched. And you've felt its presence, haven't you? It pulls at you. No matter how deep I bury it, I find myself digging it back up without realizing it. It always calls me back."

Lucien sagged against the wall. "So this is it, then?" she said bitterly. "This is how we live? Hiding in the shadows, killing to survive?"

Her mother stepped closer, placing her hand on Lucien's blood-smeared face. "Yes," she said. "The fate of the world relies on it. We stay anonymous. We move when we need to. We kill when we must. But we survive, Lucien. For the vial's sake, we survive."

Lucien shook her head, filled with a resignation she didn't know what to do with.

Her mother hesitated, then withdrew to retrieve the dagger from the ground next to the warm corpse. She wiped it clean on her sleeve and returned to her daughter.

"This will make it easier," her mother said, flipping it, catching the tip in her fingers, and pointing the handle toward Lucien with an outstretched arm. "It's sharp, precise… discreet, and has served me well. Now, it's yours."

Cassius, who had been silently observing, looked on with a hint of jealousy as his mother handed Lucien the weapon.

Lucien stared at the dagger, her hands shaking as she reached out to take it. The weight of it settled in her palm, the reality of her mother's words now enveloping her.

"I didn't ask for this," she whispered, looking into her mother's eyes.

"None of us asked for this," her mother replied. "But it's ours. And now, it's yours. Learn to carry it, Lucien. Learn to live with it."

Anger, grief, and betrayal swirled inside Lucien, building into a storm, but she couldn't find the words to speak.

Her mother stepped back, lowering her chin as she pulled her hood over her head. "Take the time you need. Process this. When you're ready, come home."

Lucien didn't move as her mother and brother both turned and walked away, the lantern light casting long shadows in their wake. The stable fell silent, save for the sound of Lucien's shallow breathing and the pattering of the ants' legs. For a long time, she stayed there, unable to move, unable to think, the vial's dark presence lingering in her mind.

15

London Turns

The morning fog curled along the cobblestones, sweeping away the remnants of the night's horrors. Lucien sat on the lip of a stone bridge, replaying the terrible images in her mind. Droplets kissed the bottom of her boots as water found its way through the rocky riverbed. The streets were quiet, save for the distant murmur of a church bell marking the end of morning mass.

Lucien pulled her hood forward. Her dark hair clung to the moisture on her forehead. Her face was pale—more so than it had been even in her sheltered life before—and luminous in the washed-out light. Her lips, once soft and pink, were now a striking crimson, flecks of dried blood clinging to the corners. Her hands rested on the cold stone ledge, pale knuckles standing in contrast to the damp surface. Her small form, wilted beneath the weight of her damp cloak, betrayed her age. She was only seventeen, but her cavernous eyes spoke of something far older.

Footsteps approached, but Lucien didn't turn to see who it was. The sound carried purposefully toward her through the fog, growing louder until Cassius emerged. The mist had darkened the fabric clinging to his shoulders, and droplets of water beaded on his wavy hair. He was taller than she by several inches, his presence looming heavily over her, yet strangely comforting.

"You've been out here for hours," he said softly, stopping a full pace from his sister. "I thought you'd try to run."

Lucien didn't look at him. Her eyes stayed on the river below, watching the gentle ripples as though they might offer some answer.

"I thought about it," she said, her voice low. "But where would I go?"

Cassius stepped closer, taking a seat beside her. He brushed off his knees and rested his forearms upon them, his gaze sweeping over the water.

"Nowhere far enough," he said. "And you'd have to come back eventually."

Her jaw tightened, her words cutting through the still air. "You sound just like her, you know that?"

"She's not wrong," he replied calmly. "I know you can sense it."

Lucien turned to look at him for the first time, her expression a mix of exhaustion and bitterness.

"When did it happen?" she asked, her voice sharper than she intended. "When did she turn you?"

Cassius exhaled, a cloud escaping his lips into the cold air.

"Not long before we traveled to London."

Lucien's stomach twisted.

"You didn't think to tell me?"

He tilted his head slightly, his calm demeanor unshaken.

"Would you have believed me?"

A sigh of frustration escaped Lucien's nostrils.

Cassius stared off into the white abyss before confessing, "She said we were going 'hunting.' Remember that? We were gone for three days? You must have been so scared by yourself for such a long time."

"I thought you both were dead." The memory of that week filled her with dread. "I thought that maybe you missed a fox and hit Mother with the arrow instead. Maybe she died in your arms, and you starved alone in the woods," she said, letting out a soft laugh.

"That's pretty bleak, Lucien," he smiled at her. "Well, we weren't hunting. Not really. She took me to a cave, deep in the woods, and told me everything. So I chose to drink from the vial."

"Chose," she muttered.

"After I woke, the visions were still haunting me. My body felt like it was going to explode, and my mind couldn't catch up." He paused, checking to see if Lucien was still angry. "Mother was scared too—I could smell that in her. She led me back through the woods to that cobbler's house. You know, the one with the round door?" Lucien nodded in recognition. "His wife was hanging their clothes in the garden, and she was my first—" He took a quick sip of air through his nose and continued. "—I didn't even realize Mother had gone into their house. As I crept over the fence, the lady just kept putting clothes on the line, not realizing how close she was to death. She didn't even scream—" His voice cut off, and Lucien waited patiently for him to finish. "—Mother came back outside, and I guess she killed the cobbler too. It was all so quiet," he said. Lucien glanced over at him, seeing his eyes beginning to well up with tears.

Her lips parted, but no words came.

Cassius leaned back, shaking off the memories that haunted him. "She knew what she was doing. She always does. You were meant for this, just like I was. Fighting it won't change that."

"Cas, I'm sorry."

"Why?" he asked, pushing down his emotions. "I'm not. I didn't want to kill a sweet old woman. But now I only take the ones that look like they'll put up a good fight."

"And that makes it okay?" Lucien questioned, softly shaking her head.

"For me, it does. This is our responsibility, Lucien. You have to find a way to live with it. Just give it some time. Whether you like it or not, this is what we are."

Lucien watched her reflection distorting in the water below.

"I feel it inside of me," she whispered. "Shifting in my veins. The rage, the hunger. It's like I'm losing myself."

Cassius was quiet for a moment, gave a nod of understanding, and then said, "You're not losing yourself, Lucien. You're becoming something else. Something more than human."

She shot him a sharp glance. "I think you mean something monstrous."

He shrugged.

"Call it what you want. But you can't deny what you feel. You've never been this alive before, have you?"

Lucien recoiled at his words, shaking her head.

"Alive? This doesn't feel like living…" She trailed off.

Cassius smiled and pointed out into the fog.

"See the people way over on the other side of the river, coming out of the church? They're going to go to the market soon, and at least half of them will be at the pub tonight. Their lives are meaningless, just flowing like water out to sea."

Through the dense fog, the steeple was barely visible. Lucien followed her brother's gesture, her gaze narrowing as she tried to focus. At first, she saw only blurred movement, indistinct shapes shifting through the haze. But then the details emerged, like looking through a veil of lace. She leaned forward, and everything sharpened into clarity. Sisters kissed each other goodbye, and men exchanged firm handshakes.

"They're so far away," she murmured, her voice tinged with awe. "But it's like they're standing right in front of me."

Cassius sighed, bellowing a cloud into the damp air.

"Like I said, more than human. It's difficult at first, but give it some time. You'll learn to embrace it."

Her voice rose, frustration breaking through.

"Embrace what? That we're cursed? That we have to live like this forever?"

He met her gaze, his expression steady.

"That we have a purpose. A responsibility. To keep the vial safe, to protect it from those who would use it for things far worse than you or I can imagine."

Lucien laughed bitterly, the sound echoing faintly in the stillness.

"For how long? Centuries? Is that how long Mother has been protecting it?"

Cassius's lips twitched into a faint smile, though the expression didn't reach his eyes.

"Yeah, I'm not sure. She's never said. I asked once, and she just smiled at me like I was a child." He paused, his voice softening. "Maybe it's better not to know."

Lucien sagged forward, her shoulders heavy beneath the inescapable truth of his words. "I don't want to be like her. I don't want any of this."

"You don't have to want it," Cassius said, standing and brushing the rain from his shoulders. "But it's yours now. And whether you believe it or not, you're stronger than you think. You'll see that soon enough."

Lucien didn't look at him as he walked away, his figure retreating into the fog.

"Come home when you're ready," he called back. "Mother's waiting. She's making biscuits," the tone in his voice rising with each word.

He almost drew a smile from her, but it flickered out before reaching its full potential. She stared at the water. The hollowness inside her mind ached, an emptiness that no amount of blood—or time—could fill.

Lucien's fists unclenched as she straightened. She felt the sharp sting in her palms where her nails had dug deep, but the pain grounded her back into the present.

I will not let this curse define me.

A plan had begun to form—a desperate, fragile thing, one tempered by a touch of resolve. She couldn't undo what had been done, she couldn't return to the life she had lost, nor live the life she had wanted, but perhaps she could find purpose.

Fragments of overheard conversations ran through her mind—stories whispered in the town square about vile beasts lurking among them. Not beasts like her or her family, but men whose actions made monsters seem tame. Men who took pleasure in the suffering of others, whose cruelty left scars deeper than a scythe's kiss.

She thought of the bastard who struck his wife in the market for choosing the wrong bread, the desperate fear in the woman's eyes as she apologized for the beating she hadn't earned; the landlord, fat from overconsumption, standing at the edge of a family's field and ordering them from their home for failing to pay their due, their cries swallowed by his cold indifference; and the thief she saw snatching a coin purse from a mother's hand, imagining the terrible groans her children's stomachs must have made that night.

But if blood was the price of survival, then she would take it only from those who deserved to lose it. The wicked. The cruel. Those who had stolen lives and shattered others. They deserved to feel the impact of the pain they inflicted, to understand what it meant to be powerless. Her hands would never be clean again, but perhaps, in this way, she would find some balance in the darkness.

Lucien stood, water dripping from her chin and hair, indistinguishable from the tears she had cried. A familiar face stared back at her from the river below.

"I'm sorry, Lucien," she whispered.

She turned from the bridge, the fog closing around her like a second skin. The city stretched before her, its labyrinth of shadows and secrets waiting. Somewhere in that darkness, she would find a way to live with herself—even if it meant walking deeper into the night.

* * *

Less than a year after her turning, cracks were already showing in her plan for justice. Rumors built throughout London like wildfire, carried in hushed whispers between women and incredulous recountings by men. Mostly-true warnings surfaced in children's songs:

Blood on the cobbles, a shadow unseen,
Prowler in the dark with hands unclean.
Run inside, cold nights bring dread.
Old man Jasper lost his head.

The first time Lucien heard that song was after the body of a stableman had been discovered, splayed out in a doorway, still holding an axe in his strong grip. His horses had alerted a neighbor to the crime. The man's skin was a pale blue, and his head rested in a pile of manure.

More than once, Lucien had witnessed the man cursing a horse and beating it in the ribs with a hammer while attempting to shoe the animal. So she went to his stable on a night when hunger was her companion.

Now, he was dead.

He wasn't her first nor her last victim. Others, equally deserving, had been found as well. Each corpse was a call to arms against an unseen predator. The townspeople watched the shadows with wary eyes, hands tightening around axes and pitchforks. After a while, the children stopped playing in the streets, their laughter replaced by an uneasy quiet. Lucien had been careful. She chose her prey deliberately, but fear in the townspeople grew, even though the dead had deserved their fate.

Every night, as she slipped through the cobbled streets under the cover of darkness, she felt the watchful eyes of the village closing in. The tension was palpable, like the crackling air before a storm. She no longer felt the fleeting satisfaction of righting wrongs in her kills—only the performative act remained, driven by hunger and rage.

One evening, as she made her way to the outskirts of town,

the sound of voices stopped her in her tracks. She pressed herself into the shadows to listen.

"It's the devil himself," an older man muttered. "A monster that walks like a human."

"A demon," another hissed. "Or worse, a witch. We've got to do something before she takes the children."

Lucien's stomach churned.

It wouldn't be long before that fear turned into action.

Lucien returned home, her mind racing. The villagers were closing in, their suspicion thick and encroaching. Her mother's voice greeted her as she stepped inside, calm and measured but tinged with frost.

"They suspect us, don't they?" her mother said, seated at the small table by the window. She didn't look up, her focus fixed on the vial resting in her palm, its crimson liquid mirroring the flickering light of the lantern.

Lucien didn't answer. She crossed the silent room and sank into a chair across from her mother.

"I've only killed those who deserve it," Lucien said, her voice filled with annoyance. "The world is better off without them."

Her mother's lips curved into a humorless smile.

"Perhaps. But the world doesn't care about your intentions, Lucien. They only see the bodies we leave behind."

Lucien looked out the window. The curse had placed the rope around her neck—a noose she once thought she could escape. But now, the town's growing fear had tightened it, ruining any chance of escape.

Her mother's voice broke the silence. "I warned you, Lucien. This is what happens when we stay in one place too long."

"Maybe you're right."

Lucien thought of the countless times they left everything

behind, fleeing in the night.

"London isn't safe anymore," Lucien said, the words tumbling out. "The whispers are getting louder. They'll come for us eventually."

She hesitated, her thoughts drifting to the stories Thomas had shared. "What if we left? Córdoba," she added, her voice soft but insistent. "It's nothing like here. We could disappear in the crowds, start over. It's a city of learning, of freedom—"

"A city?" Her mother cut her off, her tone sharp. "Córdoba is just like London—a place where secrets are currency, and trust is as fleeting as the rain."

She shook her head firmly, her fingers gripping the surface of the table. "No, Lucien. We've lived this long because we've avoided places like that. You think it's safe to hide among the masses? It's not. Too many eyes. Too many ears."

Lucien's shoulders sagged, frustration bubbling beneath her skin. "Then where? If not London, if not Córdoba, where can we go? We can't just keep running forever!"

Her mother's gaze softened, though her voice carried the weight of experience. "We go back to what worked before—small villages, places where life moves slowly, where people don't ask too many questions. Constantly moving, like when you were young."

Lucien's heart sank. The thought of slipping back into that transient life, where no place was ever truly home, filled her with dread.

"I don't want to live like that again," she said, her voice trembling. "I want… something more."

Her mother exhaled sharply, the years of running etched into her weary features.

"We don't get to want, Lucien. Not anymore. It's survival

now. You'll understand in time."

"I'll never understand," Lucien muttered under her breath, but her mother either didn't hear or chose to ignore her.

Her mother pushed back from the table and stood, the decision made.

"We leave tomorrow. Start packing."

Lucien swallowed the lump in her throat and nodded, the flicker of hope she'd clung to extinguished.

Her mother hesitated for a moment, as though searching for something else to say. But instead, she turned and began clearing the table.

As Lucien climbed the steep, narrow stairs and lay down on her cot, staring at the darkened beams above, even as she tried to imagine Córdoba's sunlit streets, the image dissolved, replaced by the gnawing certainty that her mother was right.

They were destined to run, always.

* * *

While she slept, she thought she dreamt of smoke curling around her. In her dream, she walked through a field in flames, spewing the rich scent of barley toward the sky, and her eyelids danced with an orange glow. A burning sensation filled her lungs, and she woke in a fit of coughing.

Cassius, it seemed, was already awake, yelling, "Fire! Wake up!"

The fire had already taken hold, the roar of the flames pressing in around her, punctuated by the explosion of sap popping in the dry wood. For a moment, she considered that this might still be a dream, but the vivid tenacity of the inferno rising up the walls of her small attic room was too real to be anything but.

"Mother!" she screamed as she stumbled to her feet, smoke sifting up through the planks beneath her toes. Her heart pounded, drowning out the noise as she fumbled toward the narrow staircase, her bare feet scalded by the heated floorboards.

The sight below stopped her cold. Flames licked hungrily at the kitchen walls, and the pot which hung over the fire spewed thick black plumes into the room.

The firelight illuminated Cassius, his face pale and wide-eyed as he stood near the base of the stairs.

"Lucien! Get down here. Hurry!" he shouted, his voice cutting through the din.

"Where's Mother?" she choked out as she scrambled down the stairs, the wooden steps cracking and threatening to give way beneath her.

Cassius didn't answer immediately, his gaze darting toward their mother's bedroom, where the flames raged fiercest.

"She's still in there," he finally said, his voice tight.

Lucien's stomach dropped, and her body moved before her mind caught up. She pushed past him, the heat scorching her skin as she staggered forward.

The sound of villagers reached them—angry, determined voices shouting from beyond the inferno.

"Burn it down! Send them back to Hell!" The realization cut through Lucien's panic with sharp, unforgiving clarity: this fire was no accident.

Her mother's face emerged from the smoke, eyes fierce, mouth set in a grim line.

"Lucien, get out. Now." Her voice cut through the roar of the flames as she pulled herself through the smoldering door frame.

Together, they moved toward safety, hands stretched out to navigate through the suffocating blackness.

A sharp crack split the chaos, and a beam splintered from the ceiling, crashing down and pinning their mother to the ground. She screamed as she fell. Lucien had been knocked to the ground but narrowly avoided being crushed as well.

"No!" Lucien screamed, scrambling upright. She approached the glowing beam atop her mother, her fingers scrambling desperately at the charred oak.

"Cassius, come quick," she begged. He was at her side before her plea was finished. The brother and sister heaved with their entire beings, but the beam didn't budge.

"We can get you out," Lucien cried, as hope poured out with each breath. The thought of leaving her mother here, alone, to face the flames was unthinkable.

"It's no use, Lucien!" he shouted, his voice raw from panic and ash. His hands slipped on the blackened surface, their efforts fruitless against the crushing mass.

Tears spilled freely from Lucien's face, drawing ivory streaks through the soot.

Her mother's hand reached up, shaky but firm, smearing her cheek in a fleeting, final gesture of comfort.

"You have to go," she spoke calmly, despite the pain contorting her features. Her gaze held Lucien's with an intensity that demanded obedience. "You must leave."

Lucien shook her head violently, her hands tightening around the beam as though sheer willpower could lift it.

"I'm not leaving you! I can't leave you!" Her voice broke, desperation lacing every word. Despite all her resentment, all her anger, she couldn't let her mother die—not like this.

"You must," her mother insisted, her voice softening. "Lucien, you have so much more to do. Now go." A deep sadness flickered in her eyes, a look that both calmed and shattered Lucien. "Protect it," she whispered, just loud enough for Lucien to make out the words.

Cassius firmly gripped Lucien's shoulders.

"If we stay, we all die." His voice was harsh but steady, cutting through the haze of her despair.

Lucien hesitated, her heart screaming against the truth in their words. Her mother gave her one last, pained smile before Cassius pulled his sister away. The edges of her mother's gown glowed and curled as the flames surged higher, swallowing her whole.

Outside, they collapsed into the frigid night air, the cold slicing through their blistered skin like shards of glass.

Lucien staggered, her legs buckling beneath her, but Cassius grabbed her, shaking her hard enough to cut through the fog of shock. She looked her brother in the eyes as he thrust the wooden box into her hands.

Lucien blinked down at it, stunned. The vial. She had been so consumed by the fire, by her mother's screams, that she hadn't even thought of it.

"You... you saved it?" she stammered, her voice breaking with disbelief.

Cassius's face was unreadable, his smirched features hard in the firelight.

"Of course I saved it," he said, his tone flat but laced with resolution. "It's everything."

Lucien stared at him, rubbing her thumbs along the scratches on the side of the box. A low rumbling started through her boots, and the house crashed into rubble, the sound causing her to flinch away.

She watched sparks rise and dance in the dark sky, thinking about her mother's final words. The shouts of the townsfolk couldn't be heard over the roar of the fire, but they continued nonetheless.

Cassius turned first, followed by Lucien.

A silence fell over the crowd.

The mob stood frozen, their wide eyes reflecting the hellish blaze of the inferno. Torches and pitchforks trembled in their hands, their confidence burned away by the sight before them. Lucien and Cassius staggered forward, their blistered skin streaked with soot and sweat, their tattered clothes clinging like second skins. A murmur rippled through the crowd—half-prayer, half-curse—as the impossible truth settled over them.

"They've been spared by the devil," an older voice murmured, the words dripping with superstition.

The townspeople took a synchronized step back, their weapons suddenly feeble against the unspeakable terror they had conjured. The crowd's collective fear solidified into a stunned paralysis; there was no way two figures could stand alive after such devastation.

Lucien's gaze swept over the faces—a shudder rippled through the gathering. The silence between the pair and the mob hung thick, as though the air itself conspired to trap them in this moment. But Cassius, still clutching his own burns and wounds, broke it with a low, rumbling growl. His eyes, darkened with bloodlust, locked on the retreating crowd.

"They think they can burn us?" he hissed, his voice dripping with venom. "Let's show them what fire truly is."

"Cassius, don't." Lucien's voice cracked, her own wounds

and exhaustion apparent, but her plea carried an air of authority. She stepped toward him, placing a hand on his arm. "We need to leave. Now."

But he was far beyond reason. With a violent shrug, he shook her off, baring his teeth in a snarl.

"Leave? No. They wanted death, so death they will get."

Before Lucien could stop him, Cassius lunged ahead, his movements impossibly fast. People screamed as he tore through their ranks, a blur of rage and destruction. Pitchforks and torches clattered to the ground, useless against his onslaught.

Blood sprayed, painting the dirt in crimson arcs.

"No!" Lucien shouted, running after him, but chaos had already erupted. Cassius's prey scrambled in every direction, their shouts merging into a cacophony of terror.

He moved with a feral precision, striking down anyone in his path.

Lucien stood with her mouth open as she watched him, a whirl of firelight and blood. She grabbed a discarded scythe, her hand shaking as she moved forward to stop him, the weapon feeling foreign and wrong in her grip.

"Cas!" she screamed, her voice hoarse, desperate. "You're going to destroy us all!"

Cassius paused, blood dripping from his hands as he turned to her, his expression unreadable through the haze.

"They deserve this, Lucien. They all do."

Distracted, another group of townspeople surged forward with whatever weapons they could find. Cassius met them head-on, but Lucien found herself swept into the fray. Their faces were masks of terror and fury, perverted by the flicker of the flames.

A man lunged at her with a rusty knife. She parried instinctively. The fresh wound she dealt on his inner arm sprayed her face with life. He fell back with a cry, but before she could steady herself, another figure—an older woman wielding a sickle—appeared from the crowd, screaming a prayer as she swung.

Lucien twisted to avoid the blow, but the curved edge glanced off her shoulder, slicing through her sleeve and loosing a bit of flesh. She cried out, staggering back, her grip on the weapon faltering.

"Stay back!" she gasped, her voice raw with desperation, but the mob pressed forward. A younger man shoved the older woman aside, brandishing a torch that sent embers scattering as he waved it. The flames licked at Lucien's face, the heat singeing her hair as she ducked away.

The inferno, fanned by the growing violence, leapt from building to building, consuming the town in its hunger. Smoke thickened, choking the air as shouts turned to wails and desperate cries for mercy.

Lucien fought her way to Cassius, her strength waning as her wounds slowed her movements. "Cassius, stop this! You've proved your point."

He turned to her, blood smeared across his face, his shoulders rising and falling with exertion.

"They destroyed our home. They killed her!" he roared, his voice raw with grief and fury. "I'm going to gut every last one of them!"

Lucien couldn't reason with him. Instead, she grabbed his arm forcefully and pulled him back.

"We can't stay here!" she shouted. "If you want to honor her, we leave. Now!"

For a moment, it seemed Cassius was lost to his lust for revenge, but something in her eyes—or perhaps the chaos closing in around them—made him falter.

He nodded, breathing hard, and together they staggered through the carnage, the townspeople too dead or wounded to pursue them.

The glow of the blaze loomed behind them, crackling and snapping like a living beast, but it was the silence among the fallen that sank into Lucien's bones.

16

Over and Over Again

Lucien stood cloaked in the shadows, the moonlight spilling through the thick canopy of trees, dappling her skin like ghostly veins. She gazed at the village square below, where life carried on, oblivious. Laughter and the clatter of tankards spilled from the tavern, mingling with the occasional bark of a dog and the rolling of cartwheels over cobblestones.

Dunwick was the kind of place she and Cassius had wandered through for ages. After leaving London, their lives had become an endless circuit of villages just like this one—quiet corners of the kingdom, tucked away from the grasp of time and progress. The names blurred together now, an indistinct tapestry of narrow streets, violence, thatched roofs, and wary glances cast at strangers passing through. They never stayed long before moving on. Their presence—and the sudden disappearance of neighbors—had an unsettling effect on the public. But for a while, in each village, they found anonymity.

She rubbed her shoulder, tracing the memory of where a sickle had once sliced through her flesh. The skin was smooth, unbroken, as though the wound had never existed. No scars marked her body, no evidence of the countless battles, burns, or blades that had tried to claim her life over the years. Her body healed itself perfectly, relentlessly—a prison of perfection that denied her even the smallest proof of her suffering.

She flexed her hands, marveling and hating the way they moved without stiffness, without ache, as if her body refused to acknowledge the passage of time. To anyone else, this would seem a gift, but to Lucien, it was a curse. Each perfect patch of skin served as an unyielding reminder of what she had become—and all she had lost.

Her gaze returned to the square, her sharp eyes tracking the movements of the villagers as they passed one another. A young couple walked arm in arm, their heads bent close as they shared quiet words. Near them, an older man sat on a wooden stool, his shoulders hunched from years of labor, his hands gnarled as he carved a small figure from wood. Lucien felt an unexpected pang of envy. These fleeting lives—so fragile and brief—were filled with a love she could no longer feel.

She had watched villages rise and fall, families grow and vanish. They would age, wither, and die, leaving behind only echoes of their existence—all while her body remained untouched by time. And yet, for all their brevity, their lives burned with an intensity that her own lacked. They savored each moment because they knew it was finite. For Lucien, joy, sorrow, and even rage had blurred together, worn thin by time.

The tendrils of gray and shouts rising from the tavern's chimney stirred memories of exile and torches raised in fear.

They had no name for what she was, only an instinctive understanding that she did not belong.

Lucien sighed. How many more of these nameless places could they pass through, leaving a trail of despair in their wake? The thought lingered as her gaze remained fixed on the square—this transient life of theirs, stuck between shadows and firelight. It was all she had ever known. It was all she might ever know.

A man staggered out from the tavern entrance, his movements erratic, the flush of drink darkening his cheeks. Close behind him, a woman followed—or rather, was pulled by the man's firm grip on her elbow. Her pleading words were too soft to reach Lucien's ears. As she pulled away, his hand moved too quickly, striking her across the face with a force that sent her crumpling to the ground. The sound cut through the night, and for a breath, the air stood still.

Lucien's pupils dilated, a dark pulse surging through her and shaking the ground like a beast roused from slumber.

The man stood over the fallen woman for a moment, breathing heavily, before turning and disappearing down a narrow alleyway.

Lucien moved, silent as a specter. The alley stretched before her, dark and slick with mud from recent rain. Her footsteps made no sound, her presence a mere ripple in the fabric of the night. The man stood facing the wall, retying his britches, oblivious to the shadow behind him. The stink of ale and piss clung to him like a sour fog. He muttered curses under his breath, his gait unsteady as he weaved through the passageway.

Beneath her cloak, Lucien's fingers found the small dagger, its handle smooth from centuries of use. She traced the intricate carvings, waiting. It had carried her through lifetimes, her mother's memory still sharp.

The man stumbled, pausing to regain his balance. In that instant, Lucien struck. She moved with practiced ease, perfected through centuries, the honed edge slicing cleanly through his neck. His eyes widened, confusion giving way to terror as blood spurted hot and fast. He gurgled, hands scrabbling at the wound, but Lucien was already shifting him to the ground, silencing his struggles with controlled force.

Kneeling over him, she tilted his head, exposing the cooling skin of his neck. The rage that had built inside her began to ebb as she opened her mouth, revealing the small orifices beneath her tongue, through which tendrils emerged. A shiver coursed through her as they connected to his veins, drawing the blood in a pulsing, metallic rush. The warmth spread through her, familiar and unsettling in its satisfaction.

The man's lifeless eyes stared blankly at the sliver of night sky, but Lucien's focus remained inward, on the shift rippling through her body. Heat spread outward from her core like the thaw of winter's grip. The unbearable tightness that had hardened in her chest, warping her thoughts and stealing her breath, cracked and broke free, giving way to a river of exquisite relief.

A surge of vitality filled her limbs, the burn of exhaustion swept away in a tide of borrowed strength. Her body hummed with unsettling energy, a stark contrast to the stillness of the corpse at her feet.

Lucien stepped back, wiping her mouth, her hand vibrating with the aftershock of satiation. The hunger had retracted its claws, but the reality of what she had done remained. A profound stillness settled over her—not peace, nor guilt, but relief, tinged with inevitability.

The fury would return, as it always did. The slow rise of the hunger, clawing at her insides. The wrath building. The desperate search for a face she could justify ending. The fear in their eyes as she embraced the relief, the peace—inevitable as the turning of the moon, over and over again.

The woman would rise and go home, the morning would greet her with regret and a bruised eye. And Lucien would fade back into the shadows, unseen and unremarkable.

Lucien cleaned the weapon with a swift motion and secured it at her side.

* * *

Cassius didn't just endure the cycle—he thrived in it. For him, "hunting" wasn't survival; it was a spectacle, a dance where he choreographed every step. He prowled the crowded streets with an air of anticipation that made Lucien's stomach turn, scanning the faces of unsuspecting victims, his sharp eyes calculating, lingering on those who carried themselves with strength or confidence—warriors, thieves, or anyone bold enough to meet his gaze. To him, the chase was a high, the thrill of a game where only he dictated the rules.

Lucien sat and watched as Cassius leaned against a shadowed wall, his posture casual but his eyes locked on a man at the far end of the tavern. The man was muscular, his laugh loud and boastful as he recounted some exploit to an eager group of listeners.

Cassius smiled eagerly.

Lucien had wanted to leave, but she knew the hunt was on. She watched her brother weaving through the drinkers like a hunched wolf through downed branches, his smile widening as he drew closer.

Lucien saw it—the moment the man's eyes flicked up, and up again, at the prowling beast.

Cassius didn't attack outright. He lingered just long enough for the prey to sense danger without fully understanding it. The man finally stood to leave. Cassius followed, his steps unhurried but relentless as he herded the man into the shadows of an empty alley.

She kept her distance, but was unable to look away as Cassius confronted the man. It was never a simple strike or a quiet kill with Cassius. No, he wanted resistance.

The man lunged at him, a knife flashing in the light, but Cassius sidestepped with infuriating ease. A chuckle escaped his lips, low and mocking.

"Good," he murmured, his voice almost tender. "Fight."

It was over in moments. The man's knife clattered to the ground, his strength draining as Cassius struck with precision, his hand gripping the man's neck with a casual brutality.

The leather toes of his boots scraped frantically against the cobblestones, but the defiance in his eyes faded as Cassius pulled him close. Blood flowed from prey to predator with a sickening intimacy Lucien couldn't unsee.

Cassius emerged from the alley moments later, his expression serene. The vibrant flush of fresh strength glowed in his features as he walked past his sister.

"They always think they can win," he said, his voice tinged with satisfaction. "But they never do."

He didn't ration his kills or weigh the morality of his choices; he consumed daily, recklessly, leaning into the savagery of it as though it were his birthright. Each kill wasn't just survival—it was triumph, a reminder to himself and the world that he would never be powerless again.

"Do you feel it?" Cassius questioned, his voice low, his eyes gleaming with a wild light. "The power, the invincibility? We are the storm, Lucien. Let them fear us."

Lucien said nothing, but her silence was heavy with revulsion. Where he saw strength, she saw recklessness. Where he found exhilaration, she found despair. And as the bloodlust settled in his satisfied gaze, she realized that whatever remained of the brother she once knew had been swallowed by darkness.

17

The Argument

The sun dipped beneath the horizon, casting a flash of green across the sky before settling into a warm, pinkish-orange glow. Shadows stretched across the ceiling, drawing strong lines as they stepped over the girders. Outside, the soft drone of crickets rose and fell, seemingly in harmony with the grass waving in the evening breeze.

Lucien sat at the table, her hands loosely clasped in front of her, while her mind paced. The home she and her brother shared was leagues above the cramped, makeshift lodgings of their youth. The walls were sturdy, the roof didn't leak, and the floor was lined with well-fitted planks that made a satisfying thud when walked upon in boots. The hearth crackled constantly in the corner, filling the air with the essence of pinewood.

Yet, for all its comfort, the house felt hollow, its quiet amplifying the chasm that had grown between them—a space shared only out of necessity and a curse that bound them. Meals were prepared, firewood chopped and stacked, linens washed and dried—all with the barest acknowledgment exchanged, like strangers passing on a wide road.

Light from a candle on the table danced across Lucien's knuckles while she waited. The door creaked open, and Cassius stepped inside, his broad shoulders catching the last golden rays of sunlight before he swung the door shut.

She watched as he disarmed himself and removed his cloak, setting it over the back of a chair by the door. It dripped water onto the wood.

She looked up from his careless action and blinked slowly in disdain. His hands carried crimson smudges, and the familiar scent of blood and sweat followed him inside. Lucien's stomach sank.

"You've been hunting again," she said. "So soon," she added, her voice low and damning.

Cassius turned to her, his head tilted. "We both do what we must to survive," he said with a wry smile.

"You don't need to feed so often," she countered, "or so recklessly."

His smirk faded. "Recklessly?" he repeated, stepping further into the room. "Survival isn't reckless. It's necessary."

"You call what you're doing survival?" Lucien stood, her hand gripping the corner of the table. The candle still burned below her, casting shadows off the strands of her hair onto her face.

"You're leaving bodies in the alleys, in plain sight. The villagers talk, Cassius. They're afraid. They're watching us."

Cassius shrugged, pulling off his gloves and tossing them onto the table.

"Let them watch. Let them come for me. I'll kill every last God-fearing one of them, their meaningless lives crushed beneath my boot like insects scurrying in the dark."

Lucien had had enough. "They're people, Cassius. Not insects. Each life you take leaves a hole in the tapestry of their world. Families and friends mourn their passing…" She drifted off, losing her train of thought.

Cassius stared at her, eventually raising his hands in question.

"What?" he pressed, shaking his head in exasperation.

"You can't just—"

"I can't just 'kill them'? Is that what you were going to say? Interesting." His voice turned sharp. "You think yourself a little saint because you rid the world of shit-stains in your righteous quest for purpose? You're just like me, Lucien, and you know it. We both end the lives of fathers and friends. We both see the confusion in their eyes as we suck them dry, wondering why they deserved such a cruel end."

"At least I try to live with some restraint," she snapped, her voice rising. "Despite the darkness inside me, I try to do some good."

He laughed bitterly, and Lucien recoiled.

"And where has that gotten you, sister? You think your guilt makes you noble? You can't change what we are. Torment, killing, blood, and death—that is who we are, Lucien."

Her hands balled into fists. The truth in his words hurt.

"What's required of us doesn't have to define who we are," she said, frustration filling her voice. "And your carelessness is forcing us to run faster than we need to. They're going to come for us again. And we'll have to leave, again. I'm tired, Cas. Aren't you? Don't you want to settle down somewhere longer than a fleeting season?"

"You're right," he said, pausing to let his sister enjoy a small victory.

His admission surprised her. But the fire in his eyes betrayed his words.

"Please—" she begged.

"Or… we could stay here and let the villagers' fear fester until they threaten to burn us alive. You know how this ends, Lucien."

She looked at the candle's soft flame, which sent streaks through her teary vision. She continued, hoping reason rather than emotion might have some effect.

"Not if we're careful. Not if we stop drawing so much attention. I'm not ready to leave again, Cassius. I like it here. This place—it almost feels like a home. I want it to last—"

Cassius's laugh destroyed her hope.

"Last? Nothing lasts for us, Lucien. You're deluding yourself if you think we can be sneaky little mice, only nibbling on crumbs that fall from the table. The only thing that lasts is the truth—that the blood calls to us, it always finds us, and makes us do unspeakable things."

Lucien's mind drifted to her mother's warning of an evil rising, seeking the vial.

"If you keep going on this way, they'll figure out who we are. They'll find us, and they'll take the vial—"

"Who are *they*, Lucien?" he interrupted, his voice rising with frustration. "Mother's been gone for years, and in all the time she was alive—in all the running and hiding—did you ever, once, see anyone trying to steal the vial from us?"

Lucien hesitated. He was right, and the truth of it burned. In all the years of fleeing from town to town, evading mobs, and living in constant secrecy, no one had come for them. No dark figures haunted their steps, no unseen forces clawed at their door. Aside from furious villagers chasing them with torches and pitchforks, there had never been any sign of the sinister, mysterious enemies her mother had spoken of. And yet, despite the hollow pit forming in her stomach, she couldn't bring herself to agree.

"We have nothing to fear," he said, stepping close so that every word could be felt on her skin. "And honestly, I wish an army would come for it. Maybe then I'd finally have a good fight on my hands."

"You can't mean that," Lucien said, her voice wavering as she met his gaze. Beneath the bravado in his tone, she could see something darker—anger, pain, maybe even desperation.

"The vial is our responsibility. You saw what Mother sacrificed to protect it. I won't let her life go to waste."

Cassius broke her stare, turning his head with a dismissive sigh.

"Good luck with that."

The words struck like a slap.

"I don't want to lose what's left of us," she whispered, her voice breaking as she fought back the growing lump in her throat. "But I can't keep watching you become… this."

"Then don't," he said coldly, his eyes narrowing. "If you can't stomach it, leave. But don't stand there and judge me for embracing what we are instead of pretending we're something else."

The silence that followed was suffocating, the tension between them taut as a drawn bowstring. Cassius turned toward the door, grabbing his cloak and throwing it over his shoulders.

"I'm going out," he muttered, his voice clipped.

Lucien stared after him, her breath shallow, her hands trembling at her sides. The door slammed shut behind him, the sound reverberating through the quiet house like the final note of an unfinished argument.

She sank into the chair nearest the hearth and prodded the dying embers with a log, willing them back to life. Her gaze fell on a dried sprig of lavender lying on the small table beside her—a small gesture toward a semblance of normalcy, now mocking in its simplicity. She picked it up, her fingers working methodically as she began plucking off its brittle petals. One by one, she tossed them into the coals, where they flared brightly for a moment before vanishing into ash. The scent lingered briefly, bittersweet and cloying, but it did nothing to settle the storm inside her.

Cassius's words clawed at her mind.

"Who are they, Lucien?"

His anger, his defiance—it all felt irrational. But she couldn't shake the gnawing doubt his words had planted. He wasn't wrong. For all her mother's warnings, for all the years spent running and hiding, there had been no shadowy figures chasing them, no unseen enemies trying to wrest the vial from their grasp.

The truth of it stung, but Lucien clung to her mother's conviction. Her mother's life had been shaped by a purpose so deeply ingrained it had become a burden. Was it all for nothing? Or was Cassius just too consumed by anger to see it?

Her grip on the lavender stem tightened as the questions tumbled through her mind. It snapped. She tossed the broken stem into the fire and watched it curl and blacken, the embers returning to life.

Cassius is wrong, she told herself. He has to be. But the memory of his words—the bitterness in his voice, the hollow certainty in his eyes—left her stomach in knots.

Her gaze drifted to the window, the glow of moonlight filtering through the warped glass. The village below was quiet, but she could feel its wariness, the collective unease growing thicker with every brash choice Cassius made. He was blind to it, or perhaps he didn't care. Either way, his actions were dragging them toward the brink of something she couldn't yet name.

Lucien stood abruptly, slipping her cloak over her shoulders in a practiced motion. The dim fire cast her shadow long and distorted on the walls as she moved, her steps producing that satisfying thud. She couldn't sit here, stewing in doubt. Not while Cassius was out there, driven by his anger and hunger to do something terrible—something that could destroy everything.

She paused at the door, her hand resting on the latch. A part of her wanted to let him go, to let him face the consequences of his choices. But the thought of what those consequences might be—the innocent lives he could shatter, the attention he could draw—was enough to crush the air from her lungs.

I have to stop him.

The cold night air hit her face as she stepped outside. Fog coiled through the village with ghostly fingers, muffling the sounds of families settling in for the night. The scent of rain-soaked earth lingered in the air as she pulled her hood low, melding into the shadows.

Cassius's footsteps were still fresh in the mud, leading away from the house and toward the heart of the village. Lucien followed them silently, her boots barely making a sound against the wet ground. She didn't know what she'd say when she found him—if she'd plead with him again or if she'd simply watch.

But she couldn't stay behind. Not this time.

* * *

Her steps were equally silent on the uneven cobblestones, though her brother's trail was harder to follow. The ghostly imprint of his boots on the damp stone guided her way as they led her deeper into the village. Doors were shut tight, windows dark, the town more deserted than normal.

A cat leaped down from a ledge, blocking her path. It attempted to lure a snack from her, but she stepped over it.

The boot prints were becoming fainter, nearly indiscernible with the fog dropping in the cooling night air, but she followed them still. Somewhere in the distance, voices rose and fell, muffled and frantic, though she couldn't make out the words.

The trail turned abruptly down a narrow lane. Lucien hesitated, pressing her back against the cold wall of a building as she peeked around the corner. She was certain the figure nearing the end of the alley was her brother. His steps were deliberate, and his movements signaled danger, noticeable even through the mist shifting around him.

He wove through the streets, making it almost impossible for Lucien to keep him in sight. Her breath came faster, matching the quickening rhythm of her heart as she closed the distance between them.

A sharp turn brought her to the entrance of the marketplace. The square lay empty, the stalls abandoned, their wares hidden beneath heavy tarps weighed down by stones and small pools of water. She spotted Cassius's silhouette slip between the rows, his path cutting straight toward the far side of the square.

Lucien ducked into the shadows of a cart, her eyes fixed on him. Cassius paused briefly, his head tilting as though listening, waiting for his pursuer to give her position away. She froze, gripping the edge of the cart, her breath caught in her throat.

He moved again, even faster still, his cloak swirling behind him as he passed a row of barrels stacked high against a wall. Lucien crept closer, the faint tapping of her boots against the slick stones lost beneath the muffled quiet of the night.

She lost sight of him behind the barrels. Lucien followed, her pulse hammering in her eardrums. But when she peeked around the barrels, he was gone.

She checked for traces of his scent but found none.

"Where'd you go?" she whispered under her breath.

Despite having no lead, she pushed forward, her steps less certain now, her eyes cautiously scanning the shadows. Amongst the fog, the streets wound together like a labyrinth, entirely distorting her sense of direction. Lucien wandered forward, her hand brushing against the rough stone of an unfamiliar building. The fog seemed thicker here, the air frigid, and for a moment, she thought she heard voices—distant and fleeting—but they vanished as quickly as they came.

She stopped again, straining her ears, but the night held its breath.

Breaking the silence, a high-pitched scream reverberated through the alleyway. Lucien froze, the sound chilling her to the core. It was a child's scream—desperate and terrified—carrying through the stillness with a clarity that set her pulse racing.

Her head whipped toward the direction of the sound, her thoughts scrambling.

A child? A girl?

Her legs moved before her mind caught up, her steps quickening into a run as the scream echoed again, fainter this time.

The hammering of her boots against the cobblestones was no longer silent. The mist thickened, curling around her like it wanted to pull her back. But as she came around the next corner, Lucien's blood turned cold.

Sparks from a cart full of hay, just igniting, cast flickering light across the scene before her: Cassius stood over the body of a woman, blood still dripping from his fingers. Beside the fallen woman, a small child sobbed, eyes wide with terror as they locked onto Lucien's.

A shockwave ran through her body, an anger that rose sharper and more sudden than the hunger that had plagued her for centuries.

"Cassius, what are you doing?" she hissed, her voice quivering with fury.

Cassius's expression shifted as he looked up at her, a cruel, satisfied grin curling his lips.

"What does it look like, Lucy? I'm hunting," he said, the word drenched in dark amusement. His eyes flared like the growing fire, wild and unrepentant, as he reached for the girl.

"No!"

She moved before she could think, throwing herself between her brother and the terrified child. Lucien's frantic action sent her crashing into the girl, knocking her little body back against the rough stone wall. The child's head smacked with a sickening thud. She crumpled to the ground.

Lucien's heart plummeted, a sharp pang of guilt slicing through her, but there was no time to react. Cassius lunged, fury lighting his features as he met Lucien's defiance with force.

They clashed, limbs grappling in the confined space, the fire casting wild shadows around them. Cassius's eyes blazed with a cold, manic glint as he shoved her back.

"Why so angry, sister?" he spat, his voice dripping with contempt. "They're nothing more than food. Every one of them."

The desperation in her eyes met the ruthless fire in his.

"How can you say that?" she gasped. "How can you look at her and see nothing but prey?"

She gestured toward the girl while brushing out the fire dancing on her sleeve. The child's still form sent a rush of memories flooding into her mind—laughter shared under the yew tree, moments when young friendship had felt real, hearts fluttering beneath flushed cheeks.

Cassius's grin widened, teeth bared in a mockery of joy.

"Why should I see anything else?" He leaned in, his voice lowering to a taunting whisper. "They're frail, selfish creatures, clinging to lives that mean nothing. We're beyond them, Lucien. We were born to rule this way."

He leaned back, throwing his hands in the air as if he were the king of Norway.

A shudder ran through her, not from fear but from the realization that Cassius was lost to her. The brother who once guided her, who understood their shared pain, was gone. In his place stood a being consumed by hunger, devoid of compassion.

"Look what you've become, brother," Lucien said, her voice steadying as the truth settled over her. "Once, not long ago, you felt remorse for the pain you caused. You may deny it, but I saw it in your eyes when you told me about your first kill. That woman didn't deserve what you did." The fire roared louder now, causing Lucien to raise her voice to ensure she would be heard. "Is there nothing left in you that remembers who we were before all of this?"

For just an instant, his expression faltered, a flicker of something that might have been doubt, but it vanished as quickly as it appeared.

"Who we were?" He laughed, a sharp, hollow sound. "This is who we are now. We take what we need, and we survive. It's the only thing that matters."

Lucien's jaw tightened as the realization struck her: Cassius wasn't just lost to the hunger; he reveled in it. He had let it consume him, stripping away anything human that might have lingered in the corners of his mind.

"Is survival all that's left for you?" she asked, eyes narrowing. "What's the point if you cause nothing but fear?"

Cassius's grin widened, feral and unrepentant.

"They're afraid of us because they should be. We've become what they can't fight, what they can't control. We're their nightmares made real."

"No, Cas," Lucien whispered, the bitterness in her voice edged with sadness. "You're the reason they have nightmares at all."

His eyes darkened, any hint of brotherly affection burned away.

"Rightfully so."

With a roar, he lunged, but Lucien was ready. In one fluid

motion, she sidestepped his charge, grabbed the discarded pitchfork glinting in the firelight, and drove it into his side. With a fierce shove, she forced him back into the flames, which leaped with hungry hands to claim him.

"Lucien, stop," he choked out, the defiance in his eyes dimming, replaced by a glimmer of something almost human. "Please."

Tears stung her eyes, but she held firm. "I'm sorry, Cassius," she whispered, her voice breaking. "I can't let you destroy what little good is left in this place."

With a final, shuddering breath, she forced him deeper into the fire, the flames surging with an intensity that choked the alley with smoke. His screams tore through the night, searing into her memory before being swallowed by the raw ferocity of the burning wreckage. The heat licked at her face, blistering her skin. Pain shot up her hands and forearms, the searing agony urging her to let go, but she held on, her grip unyielding, until his charred body stopped resisting.

Her fingers released the pitchfork, its long handle now fully consumed by flames. The pitchfork remained embedded in Cassius's burning body, a grotesque monument to her desperate act. The acrid stench of burning meat filled the air, and distant shouts of villagers broke through.

Lucien staggered back, looking at her burned hands. The skin of her palms had stayed on the handle.

She turned to see the child she had tried to save—unmoving, but clear of the fire's reach. Behind her, the flickering light of the inferno continued while the ghost of her brother's screams still echoed in her ears.

Another sound approached from the shadows beyond the firelight—hard boots, moving fast. Lucien's head snapped up, her heart pounding as the sound grew closer, each step pushing into the carnage.

Through the drifting ash, a figure emerged—a man, his face etched with sharp lines, his dark eyes locking onto hers.

For a moment, neither moved, the space between them heavy with unspoken tension. The glow of the fire cast shifting patterns across his face, but there was no mistaking the intensity in his gaze. Her instincts screamed at her to move.

Without a word, she turned and bolted into the night, her steps uneven but fast as she disappeared into the shadows. The searing pain of her burned flesh was nothing compared to the torment in her mind—a heavy, unshakable burden of the brother she had lost and the girl she could not save.

III

Part Three

18

The Blacksmith's Daughter

The setting sun behind the rolling hills bathed the sky in deep hues of pink and gold. Alice hurried through the tall grass behind their family cottage, a small bucket of grain swinging at her side. The cool, early evening breeze rustled the blades of grass, carrying the redolence of iron from her father's forge along with the earthy musk of the fields. The soft cluck and chatter of chickens greeted her as she neared their pen, tucked beneath the shade of a sprawling oak tree.

Alice circled the flock, her fingers scattering grain as she walked. The chickens followed her, clucking their gratitude as they pecked eagerly at the feed. She smiled, humming softly to herself, her melody blending with the light rustle of leaves overhead. The breeze tugged at her frayed linen dress, its hem stained with mud from her earlier adventures in the fields.

After making it halfway around, she noticed a mess of feathers strewn across the dirt. She stepped closer and saw the head of a hen lying absent its body. The grisly sight surprised her, but she knew it was part of farm life.

Every animal has to eat, she thought.

When the bucket was empty, she stood, brushing her hands against her apron and glancing toward the cottage. The warm, golden light of the forge spilled from the open door of the workshop, casting sporadic shadows on the ground.

She walked back across the yard, her bare feet brushing against the dewy grass, the familiar sounds of the evening wrapping around her like a favorite blanket.

Near the cottage, her father's silhouette stood framed by the firelight in the workshop. Edmund's broad shoulders moved with precision as he hammered a white-hot piece of iron, each strike ringing out in sharp, pulsing clarity. Sparks flew in bursts, illuminating the deep grooves of his face—the lines of a man who had worked tirelessly for his family.

Alice lingered in the doorway, her arms wrapped around herself as she watched him work. The steady clang of metal against metal was the heartbeat of their home, its constancy reassuring her in ways she couldn't yet put into words. She felt the pull of the heat emanating from the forge, a sense of safety that only her father's presence could bring.

"Papa!" Alice called.

Edmund looked up from his work, the stern lines of his face softening into a comfortable smile. The firelight cast a warm glow across his features, shimmering on the sweat twinkling on his brow. He wiped his forehead with the back of his arm, leaving a dark smear behind, and raised a soot-stained hand in greeting.

"Hello, my little bird," he said, his voice deep and affectionate. There was a roughness to it, but his posture eased as his gaze met her stormy blue eyes, twinkling with affection.

"A fox got one of our chickens again," she said, seemingly

unfazed by the loss.

"Ah, that's too bad. Was it Eggbert the Unready?"

"No. Feathergail the Fowl, I think."

"She was a noblewoman."

Alice laughed, and so did Edmund.

"I'll bring them inside after I'm done here."

"What are you making?" Alice asked, stepping into the open doorway. She craned her neck to see the incandescent piece of metal resting on the anvil, her small hands gripping the doorway.

Edmund's smile widened as he picked up his hammer again.

"A new plow blade for Mr. Carter," he said, gesturing toward the iron with a nod. "The old one broke, and he needs it for his fields by morning."

"Why does it glow like that?" Alice's eyes widened, asking the same question she had a dozen times before.

Edmund chuckled, the sound warming Alice's heart.

"Because it's hot. When metal is heated in the forge, it becomes soft enough to shape. See how I hammer it here?" He demonstrated—like he had a dozen times before—striking the iron, the clang ringing through the air and sending sparks flying. "This shapes it into what it needs to be. Then, when it cools, it will harden into the right form."

Alice watched, enraptured, as her father's strong hands worked the metal, each strike deliberate and controlled.

"It looks like fireflies," she said softly, watching the sparks dance and fade into the air.

Edmund paused for a moment, glancing at her with a grin.

"It does, doesn't it? But fireflies don't really burn, little bird. This does." He reached for the tongs and lifted the luminous metal, letting the heat radiate toward her. "Feel that?"

Alice stepped back instinctively, her eyes widening. "It's hot!"

He laughed again, setting the hunk of metal down carefully.

"That's why you stay back. It's not something to play with, my girl. It's something to respect."

Alice nodded solemnly, tucking a stray curl behind her ear. "Will you show me how to do it one day?"

Edmund's gaze softened, and he crouched to meet her eyes, the hint of a smile tugging at his lips.

"Maybe one day," he said, his voice kind but firm. "When you're older. For now, your job is to keep me company and remind me not to work too late."

Alice giggled, her worry melting away.

"You always work too late."

Edmund straightened with a mock groan, his hands resting on his hips.

"And who else will keep this little village running, eh?" He winked, turning back to the forge. "Go on now, little bird. Tell your mother I'll be in soon."

She lingered for a moment, watching as he returned to his work, his silhouette framed again by the warm light of the fire. Another hard whack of the hammer sent a large burst of sparks flying.

"Sard me!" Edmund shouted, dodging the molten metal, not realizing his daughter was still watching him.

Alice clucked in delight. Taking the expletive as her sign to leave, she turned and skipped toward the front of the house, where her mother, Edith, was tending the small kitchen garden. The air was filled with the fragrance of herbs and freshly turned soil.

Alice approached her mother, who knelt beside a basket

filled with freshly gathered herbs. Pale sprigs of chamomile peeked out from the wicker weave, their soft, calming aroma mingling with the crisp evening air.

Edith smiled when she saw Alice skipping toward her. The girl didn't have a care in the world.

Edith's light-brown hair, pulled back into a loose braid, glimmered in the last golden rays of sunlight, giving it a warm, honeyed glow. A few stray strands framed her freckled face.

"Finished helping your father already? So you've come to 'help' me?" she asked in a joking, sing-song voice.

"Yes," Alice replied, the vowel rising to the sky.

Alice leaned forward, peering into the basket with un-abashed curiosity. The fragrant mix of marjoram, sage, and thyme held her attention, and she ran her fingers along the rim of the basket as though tempted to pluck a leaf.

"Can I help you pick them?" she asked eagerly, her eyes bright with the hope of being useful.

Edith laughed softly, the sound light and breezy, easing the day's quiet weariness. She reached out and tucked an errant curl behind Alice's ear before ruffling her hair.

"Not tonight, little one," Edith said, her tone playful but firm. "The stew is nearly ready, and these herbs are the final touch."

Alice's face shone with excitement at the chance to add the fresh herbs to the boiling stew; the change in smell with their addition was one of her favorite things.

Her mother handed her the basket of herbs and whispered softly, "There's something else you can do as well. Would you please set the table for us? You always do it so beautifully, and I'll be in shortly."

Alice brightened at the praise, her small hands clasping

together.

"I'll make it perfect!" she declared, spinning on her heel to dash toward the cottage.

Edith watched her go, a fond smile playing on her lips. Her fingers moved absently to the edge of her apron, tracing the intricate embroidery she had stitched years ago. Her gaze lingered on the retreating figure of her daughter, her heart swelling with the bittersweet ache of love—so fierce, so consuming, that it sometimes frightened her.

Alice was their only living child. In a world often shadowed by uncertainty, Edith delighted in her joyful presence.

* * *

The door moaned as Alice pushed it open, the hinges worn from years of use. Inside, the warmth of the hearth wrapped around her like a blanket. The fire hissed, sending steam up the stone chimney and casting flickering shadows that made the room feel alive. The wooden beams overhead creaked, the familiar sound speaking of the cottage's age and the countless evenings they had spent under its roof.

Alice carried the basket to the hearth, her steps light with purpose. She placed it carefully on the small table beside the simmering pot, inhaling the richness of the stew. Reaching into the basket, her small hands deftly pulled out a sprig of thyme.

"Just a pinch," she murmured to herself, mimicking her mother's careful instructions from times before.

Leaning over the pot, she dropped the leaves in one by one, watching as they swirled into the bubbling broth, releasing their fragrance into the air. She tossed in a handful of marjoram just for good measure.

Satisfied, Alice stepped back, her cheeks flushed from the glow of the fire. She turned her attention to the table, picking up the wooden bowls and carved spoons from the sideboard and carefully arranging them in their places.

Edith stepped inside the cottage, brushing the last traces of dirt from her hands onto her apron. She paused, her gaze falling on the table, where the wooden bowls and spoons were arranged with precision.

"Looks perfect, my love," Edith said warmly as she walked to the pot, reaching for the ladle to give the stew a final stir. The orange brilliance of the fire bathed her face, accentuating the soft lines around her eyes. Her dark brown eyes caught Alice's as she turned, her expression brimming with pride.

Alice beamed, her small fingers straightening one of the spoons.

"The herbs made it smell even better," she said brightly, glancing toward the pot as if the stew might respond.

Edith nodded. "You have a good nose for cooking already," she teased, brushing a hand along Alice's shoulder. "Soon, you'll be making the whole supper yourself."

Alice's laughter rang out, light and carefree, as she picked up the basket of remaining herbs and hooked it on a peg by the door.

"Maybe tomorrow?" she called over her shoulder, her voice brimming with excitement.

Edith smiled, her gaze following her daughter before returning to the pot. The room felt complete. Like most nights, it was filled with the simple comforts of their shared life, where even the smallest moments carried the air of love and care. For now, the world outside seemed far away, and the safety of their home wrapped them in its quiet embrace.

The peaceful moment was broken by a sudden, sharp knock at the front door. The sound echoed in the small space, cutting through the warmth and releasing a ripple of unease. Alice's hands stilled, the spoon she held hovering just above the table.

They exchanged glances, a touch of concern crossing Edith's face.

The knock came again, louder this time, insistent.

Edith wiped her hands on her apron. "Stay there," she said softly, but her tone left no room for argument. Alice's heart fluttered as she nodded, watching her mother move to the door.

Outside, the light of the forge flickered, casting long shadows that wavered in the breeze, followed by the clanging of Edmund hastily setting down his tools. Beyond, the village lay shrouded in the deepening blue of twilight, unaware of the shadows creeping closer.

Edmund's heavy footsteps approached through the back door leading to the workshop, boots thudding against the wooden floor as he entered, wiping his hands on a rag.

His brow furrowed as he looked between Edith and Alice.

"Who could that be at this hour?" he asked, his voice low and steady, laced with a touch of concern.

Edith's fingers hovered over the latch, the urgency of the knock still vibrating in the air. She glanced back at Edmund, drawing reassurance from his solid, familiar presence. His eyes met hers, alert and unwavering—a silent promise that whatever came next, they would face it together.

The knock came again, more frantic this time, echoing through the small cottage like a cry for help.

Edmund stepped forward and placed his hand on Edith's

shoulder before moving past her to open the door.

A gust of cold night air swept into the room as Edmund pulled the door open. A man stood framed by the darkness outside, his face pale, sweat beading on his brow despite the chill. His wide, bloodshot eyes darted between Edmund and Edith as he gasped for breath.

"It's my wife," he managed, his voice raw and desperate. "Please, she needs your help. The child is coming."

Edith's face softened, the practiced calm of a midwife taking over as she placed a hand on Edmund's shoulder.

"Give me just a moment—" she said, moving to gather her satchel from its hook by the door.

Fear gripped the father-to-be's face. "It's the cottage with the blue door. The other side. To the north!" His exasperation spilled out.

Before she could reply, he had already begun his retreat back to his wife.

Alice, who had been watching with wide eyes from beside the table, felt her heart leap.

"Mama, can I come too?" she asked, her voice bright and hopeful. The promise echoed in her mind—Edith had said she could come along the next time there was a birth.

Edith hesitated for a heartbeat, glancing between Alice and her husband. Her gaze softened as she took in Alice's eager expression, the lantern clutched in her small hands.

"All right," Edith said, her voice gentle but firm. "But you must stay close and do exactly as I say."

Alice beamed, the thrill of being included pushing back the shadows of apprehension creeping into her mind. She reached for the small lantern on the shelf, the flame sputtering and casting a golden twinkle that danced across the room's wooden beams.

Edith looked to Edmund, who nodded once, his jaw still clenched as he attempted to ease his worry.

"Go. I'll try to save some stew for you," he said with a wink, his words as solid and reassuring as the forge's steady heat.

Mother and daughter stepped hand in hand into the cool embrace of the night, where the village of Dunwick lay in hushed stillness.

19

The Alleyway

They ran. Alice held the lantern high, the oil vessel swinging violently. Wild beams of light flared erratically, casting jagged angles across the stone and timber walls. The random illumination turned Edith's stomach—though she always felt a touch of nausea before a birth.

* * *

Last spring, she gave birth to their son. His body was limp when Edmund first held him. He never took a breath. Edmund didn't speak for weeks. She often thought of the boy who never was—especially while tending her garden. His body lay beneath the soil, giving life to the fresh herbs, a quiet reminder that some good might still come from her torment.

* * *

The satchel at Edith's side swung rhythmically. Her determined stride masked the unease gnawing at her heart. She held Alice's hand tightly, guiding her daughter through the night.

"A bit faster, little one," Edith whispered.

Her voice was warm but clipped, as though speaking more to herself than to Alice. The words were meant to urge her daughter forward, but the way Edith's gaze darted between the shadows sent a ripple of worry through Alice.

It wasn't her imagination—something was wrong.

They turned left, moving past a hay cart, the tall stone buildings on either side looming oppressively, their edges dissolving into the darkness above. The air was colder here, biting at Edith's cheeks and slipping beneath the folds of her cloak. They halted momentarily, and Alice lowered the lantern to her side. The small circle of light at their feet did little to confirm whether they were still heading north.

A quick sound, like the scuff of leather against stone.

Alice's grip on her mother's hand tightened.

Just ahead, the lane opened into the empty town square. The cottage with the blue door was just a right-turn-at-the-square-and-a-short-run-up-the-hill away. But something blocked their path.

A figure—half in shadow, half bathed in the silvery light of the moon—stood guard. It did not move.

Edith stepped forward, taking the lantern from Alice and guiding her daughter protectively behind her. The laboring mother needed her, and they could be at her side in minutes.

"Stay behind me," Edith murmured, her voice so low it was almost a growl.

The steel in her tone made Alice freeze, her heartbeat thundering in her ears as she peeked around her mother's side. Edith raised the lantern in front of her, illuminating the space, but the figure's face remained shadowed.

"Who's there?" Edith called, her tone demanding an answer. The question spewed into the misty dark of the village square.

Silence.

Only the rustle of wind through unseen crevices.

"Sir, please," Edith said, urgency lacing her voice. "There's a woman who needs my help. Let us pass."

Then the figure shifted—barely, but enough for the moonlight to catch its face.

"God, save us," Edith whispered.

Its grin was unnaturally wide, stretching too far across its face, the pale white of its teeth illuminated by the light. Something dark dripped from its chin, falling in slow drops that splattered against the cobblestones below.

It took a step forward.

The lantern flickered violently, its light distorting the shadows into writhing, living things. Alice clutched her mother's dress, whispering, "Mama… what is that?"

Edith didn't answer. She shifted slightly, bracing herself for something inevitable.

Her voice, when it came, was cold and unyielding.

"Alice, run."

Alice obeyed, her feet flying around the corner. But something made her glance back.

Her mother hadn't followed.

Edith stood frozen in place as the figure advanced, its footfalls echoing like the toll of a bell.

The lantern slipped from her grasp.

Glass shattered.

Flames leapt to life, licking up the dry hay stacked nearby.

The man's shadow stretched, towering and monstrous, as he lunged.

Everything slowed.

Alice saw her mother raise both arms—a final act of protection.

The fire roared.

And Alice's scream tore a hole in the night.

20

The Blacksmith

Edmund sat alone at the table, scooping the last remnants of stew from his bowl, the spoon scraping softly against the wooden surface. He sat back and stretched his arms above his head, taking in a long breath to settle the warm fluid and meat swirling in his gut. He had eaten too much. A long day of hammering often ended this way, but usually with the inclusion of his wife and daughter sitting across from him, laughing about something odd from the day or a good joke.

What is brown and sticky? A stick.

Edmund's full belly bounced as he thought of Alice telling that joke again and again—each time as though it were the first.

He glanced at the two empty bowls across from him, still dry and untouched. They had left not long ago, but their quiet absence unnerved him.

The fire burned steadily, casting a golden luster through the cottage and silhouetting the pot still hanging above the coals. Edmund rose, taking his bowl and moving toward the hearth. He lifted the stew pot by the handle and set it aside, away from the direct heat. Though the iron was quite hot, his calloused hand was unbothered, his mind already shifting to thoughts of the forge. Tomorrow's work loomed ahead—the plow for Mister Carter only required some final touches, then he'd be on to repairing shoes for the stableman. It was honest work and good pay. The quiet routine of his life steadied him, a pace as predictable as the village itself.

But then it came—a sound that cleaved the night in two.

Sharp, high, and filled with terror.

Alice.

The bowl slipped from Edmund's hand, clattering against the floor, sending remnants splattering across the wood. He was at the door in an instant, yanking it open with such force that it slammed against the wall. The night air rushed in, biting at his face and bare arms. His eyes scanned the darkness frantically, the warm light of the cottage spilling onto the dirt path outside, casting long shadows.

The silence that followed was louder than the scream itself, an unbearable void that sent his mind racing. The cry echoed in his ears, wrenching him out of the warmth and into the cold.

"Edith? Alice!" he shouted, his voice raw and desperate, thundering over the stillness of the village.

He stepped onto the path, his boots crunching against the frost-kissed ground as he strained to listen. Somewhere in the distance, a muffled rustle stirred the air, followed by the low, ominous howl of the wind threading through the trees.

And then he saw it—flickering orange light, like a distant ember, rising from the north end of the village. Smoke coiled upward in the pale moonlight, its wind-blown tendrils cutting across the star-streaked sky.

"Edith! Alice!" he called again, his voice breaking as he stumbled forward.

Taking the path to the east, while less direct, might save some time. The stench of smoke grew sharper. His breath came fast and shallow, his heart pounding against his ribs as the stew sloshed in his stomach.

The distant glow brightened, casting jagged shadows against the sides of the nearest cottages as Edmund cut between the weathered stone buildings. The lanterns hanging outside doorways dimmed as he passed, as though the world itself were retreating from the menace that loomed outside.

Voices argued—a woman's voice, but not Edith's, and a man's. The quiet village seemed to shrink around him as he pressed on. Its narrow alleyways twisting and bullying him, just as the memory of Edith's scream had.

A man cried out in agony.

"Please, no," he whispered, the words barely audible over his hurried footfalls as fear clawed at his throat.

He was nearly there. People were beginning to emerge from their homes, eyes wide and faces pale with shock. The fire blazed, fierce and hungry, illuminating the street in a hellish scene. Flames curled up the side of a building, reaching toward the sky, while sparks danced like fireflies on a summer night. The sweet scent of burning hay mixed with the grit of soot, stinging his eyes as the shouts of villagers merged into a chaotic roar.

Edmund's stride faltered as he turned a corner and came face-to-face with the inferno. He moved in, driven by love and fear.

A body, too large to be a woman or child, leaned against a

burning cart. The fire had devoured the poor soul and moved on to the surrounding buildings. The corpse was charred beyond recognition, the flesh blackened and cracked, with tendrils of steam and the stench of overcooked meat still rising from it. A pitchfork jutted from the man's abdomen, its handle scorched, the tines embedded deep as if pinned by a vengeful force.

Edmund tore his eyes away, bile rising in his throat as he stumbled past the gruesome sight. Whoever the man had been, there was no saving him now. Clenching his jaw, he pushed through the smoke, each step heavier, the fire's roar growing louder in his ears.

Edmund's gaze darted through the swirling haze, searching desperately for any sign of life. His heart sank as his eyes landed on Edith, lying on the ground, unmoving, but out of the torrent's reach.

Her darkened hair was splayed out like ink on stone. He knelt beside her, placing his fingers beneath her nose. She wasn't breathing. He desperately hoped for a pulse, but when he touched her neck, it was wet. And beneath the sticky mess, he found an open wound, two fingers wide.

"Edith…" The name escaped him in a breathless whisper, choked with disbelief and grief.

But where's Alice? He thought, frantically scanning the surroundings of his beloved.

Behind him, against a wall, Alice's small form lay crumpled, a smear of soot streaking her pale face. Edmund shifted to her side, placing his fingers firmly against her dry neck. A pulse— weak and fragile, but there. Relief flooded him, sharpening his focus.

"I need help here!" His voice cracked as he gathered Alice

into his arms. Her breaths came in shallow, uneven gasps, eyes half-lidded, barely clinging to consciousness. Her small body, normally so full of life, felt impossibly light and fragile.

"Hold on, little bird," he whispered, a plea wrapped in panic.

Movement at the corner of his eye—a shadow at the fringes of the firelight's reach. For a brief moment, he saw her: a woman with dark hair, eyes glinting in the flickering light. Her hands were red, dripping with blood. She stood still, taking in Edmund's torment. Then she was gone.

"Come back!" Edmund shouted. But she did not return.

"Help!"

His voice was swallowed by the chaos around him. The woman was gone, leaving only questions and the burning imprint of her face seared into his mind.

Edmund spun back toward the alley, Alice's arms swinging lifelessly at his side.

"Someone, please!" he cried.

A tall figure emerged from the thick gray wall—a burly man covered in ash, his face grim and determined. The man knelt beside Edith without hesitation, his sharp gaze taking in the scene.

"I'll carry her," he said. His steady voice was the lifeline Edmund needed. "You take the little one to the doctor's house. You know where it is?"

"Yes," Edmund replied, shifting Alice's body higher into his arms.

"Good," the man said, already moving to lift Edith's lifeless body with surprising care. "Go. And don't stop for anything. I'll be right behind you."

Reluctantly, Edmund spared one last anguished glance at Edith before turning toward the street. Alice stirred in his arms.

He whispered, "Hold on a little longer."

He ran, his boots striking the uneven cobblestones with sharp, jarring thuds. Figures emerged from their homes, shouts echoed in the distance, the world a clamor of panic that felt both near and far.

The weight of Alice in his arms grew heavier with each step, her shallow breaths a fragile thread pulling him forward.

"Stay with me, little bird," he muttered, his voice cracking as though the words alone could keep her alive. His legs trembled with each step, muscles screaming in protest, and his arms ached under her bones, but he pressed on, the doctor's house drawing closer with every agonizing stride.

At last, the timber-framed row house came into view, and relief surged through him, sending a fleeting tremor through his limbs before urgency took hold once more. Momentum threw his body at the door, shoulder-first. The thick wood rattled on its hinges as he pounded the side of his fist against it.

The door burst open under the impact, swinging wide to reveal the doctor already standing there, as if he had been waiting. His face, lined with age and wear, was calm but alert, his eyes immediately landing on Alice.

"Inside, quickly!" the doctor barked, stepping aside without hesitation.

Edmund stumbled through the doorway, cradling Alice protectively.

"She's barely breathing," he managed, his voice a raw plea as the doctor shut the door firmly behind them, sealing out the chaos of the night.

* * *

The doctor's hands moved with practiced urgency, fingers checking Alice's pulse, tilting her head gently to inspect the wound at the back of her skull. The moment stretched long and taut, filled only with the frantic thud of Edmund's heartbeat and the rustling of feet on wood.

"There was a fire... and a woman..." Edmund's voice faltered as he tried to piece together the chaos. "And a man. I saw—"

His words were cut off as two villagers pushed into the room, their faces grim. The larger of the two carried Edith's body inside. Her dress was stained with blood—some still slick and fresh, some dried by fire until it was nearly black.

"Place her there," the doctor said, gesturing to the bed. "I'll check her in a moment."

But the man shook his head, his eyes dark and filled with unspoken grief.

"It's too late. Her throat..." He didn't finish—he didn't need to.

Still, he placed her on the bed.

Edmund's gaze locked onto Edith. Shadows danced across her face, softening the sharp lines of reality. He knelt beside her, and for a fleeting moment, he refused to believe it, waiting for her to speak, to scold him for worrying too much. But truth spoke instead.

Just hours ago, Edith's freckled nose twitched away a fly as she lovingly plucked herbs—placing the unblemished ones in the basket, casting the others aside—while speaking kindly to her daughter, and the sun set on the hills. Now, she was dead.

His heart revolted, threatening to drag him under, but there was no time to grieve. Not now. He tore his gaze from Edith, forcing down the lump rising in his throat.

Alice.

He turned back to her—the last fragile thread of his shattered world.

The doctor's hands hovered above her, stilled. He met Edmund's eyes, the finality in them like a punch to the nose.

"I'm sorry. She's gone."

21

Fallout

The following days were filled with numbness and the taste of salt.

Edmund finished the plow blade. Mister Carter brought a pie, baked by his wife. The stableman—though not the same man who had originally requested the repair—collected the horseshoes without looking Edmund in the eye.

A timid rap on the door signaled the delivery of yet another loaf of bread, a pot of stew, or dried meat wrapped in cloth. The neighbors who knew him left their gifts and were gone before he opened the door. Others knocked repeatedly. He would wait until the husband urged his wife away, only rising to gather the food after they were long gone.

At night, he sat in the dark and stared at nothing.

One morning, the brave men who had come to his aid stood at the door. On that wretched night, they had walked him home, afraid he might throw himself into the river. They didn't fault Edmund for mentioning the idea.

They helped him into his coat, their eyes avoiding his, as if afraid his grief might spread to them. The walk to the burial site was slow and short.

How long had it been?

A week, surely, though reason whispered it had only been days.

Edmund stood before the gathered crowd, two mounds of dirt at his side—one large, the other much smaller.

More people than he had expected encircled the graves. They all looked at him. Waiting. He wasn't sure what to say, but he rightly assumed they would continue staring until he spoke.

He cleared his throat and glanced up through his eyebrows. They were still staring.

"Uh, well," he began awkwardly. "Thank you. Thank you for being here. Thank you to those of you who brought me food."

He looked up but avoided their eyes before bowing his head toward the ground.

"Edith is… she was, my rock. Her kind voice brought many of you peace as you welcomed your newborns."

Edmund scanned the crowd for the man who had stood in his doorway, pleading for Edith's help. He wasn't there.

"She brought me peace as well. I was lucky enough to have her by my side for the past ten years or so. When I'd come in from working all day, her smile was always there to greet me. Now, she's gone to be with her Lord, and I'm sure she's greeting the angels with that smile as well."

The words didn't feel right, but he said them anyway. He shook his head, closed his eyes, and inhaled for what seemed like an eternity before he could draw enough courage to say her name.

"Alice…" he choked. His eyes flooded. He swallowed hard.

"*My little bird.* She was always flying around, just trying to catch a glimpse of what you were doing. She smiled a lot too—oh, God."

He thought he might be done speaking, but someone rested a hand on his back. After a long pause, he decided to continue.

"She was taken from me—they *both* were—so… *violently.*"

The crowd shifted uncomfortably.

A scream waited, buried in his lungs—a chance to cry out and release the hatred he held inside. Instead, he pushed it down and fixated on the image of the woman whose hands dripped with his wife's blood.

"Go home," he muttered.

As the crowd began to disperse, the burly man offered to help. Edmund waved him off, picked up the shovel, and drove it into the dirt.

* * *

Days dragged on, each one filled with a dull, relentless ache. He watched the sun rise, though no birds sang.

drip

He swung his hammer, though his hands were blistered and raw.

Drip.

He sat and ate, though the food was bland.

DRIP.

And he stared at nothing.

I'll make her pay for what she's done.

* * *

Arriving in London, he found the city shrouded in tension, every step echoing off the cobblestones like a secret waiting to be discovered. The streets that should have been alive with market chatter and the bustle of merchants were subdued.

He hadn't brought more than he could carry. The only required item was the axe tucked into his belt, sharpened so finely that, out of caution, he covered it with a leather sheath.

He moved through the marketplace, his eyes scanning faces, his ears attuned to every snippet of every anxious conversation.

"The constable says there's nothing to fear, but more bodies keep turning up," a woman muttered, clutching her shawl tighter around her shoulders as though warding off a chill.

"Well, it's been a while since the last one," her companion replied. "We've started unboarding the windows during the day."

"We're getting on a boat tomorrow. Stephen has family in France," a young mother said, cradling her infant as she selected a loaf of bread.

Certain that he was in the right place, Edmund found an inn, rented a room, and ordered a bowl of pottage from the alewife.

A bearded fellow sat alone at a table meant for many. Edmund recognized the pain in his eyes. The man was older— by perhaps twenty years.

Despite the room being empty, Edmund set his leather jack of ale down across from the man and took a seat on the long wooden bench.

The man glanced at him, wary.

"Edmund," Edmund said.

"Harold," Harold replied.

The alewife brought the pottage and set it in front of Edmund. It smelled of barley and carrots.

"Are you just passing through?" Edmund asked. "Seems ugly out there."

"Yeah."

"Do you know anything of the demon people are speaking of?"

Harold's eyes twitched uncomfortably, as if a long brow hair had gotten stuck—first the right eye, then the left, then both.

"Sorry, I didn't mean to upset you. It's just—" Edmund hesitated. "My wife and my daughter. They were murdered by her."

"Her?" the man probed.

"Yeah. I don't think she's actually a demon, though. She looked... normal, I suppose. Dark hair, about down to her shoulders, average height, dressed in a cloak. Terrible eyes..."

Harold had opened his eyes fully now, listening intently.

"...they were so cold. She ran off, but I couldn't follow her—"

"Me father," Harold interrupted. "Kept the lord's land free of rats and foxes—set traps, chased off vermin an' such. Hard work, an' he was there most nights, makin' sure the grain stores and chickens weren't chewed through."

"Okay..."

Harold nodded and continued. "The old lord weren't too bad, bit of a bastard, but the lady—she'd scream about a rabbit in her garden, always threatenin' to feed Pa to the wolves if he didn't catch it, while eatin' bread that didn't have maggots in it 'cause of him."

He took a large gulp of ale to clear the gravel in his throat.

"Well, he was fixin' a fox trap one night, an' somethin' didn't feel right. It was that kind of quiet before a storm, you see? An' out in the woods—'bout ten paces off, he'd say—he saw two pairs of eyes, glowin'. At knee height, he'd say. Now, wolves were a real problem—not as much as the foxes—but a farkin' terrifying problem when you're alone at night. So he picked up a stone and tossed it at 'em—just missed, on account of the stone bein' heavy.

"The wolves didn't run. They just stood there, starin' at 'im from the dark. He gave a big ol' whoop, tryin' to git 'em to git. Those farkin' eyes…" Harold trailed off, his own eyes turning redder and glassier.

"What happened?" Edmund pressed, a hint of urgency creeping in.

Harold let go of his ale and held out his hand, two fingers pointed directly at Edmund.

"They rose."

He lifted his pointed fingers above his head, so high he lost his balance even while seated. He dropped his arm and barely kept himself from falling backward off the bench.

"Me father, he ran off, an' never went back."

"Terrifying," Edmund said, hoping Harold got the sarcasm.

"You're not listenin'! Me father never went back, but he 'eard from one of the servants that the lord and lady were murdered that night. Not by no wolves, tho'. Wolves don't cut yer neck and drain yer body dry."

Edmund's jaw tightened.

"I see. And this lord…"

"De Vaux. Lord Alric de Vaux."

"He was here in London?"

Harold nodded.

"Where?"

"'Cross the river an' up the hill. An estate, deep in the woods. But mark my words—leave it be. You'd do well to leave London in'tirely before it's too late."

"Thank you, Harold."

Edmund slid his ale in front of Harold as he stood. He left the pottage where it was and patted Harold on the shoulder before heading upstairs to his room.

Leaving London was not an option. He knew where he was headed, and he knew he would not turn back until the woman who had shattered his life paid for what she had done. But he thought it would be best to wait until morning to confront her, lest the shadows keep her hidden from him. A good night's rest would restore him for what lay ahead.

22

Lucien's Grief

The village behind her rose to life in a mix of shouts, crackling, and firelight. She kept her hood low as she fled. Doors creaked open, revealing cautious eyes whispering in the shadows, as though the village sensed danger but dared not confront it outright.

Lucien's heart raced as her mind searched the visions of the girl, motionless on the ground, for signs of life—for some sign she had still been breathing. Then there was the man who emerged through the smoke. Their eyes met for the briefest of moments, and Lucien was certain she had seen him before.

The chill of pre-dawn clung to the village, and the cobblestones beneath her feet were slick with dew. She pulled her hood lower, quickening her pace. Every step put distance between herself and the nightmare in the alley, but it wasn't enough. It would never be enough.

Her boot slipped in the mud as she climbed the gentle slope to her home. Relief and dread knitted together as she approached the door. The sound of distant voices, frantic as they struggled to put out the flames, reached her ears. The scene would no doubt spark questions, followed soon after by rumors, then a mob.

The familiar creak of the floorboards beneath Lucien's boots echoed too loudly in the stillness. The embers had died, and the room was cold.

Her eyes scanned the room, landing on the small wooden box on the table. The box that had once been her mother's constant companion—the one her mother had guarded as if the world depended on it, the one she had left under her own bed that morning—now rested before her, its pull as relentless as ever.

Her cloak, heavy with ash and the night's horrors, hung awkwardly from her shoulders. The edges were burned and frayed, and as she reached to remove it, the fabric tore beneath her fingers. She let it fall to the floor, a ruined, useless shell. Her skin was unmarred, the burns already healed. She touched her arms gingerly, her fingers grazing the smooth flesh where scars should have been.

Lucien approached the table, the box glowing with a familiar, faint light. She hesitated, her hand hovering above the lid before she pressed her palm against it. The cool wood steadied her. When she opened it, the vial lay nestled inside, untouched and unyielding.

The crimson liquid swirled, reaching deep into her being and gripping her heart with invisible fingers. It was more than just an object to be protected—it was a curse, a relic of power that had shaped her family's history and shattered her future.

Lucien shook her head and shut the lid. She grabbed a light blanket from the chair, wrapped the box in cloth, and tucked it into her satchel. She had no choice—it was coming with her.

Her gaze swept over the remnants of the life she had cobbled together, a veneer of normalcy that had barely concealed the truth of what she and Cassius were.

The events of the night replayed in flashes—Cassius's eyes reflecting bright flames, the crack of the girl's skull against stone, the pain of her skin bubbling under the heat of the flames, the look on the man's face as he cried for help.

Lucien thought of the life the girl might have had, as though willing it into reality, but there was no time to dwell on it. The villagers would find her. They would talk, and eventually, they would come.

With the satchel secured over her shoulder, Lucien stood in the middle of the room, her gaze lingering on the silent hearth. This house, this village, had been a fragile attempt at permanence, and now it was slipping through her grasp like all the others.

As she turned toward the door, her thoughts shifted to London. She knew of a place there, a small sanctuary where she could disappear for a while, regain her strength, and decide what came next. It wasn't safety—nothing was—but it was far enough from the storm brewing in Dunwick.

* * *

London loomed in the distance, its solid lines enveloping the glow of scattered lanterns, blurred by the thick mist settling over the city. The sprawl stretched further than she remembered. When her mother had died here centuries ago, the city had been a patchwork of uneven streets—bustling but crude. Even fifty years ago, when she and Cassius had last stepped foot on London's streets, it had been a chaotic expanse, spreading unevenly like roots searching for fertile ground. Now, it was something altogether different—a sprawling labyrinth of ambition and power.

The wooden walls that had once attempted to keep its residents safe had been replaced by towering stone fortifications, punctuated by watchtowers that loomed against the night sky. The hum of voices and the creaking of cartwheels clamoring over cobblestones reached her ears, muted by the fog yet still alive—a testament to a city that never truly slept.

As she approached the gates, Lucien ducked her head, hiding her face in the shadow of her hood. The guards stationed at the entrance barely glanced at her, their attention dulled by the long hours of their watch. She passed through the archway unnoticed.

The stench of the city hit her immediately—a pungent mixture of damp stone, decay, and refuse. It was familiar but sharper than before, like a memory turned cruel. The streets were lined with buildings whose jagged rooftops cut into the mist like dark teeth. And yet, beneath the changes, the city's essence remained—the ambition, the greed, the quiet desperation of its people. It had always been a place that consumed as much as it gave.

Shadows danced in the glow of lanterns, creating fleeting illusions of movement in every corner.

She moved quickly, her boots skimming across the uneven streets, avoiding the occasional gaze of men stumbling through the night.

Lucien's steps faltered as she crossed a square she barely recognized. A fountain stood at its center, its base adorned with freshly carved reliefs of archers fending off dragons, though the worn stone steps remained untouched. She paused, brushing her fingers along the cold carvings.

The last time she had stood here, it was with her brother. A street performer had juggled knives while onlookers crowded around, laughing uneasily and clapping for the man who narrowly avoided death by his own hand. Cassius had smiled at her when the man bowed—perhaps the last time a genuine smile had crossed his face.

She pressed on, adjusting her satchel and quickening her pace. Her path wound toward where the stone streets ended. The muffled echoes of the city receded as fields and open stretches replaced the crowded buildings. Her boots crunched softly against the dirt, the air growing cooler and fresher as she left London's oppressive confines behind.

The fields soon gave way to the edge of a forest, and within the hour, the forest gave way to the iron gates of the estate.

Beyond the gates, the house loomed, its silhouette familiar yet altered by time. The stone walls were streaked with lush greenery, the once-pristine windows dulled and fractured. The estate's grounds, once meticulously kept, were now wild—the hedges overgrown, the garden consumed by weeds and wildflowers.

Cassius and Lucien had watched the previous owners for weeks. The lady's constant demands, often followed by the back of her hand, had left the youngest servants in tears nearly every day. The rest had long since lost the light in their eyes— beaten out of them, leaving only husks that muttered *yes, Madam* as they moved to obey.

Everywhere he went, the lord's hulking presence quickened the staff's pace and sent their eyes downward as they shuffled out of his way. Cassius had admired the respect he commanded, unconcerned that it was driven by fear. The childless pair's ignorance of the predators stalking them had almost been insulting. But by now, Lucien and Cassius were used to it.

* * *

One moonless night, Lucien and Cassius struck with the precision of shadows. They slipped past the guards stationed near the gates, their movements soundless and deliberate. Not a single footstep betrayed them, and the dim light from the servants' quarters cast no trace of their passing. The staff slept soundly in their rooms, unaware of the danger threading its way through the estate.

The lord and lady didn't have a chance to scream. Cassius pressed his hand over the lord's mouth, his other arm pinning him against the headboard with an ease that unsettled Lucien even then. The keen point of her weapon slid beneath the lady's trachea and out the front. Air sucked in through the gaping wound and sprayed droplets of blood across the sheets as it came back out. The metallic scent filled the room, overwhelming the lavender perfume lingering on the linens. By the time dawn broke, the estate was silent, save for the whisper of the morning wind brushing against its empty halls. They had left in silence, leaving no trace of their presence—except for the bodies.

The staff abandoned the estate, leaving the corpses to rot where they lay. Not a single foot crossed the threshold again. Stories took root among the townsfolk like weeds, each more elaborate than the last. Some claimed the family had offended a witch and that her curse had come for them in the night.

Others swore they'd seen eyes moving unnaturally beyond the walls, creeping closer with each retelling. The estate remained untouched. No one dared claim it—not the distant cousin, not the servants, not even the most desperate of thieves.

A year later, Lucien and Cassius returned.

The house was shrouded in decay, the once-pristine estate now a hollow shell of its former grandeur. The shutters groaned in the wind, their edges splintered and rotting. Weeds choked the pathways, and ivy climbed the walls, creeping into newly formed cracks. The air carried a stillness, as if the house itself were holding its breath.

Lucien hesitated at the gate, her eyes tracing the familiar lines of the stone façade, now softened by time and neglect.

"They truly abandoned it," she murmured, her voice barely audible.

Cassius smirked, his hands resting on the rusted bars of the gate.

"They're afraid of the shadows. It's ours now."

Inside, the air was thick with dust, motes swirling in the dim light filtering through the cracks in the boards. Lucien ran her fingers along the surface of a once-polished table, leaving a streak in the grime.

For weeks, they worked to restore the house—not to its former glory, but enough to suit their needs. Lucien cleared the weeds from the garden but left the ivy.

The estate became their sanctuary, hidden in plain sight. The stories of curses worked in their favor, keeping curious eyes and prying hands far away. For decades, it served as a haven—a place where they could rest, regroup, and pretend, if only for a little while, that the world wasn't always hunting them.

* * *

Lucien pushed open the rusted gate, the groan of metal breaking the stillness of the night. The iron was warped, its once-proud design now bent and jagged, like the ribs of some long-dead creature strangled by nature. Beyond it, the garden stretched in chaotic disarray, the wild growth having entirely erased the path to the entryway.

She stepped through the gate, her boots crunching against the gravel, and paused. Memories hovered at the edges of her mind, flickering like phantoms in the pale moonlight. She could almost hear the echoes—their laughter ringing across the garden, the whispered plans for their next hunt, the brief moments when Cassius had been her brother in more than name. Those memories felt like another lifetime, a world away from the hollow ache that now defined her.

The house loomed ahead, its windows staring back at her like empty eyes. She reached the heavy wooden door, the grooves of its carvings worn smooth by time. The metal latch was cold under her fingers, resisting as she pressed down.

She stood in the doorway, her breath steady but shallow, taking in the familiar sight of the grand entry hall. The house was as she remembered, yet it felt utterly foreign. Her fingers grazed the door frame as she stepped inside.

She traced a path through the familiar corridors. The estate was no longer theirs, not really. It belonged to the shadows now, to the silence that had settled over the rotted furniture and cracked floors. The air hung heavy with dust, each step kicking up swirls that danced in the shafts of moonlight streaming through shattered windows. But for tonight, it would be enough. It was shelter, a reprieve from the darkness outside—and the storm within.

Lucien's steps quickened as she ascended the stairs to her chamber. The fractured windowpanes allowed slivers of moonlight to spill into the room, pooling on the cold stone floor. The pedestal stood in the corner, bathed in pale light, its surface bare but still commanding a presence.

She stood before it, her gaze lingering on the empty slab. Cassius had built it the last time they were here, insisting the vial needed a place of reverence. She had mocked him for the effort, calling it a monument to their curse, but now, in the emptiness of the house, it felt like the only thing that truly belonged.

Lucien knelt, sliding the box free from the satchel she carried. The carvings along its edges moved, their intricate patterns seeming to shift and ripple beneath her fingers. She clutched it to her chest for a moment, the gravity of it both physical and symbolic—a burden passed through generations.

Her gaze shifted to the pedestal. She traced its edge lightly with her hand, her mind flitting back to the countless nights Cassius had spent shaping it.

"Because it's what made us," he had said when she questioned him. She hadn't understood then, and now, years later, she still wasn't certain she agreed with his reverence.

With deliberate movements, she placed the box atop the pedestal, the wood settling into place as though it had never left. The room felt colder somehow, the air heavier, as if the vial itself recognized its return. She stepped back, her eyes fixed on the box, the hollow ache in her chest deepening.

The vial wasn't just a keepsake of her past; it was the embodiment of her curse, her inheritance. And though it remained sealed within the box, its presence was palpable—a silent reminder of the chains that bound her.

She turned away, the moonlight casting long shadows that seemed to follow her as she crossed the room. For now, she could rest. But in the shadows of her mind, the questions remained, circling like vultures over a dying flame. Could she survive this existence? And more terrifyingly, did she even want to?

"How many?" she whispered into the dark as she paced the room. How many lives had she taken just to stave off the hunger that grew sharper with each passing year? At first, it had been bearable, a choice she told herself she could control. But over time, the craving devoured her will, replacing her with a creature she scarcely recognized. Her mind filled with faces—pleading, terrified, lifeless. Many had deserved it; more had not.

Anger boiled in her veins, but not the familiar rage born of hunger. This was something deeper, a seething hatred for her mother, who had bound her to this fate, and for Cassius, who had reveled in it. She should have left for Spain when she had the chance.

She thought of the song her mother used to hum by the fire.

Undar måna's vigil thur,
Jhalan dansar, sufi mur.
Håmran fayad, 'vur narra dyr,
Sirr'an fi layl thura myr,

Ay, warda min, threnn an'mir,
Riyah'sa håmla, ard tajir
Lakin qalb harib, khafa ghana,
Jeldi firar, a'nan fa'ine

The tune had once brought her comfort—until she learned the meaning of the foreign words.

> *The stolen gift beckons,*
> *Shadows dance, whispering loss.*
> *Our cursed hands, never clean,*
> *No absolution will ever be found.*

> *Oh, my rose, this endless burden,*
> *Evil seeks us, but never finds.*
> *Through their suffering, and in ours,*
> *We endure, this is the price.*

It was a warning, a promise of the darkness that came with power, meant to prepare them for the tragedy of eternity.

A sob pressed against her lungs, and she clamped a hand over her mouth to stifle it. Centuries of violence, of blood staining her teeth, of stolen lives and justifications—more than any melody could ever have prepared her for.

Rage had contorted her brother's face, warping him beyond recognition, consuming him whole. Lucien avoided the eyes that would stare back at her from the polished silver mirror on the writing table, afraid she now bore the same visage.

Her gaze drifted across the room to the pedestal, a solitary figure standing vigil in the faded glow of moonlight. Atop it, still cradled within the worn wooden box, lay the vial—her mother's gift, her curse. The liquid inside was as full as the day she had first been forced to drink it.

It sat there as a tribute to her mother, a relic of the past she could never escape, a constant reminder of the chain that bound her. The polished glass seemed to whisper with her mother's voice, an echo of choices made for her, of paths she had never wanted to walk.

The final verse—*Through their suffering, and in ours, we endure. This is the price*—lingered in her thoughts. Her mother had understood. She must have known what she was passing on—the dark legacy that would corrupt and mangle her daughter's life.

Lucien's eyes welled with tears she hadn't allowed herself in centuries. The faces of those she had drained to quell the endless hunger plagued her, eyes wide, accusing. Each one left an indelible mark on her soul, a stain she could never cleanse.

Her mother had chosen this life, running from shadows while embodying darkness. And Cassius—how easily he had embraced it, reveling in the power while she clawed for control. The last time she had seen him, swallowed by the fire's embrace, she had turned away, unable to watch as the flames consumed him.

Fire seemed to be the only end for their kind. She had seen it in her mother's death as well, the inferno that reduced her to ash and memory. The heat, the finality of it—death by fire was apparently irreversible.

And yet, doubt whispered through Lucien's mind, a taunt that eroded her certainty. She had survived what should have killed her countless times—why not him? Was it possible that Cassius had found a way, that he lingered in the shadows now, waiting for revenge?

The thought sent a shiver racing down her spine. She still felt the vial's pull, the promise it whispered, a power as cursed as it was seductive. Whether Cassius was out there—a phantom of her guilt or a specter with substance—she would find a way to end it. This curse, this life that had bound her, had stretched the limits of her humanity to a breaking point. Perhaps it was time for the peace her mother had found—a final release beyond the perpetual night she endured.

A sharp noise shattered her thoughts—a creak of the iron gates being pushed open. Lucien's muscles tightened as she strained to listen, every nerve tingling. Another sound followed, closer this time, reverberating through the foyer.

Her mind leapt to her mother's warning of the "evil people," seeking to "raise an army." Could her mother have been right all along? The possibility sliced through her, equal parts dread and anticipation.

Instinct took over, and she melted into the shadows. The silence covered her, broken only by the pounding of her heart.

A third sound—a floorboard groaning under the pressing weight of a step. She held her breath and adjusted her grip on the dagger. She was ready to confront whatever monster had come for her.

23

Edmund Continues

Sleep didn't come easily that night, but cradled by the murmur of the river just beyond his window, Edmund found some rest.

He dreamed of sun-bathed fields, and laughter bubbling up from deep within his soul as he spun Alice around, her delighted squeals ringing out like a song. Edith watched from the porch, her eyes soft and filled with a love that anchored him. He sat beside his wife and she placed her hand on his knee.

We miss you.

I miss you.

Find us.

I will.

The world was whole, unmarred by grief, framed in the golden light of a life he yearned to reclaim.

Clouds covered the dying sun, and Alice fell to her knees, sobbing. An icy chill blew Edmund back, and Edith was gone.

Shadowy figures crept from the tree line. Deep hoods covered their faces.

Alice looked toward the sky, her arms pinned back by an unseen force.

Her mouth opened wide in a silent scream as the sky pulled apart.

Blood rained down from the heavens, followed by a sharp shriek—a thousand voices crying out at once—that rattled Edmund's bones and pierced the veil between sleep and waking.

Edmund jolted upright, heart thundering as he tried to shake the vision. His breath came in ragged gasps, sweat beading his brow and trickling down his temples. For a moment, the only sound was the frantic pounding of his pulse, completely obscuring the river's gentle lapping. He sat in the dark, wondering if those screams were just a cruel twisting of his mind, or if they had come from outside, carried on the night air. His skin prickled, a cold shiver running down his spine.

Fully awake now, he forced himself to stand, shaking out his arms and turning his neck to break up the deep knots. He lit the lamp on the nightstand, and light spilled across the rented room, flashing off the cutting edge of his axe and into Edmund's eye. Ducking out of the beam, he retrieved the weapon from the chair and spun it while he paced back and forth across the small room.

The movement did little to quell the gnawing unease in his gut. Though it was likely hours before the sun would rise, he quietly headed down the stairs, through the pub, and out into the dark.

The path ahead, lit only by the lantern's thin glow, was pure black beyond its reach, the night air thick with the whispers of unseen things echoing his hurried steps. Each stride carried him closer to the estate, closer to the heart of whatever fate awaited him there.

He could still feel the ghost of Alice's laughter, Edith's touch—a cruel reminder of what had been, and could still have been, if not for her.

The wind picked up, a low, mournful sound that whistled through the reeds and branches. Edmund pressed on, grief and determination driving him forward into the unknown.

* * *

A fortress of shadows loomed ahead. The ancient, gnarled trees reached skyward, their weathered limbs warning him to turn back, while the lantern's light illuminated the uneven puffs of mist coming from Edmund's lungs.

The hoot of an owl cut through the silence, sharp and sudden. Edmund's heart stuttered, and his fingers tightened around the axe handle, knuckles whitening. He scanned the path ahead, straining to catch a glimpse of the night sentinel. The silence that followed was almost sentient, as though the forest itself were holding its breath, waiting for him.

The crunch of dried leaves and twigs echoing in the silence led the way as he carried on. It was as if every sound he made was calling him to something just beyond the light's reach.

A rustle to his left snapped him to attention. He froze, pulse thundering in his ears, and stilled his lungs. The noise came again, this time from behind—closer, more distinct. Footsteps.

Edmund spun, axe raised, the lantern's light casting a swinging halo that only deepened the darkness beyond. The forest swallowed his frantic gaze, the branches shifting as if mocking his fear. The silence returned, deeper now, punctuated only by the whisper of the wind through the trees. His muscles tensed, expecting the sudden rush of movement or the glow of eyes rising from the brush.

A shadow moved, and his heart leapt to his throat. He crouched and set the lantern on the ground beside him, gripping the axe with both hands, readying himself for whatever emerged. The shape resolved into a slender form, stepping gently into the lantern's golden light—a deer. Its eyes were wide, deep pools that reflected the firelight, catching him in a gaze so calm and unafraid that it rooted him in place. The tension in his chest loosened slightly, replaced by an inexplicable sense of connection.

For a moment, Edmund and the deer stared at each other, the forest's menace giving way to a new stillness. The creature's calm exhales were visible in the cool air, mingling with his own in fragile wisps. There was no fear in its eyes, only a soft curiosity, as if it had appeared to remind him that not all things in the dark meant him harm. He let out a long, shaky sigh, the tautness in his limbs easing as the adrenaline ebbed.

The deer blinked once, then turned and bounded silently back into the woods, its form vanishing into shadow as if it had never been there. Edmund shook off his fright and returned the axe to its sheath. The fear that had gripped him moments before felt distant, almost foolish. He retrieved the lantern, its glow now lighting the path ahead once again. The wind sang through the branches, and with each step forward, he felt the forest watching—but no longer as an enemy. He pressed on, lantern held high, the estate looming somewhere ahead, waiting.

* * *

At last, the estate rose before him, a looming silhouette against the night sky, half-veiled in the low fog that clung to the ground like a shroud. The structure was massive, its stone walls wrapped in thick, knotted vines, resembling interwoven fingers holding up the crumbling façade. The windows, once proud and framed with intricate carvings, now stared out like hollow eyes—dark and unfeeling. The sprawling estate must have once been glorious, but time was a cruel mistress. Yet, it stood defiant, as if challenging the world to see through the decay to its former glory.

Edmund paused at the edge of the clearing. His gaze swept over the wild garden, where overgrown topiaries hinted at the forms they once held. He imagined the estate filled with life—groundskeepers and guests walking the gardens, the halls echoing with laughter, or perhaps the shrewd demands of the lady of the house. Now, it exuded a silence so profound it pulled the warmth from his bones. The estate was both a mausoleum and a monument, a testament to past beauty twisted by secrets too dark to bear the light.

Wind blew over the ivy, rustling the leaves, making it look as though the estate itself were gasping in the night air. The carved stone gargoyles perched above the arched entry sneered at him, their expressions frozen in grotesque mockery, as if they alone knew what dreadful secrets the walls concealed.

The cold gust pushed against Edmund, shifting his stance, and he momentarily thought the hooded figures from his nightmare might have been creeping up from behind. They weren't, but the screaming from the heavens flooded his mind.

Squinting his eyes tightly, he pressed them away, replacing them with the fond memory of Alice's laughter and Edith's hand on his knee.

"I'll see you soon," he whispered into the dark.

He opened his eyes, his vision now blurred with rage as he considered the monster inside. The cruel beast that had taken everything from him—he would reduce her to a pile of mangled flesh and bones—deserved her fate.

The gates groaned as he pushed them open, the cold metal scraping against stone, resonating into the hollow silence. Edmund's pulse quickened. This place, this hollow shell that mirrored the emptiness inside him, would soon be filled with wails of agony.

* * *

The gargoyles watched as he pushed the door open, the rusted hinges slicing through the silence. Wind moved past him as he stepped inside, snuffing out his lantern with a hiss. Darkness wrapped around him, thick and impenetrable, pressing down like the hand of an unseen giant. He stood motionless, straining to hear past the hammering of his own heartbeat.

The old timber pillars groaned under the magnitude of years and secrets. Statues lined the foyer, their outlines barely discernible, yet he sensed their stares. Drapes hung over the windows, heavy and unmoving, shrouding any hint of moonlight that might have eased the darkness.

Edmund clenched his jaw, lifting the axe in his hand, its familiar presence a small comfort. The silence was suffocating, broken only by the distant moan of trees bending in the wind. His boots creaked against the ancient floorboards, each step sounding louder than it should, as if the house itself were listening.

A shadowy, almost imperceptible noise made the hairs on the back of his neck rise—a soft rustle, a shift in the dark. He froze, muscles tensed, every nerve alight with instinct. The air pulsed with anticipation. His eyes darted, seeking movement, but the shadows refused to confess.

He exhaled slowly. The emptiness beyond the foyer loomed, vast and eerie, devoid of life yet charged with a presence that made his skin prickle.

Something was here.

Waiting.

Watching.

He took another step inside. The door groaned shut behind him, and dust fell off the curtains.

Edmund crept further into the dark, carefully pulling in air through his nostrils so as not to make more noise than necessary.

A sharp pain erupted in his side.

He broke the silence with a pained shout, clenching the muscles over his ribs. His agony was swallowed by a soft hand that clamped over his mouth from behind.

The metallic spark of blood filled his senses as the blade plunged into him again, sending fire lancing through his body. His vision blurred with agony, and he strained at his captor in futile resistance.

"This ends here, brother," a voice whispered behind him, spite and grief intertwined.

The hand pressed harder, muffling his strangled cry as the pain tripled, stealing his strength.

The presence behind him, breathing heavily with rage, hesitated for only a fraction of a second. It was enough. With a burst of desperate energy, Edmund wrenched free just enough to let out a hoarse shout, his voice cracking the oppressive silence. The hand fell away, and he stumbled forward, swinging his axe behind him, collapsing against an old, dust-covered table that shuddered under his weight.

The attacker, a shadow within the shadowy room, went still. For a heartbeat, the tension stretched taut—an eerie pause where time hovered on the verge of breaking. The figure stepped into a thin beam of moonlight filtering through a cracked window, revealing dark eyes wide with confusion and something close to shock.

Edmund's knees buckled as pain surged anew, his strength failing. He crumpled to the floor, the room spinning around him. His vision blackened, the last thing he saw was the woman he came to kill, standing frozen, dagger clutched in hand.

24

The Confrontation

This wasn't what he thought death would feel like. Angelic beings hadn't pulled him toward a light, nor had his wife reached out to receive him.

Instead, he heard the hum of a sad tune.

Edmund blinked open his eyes to see the blurred lines of wooden beams above him. His head rested on a lumpy pillow, and he found himself lying in a bed. The scent of aged wood lingered in the air, mingling with the fragrant notes of lavender. A lantern's flame sizzled, and the room groaned as a gust of wind pressed on the ancient building. His gaze traveled across the room, pausing on a tapestry of rolling hills hanging from the wall above a cracked chair. A small table at his bedside held the remnants of bandages and a bowl of water, tinged pink from blood—his blood. The realization struck him hard, sending a wave of nausea rolling through his gut.

He moved to stand, but pain lanced through his side. The breath he expelled came with a grunt, which echoed off the stone walls. His pulse pounded, matching the erratic beat of memories—shattered images of the estate, shadows shifting, a glinting blade cutting through the dark into his torso.

Edmund's brow furrowed, his breath faltering as the room shifted into focus.

Then he saw her.

The woman stood at the far end of the room. He was certain it was her—*the shadow in the chaos, the destroyer of all he loved,* now melodically humming just five paces away. But for the first time, he truly saw her as she was in the wavering lantern light. Young. Almost beautiful. Her sharp features, pale even in the warm glow, held an unsettling stillness, as if stone had been carved into something too perfect to be real. Her dark hair, damp with sweat—or was it blood?—clung to her temple, and her eyes—deep, dark, unreadable—were not the eyes of a mindless killer. They were something else. Calculating, perhaps? He couldn't tell, and that only stoked his anger.

She wore dark trousers and a linen shirt, sleeves rolled to the elbow. Blood stained the fabric—his, and likely hers. Above her wrist, nearly to her elbow, a gash—a deep, clean wound from his axe—but it didn't bleed.

This was the creature he had come to kill. And yet, standing here now, she looked nothing like the beast he had imagined. That made his hatred burn hotter.

She was studying the vial, eyes locked on it with an intensity that bordered on obsession. The light outlined her face in shades of shadow and amber, and he saw something in her expression that made his heart twist—sorrow, resignation, and a deep-rooted exhaustion.

He looked for his axe, but couldn't find it. He swallowed, trying to push back the tide of confusion and anger rising within him.

"Who… who are you?" he managed, his voice a rasp that betrayed the fear and fury simmering beneath.

His voice must have taken some time to cross the room because she continued looking at the vial. The moment passed, and Lucien's eyes darted up, wide and briefly unguarded, before settling on Edmund with renewed wariness. She drew a quick breath, fingers tightening around the vial before setting it down on the table with a deliberate motion.

The liquid swirled inside, casting red patterns that flickered across their faces.

"I didn't think you'd wake so soon. I'm Lucien," she said, voice low and steady, though it carried an undercurrent of unease.

Edmund said nothing but watched as she took a step toward him, now truly seeing her eyes for the first time. The hollowness within them spoke of pain and sleepless nights.

Edmund's eyes narrowed, and his breath came faster, each exhale pushed out in a grunt as the storm built inside him.

"Did you look into their eyes before you killed them? Did you see the fear? My wife, my little girl—how could you, you *demon*?" The echo of his daughter's laughter, warm and innocent, clashed violently with the silent, cold stillness of her lifeless form lying on the doctor's bed.

Lucien flinched, a subtle twitch that barely broke the mask of sorrow she wore. But it was there, and it gave Edmund a sick satisfaction—the only power he could claim from the bed where pain kept him prisoner.

Here it was, right in front of her. The result of the terror she had inflicted for centuries. Broken by grief, covered in pain, a man left behind to endure the loss of his family.

His fingers curled into fists, nails biting into his palms.

"You're a monster," he spat, the word soaked in venom. "A demon in human skin, preying on the innocent!" Sadness and confusion entered his mind. "Why would you kill them? What did they do to deserve that?"

Lucien's jaw tightened, and for a heartbeat, she looked away, unable to bear the raw accusation in his voice. Silence fell heavy over the room, broken only by the shifting of bandages over fresh wounds and a groan as Edmund fought to sit upright.

"You're right. They did not deserve it," she said, each syllable deliberate. "I didn't kill them. That man on the cart—he *killed* them. I came to stop him, Edmund." Lucien's eyes shifted as she relayed the half-truth, but Edmund didn't notice.

His eyes widened; surprise flew across his face before hardening once again.

"How? How do you know my name?"

Lucien's expression remained resolute.

"My brother talked about you. I believe he envied the life you have—*had*," she corrected herself.

"So he murdered an innocent child and a woman on her way to—*Do you fucking know why she was out there that night?*"

Lucien stared blankly back at him.

"She was on her way to deliver a baby," he said slowly, ensuring she heard every word. "But instead, the infant came out with the cord around its neck, and the father had to bury it in the garden on account of it never taking its first breath." Vitriol spilled across the room. "All this because he was jealous of me?" The fire in his eyes nearly burst out as he waited for her to speak.

Lucien's eyes glazed over as she nodded, etched with a grief that seemed to echo his own. She spoke, barely above a whisper, as if saying his name would summon his ghost.

"His name was Cassius," she admitted, the weight of her words pulling her shoulders down. "He *was* my brother—" She hesitated, the word sticking in her throat as though it tasted of ash. "But he became something monstrous. He killed them to get at you."

Edmund's head tilted as Lucien continued.

"He saw that you loved them, and he knew a blacksmith would surely be strong, but he wanted you angry. He wanted a man fighting with nothing left to lose." She pointed toward the vial she had set on the table. "He became a monster, driven by rage brought on by the blood in that vial. I tried to stop him before he could reach your fam—" Lucien's words caught in her throat, "before he could hurt anyone else."

The room felt colder, the warmth of the lantern doing nothing to ward off the chill rippling over Edmund's skin.

"You're telling me that he killed them to bring about some sort of sick brawl with me?"

"Yes," Lucien whispered, the single word ripe with agony. "And I failed to stop him in time." Her eyes shimmered, no longer with the threat of tears but with the kind of guilt that had long dried to stone.

"I wanted to save them, but I was too late. When I saw what he had done, I drove him into the flames with a pitchfork and held him there until he stopped moving. I'm so sorry, Edmund," Lucien said, her voice almost pleading.

Edmund stared at her, the pieces shifting painfully in his mind. The rage that had fueled him dulled to a hollow ache, replaced by the uncertainty of a man standing on the brink of an abyss. The silence stretched, their shared grief binding them in a fragile, uneasy truce. For a fleeting moment, rather than enemies, they were two souls bound by the pain of what they had both lost.

Edmund's fists unclenched, the tension in his body giving way to a bone-deep weariness. He glanced at the vial, its blood-red liquid catching the light.

Lucien's eyes didn't waver, even as disbelief and anger marred Edmund's expression.

"What Cassius was—what I am… is something that defies belief, but you must hear me out—"

"What *you* are?"

Lucien noticed the pulse at Edmund's temple quickening as he continued.

"I don't care what you are. You think I'd believe there's any reason that could justify what he did?"

Lucien's gaze softened, haunted but determined.

"I don't ask for your trust, only that you hear me. I have lived lifetimes, watched kingdoms rise and fall, seen the world change over ages. And through it all, that"—she nodded toward the vial—"has cursed my family."

Edmund's eyes flicked to the vial, a mix of dread and an unexpected pull that stirred deep within him, like a whisper brushing the edge of his consciousness. The crimson liquid seemed aware of his gaze, tugging at something primal and unspoken.

"You said *ages*? How long?" His voice was raw, skeptical but tinged with an unsettling intrigue despite himself.

"Too long," Lucien admitted, a shadow passing over her features. "Centuries that blur together. The blood in that vial holds power—immortality, yes, but at a price that corrodes the soul and corrupts the mind.

It binds, it consumes, and causes us to kill, endlessly. I

have tried to destroy it, to end it, but it cannot be undone. It replenishes itself, an endless cycle of torment."

Edmund's laugh was sharp, edged with hysteria. "Immortality? This is madness. You speak of legends, tales to frighten children, nothing more."

"Do I?" Lucien retrieved the vial. The liquid inside sloshed slowly, as if stirred by unseen forces. She released the latch with a deliberate flick, the metallic snap sharp in the quiet.

Tilting the vial, she let a few drops of its contents fall onto the wound Edmund's axe had carved into her forearm. Hours old, it had already begun to mend—muscle reknitting beneath the surface—yet the skin remained split, raw and open.

Each drop slithered across her skin, sinking into the wound as if drawn by unseen hands. The torn flesh sealed itself, the last traces of injury vanishing until only smooth, unblemished skin remained.

He stared, stunned into silence, the air between them heavy with the impossible truth. His gaze met hers, and the doubt in his eyes began to erode under the weight of what he'd witnessed.

"Then you… you really—"

"I'm not lying to you," Lucien said, the conviction in her voice echoing in the room.

"I am bound to this curse, as Cassius was, as were others before us. It brings strength, longevity—but robs you of everything else."

She placed the vial back on the table, and Edmund's eyes followed its movement.

"And now," her eyes darkened, and she tilted her head toward Edmund, "it is up to us to make sure it never claims another life."

25

The Plan to End It

"Us? No. There is no *us*. Your brother killed my family, and if I presume correctly, they weren't the first."

Lucien shook her head.

"And you're bound to this 'curse' as well?"

She nodded.

"So there's a century's worth of blood on your hands *as well?*"

Her eyes looked down at the floor and stayed there.

"There's no *us*."

She drew in a slow breath and replied, "I'm not like him. When I was younger, long ago, I had friends, and I was happy. They loved me, and I loved them. But my mother—she forced this on me. While I slept, she poured the cursed blood into my mouth. I didn't want this, I didn't ask for this, and I want it to end."

Lucien told him how she fled—how she tried to leave it all behind—and how she fought to resist. She told him about the man in the barn, how her mother teased the blood from his neck to entice her.

Tears fell from her face, and Edmund put on his shirt.

Edmund spoke. "Then why hold onto it? Why not pour it out and be done with it?"

Lucien retrieved the vial and returned to Edmund, weary resignation etched into her face. Without a word, she unlatched the lid and tipped it over, letting the viscous fluid spill onto the table. It pooled for a moment, then slithered outward in thin, searching trails, as if looking for something—or someone. It slipped over the edge, dripping onto the floorboards before seeping through the cracks and vanishing into the dark below.

Edmund's gaze followed the blood's path, but as soon as the last drop left the vial, an impossible thing happened: the vessel began to refill itself, the liquid swirling anew, as though drawn from a bottomless well.

"What… how is that possible?" he whispered, the ember of hope snuffed out by the relentless truth, replaced by a dangerous curiosity that unsettled him.

"It doesn't end," Lucien said, her voice hollow, the practiced acceptance of centuries laced in her tone. "It regenerates itself, bound to a power deeper and older than you or I can fathom."

Edmund's jaw clenched, his frustration boiling over. He pressed his palms to his temples, then dropped his hands, fingers splayed as he struggled to think through the impossible. "Then destroy it. It's just glass, isn't it?"

Without hesitation, she reached for a bust of an unknown aristocrat perched on a shelf. Her fingers tightened around it, and with fierce determination, she brought it crashing down onto the vial. The bust shattered instantly, fragmenting into jagged pieces that scattered across the floor, but the vial remained unscathed, standing defiantly amid the wreckage.

The room fell silent in the wake of the noise, the air charged and tense. But the vial sat there, untouched, unchipped, gleaming as if mocking their attempt.

"It isn't just glass," she said, her voice low, each word carrying the weight of both defeat and defiance. "It is bound by something that even I have yet to fully understand. I have spent lifetimes trying to break it, to shatter its hold, but it resists everything—fire, stone, the sharpest edge. Nothing can harm it.

"I've tried to hide it as well—to bury it deep in the earth," Lucien said, a weary smile tugging at her lips, devoid of joy. "But it finds its way back to me, always. It calls to those who seek power, those willing to pay any price."

Edmund stared at the unyielding vial, the grim realization settling over him like a shroud. Yet, even as dread coiled in his gut, the vial seemed to purr with a silent promise, a temptation that slithered through his veins, leaving his pulse pounding in his ears.

"Then what hope do we have?" The question lingered, spoken as much to himself as to her, the room's silence offering no answer but the steady, menacing thrum of the liquid that refused to die, its allure pressing on him like an unspoken challenge.

Lucien's gaze shifted away from the vial, the hard lines of her face softening as memories flooded back, old wounds reopening in the silence. She sat on the bed, folding her hands in her lap, fingers intertwined as though holding herself together.

"There was a time when I believed I could wield the power without falling to its darkness," she began, her voice measured, each word carefully chosen. "When I first realized what the blood could do—its ability to heal, to grant strength beyond human limits—I told myself it was a gift, a tool to right wrongs, to dispense justice where the world had failed."

Edmund's eyes narrowed, suspicion etched into every tense muscle of his face.

"Justice?" He couldn't keep the bitterness from his voice. The sting of loss, of what he had witnessed, made the word sound like a cruel jest.

Lucien met his gaze, unflinching, the truth stark in her eyes.

"Yes, justice. Do you know why this place is empty?"

Edmund tilted his head.

"The lady beat her servants, and the lord forced himself on the youngest ladies among them. So I put an end to that. As I put an end to countless others who had done unspeakable deeds. I was the blade that cut where justice could not reach. Even as the blood tied me to its curse, I was preventing more suffering."

She paused, looking past Edmund as if seeing through the walls of the room into centuries past. Her voice grew quieter, burdened by guilt.

"But power is never content to be wielded without cost. It whispered, changed me in ways that felt subtle at first. I started justifying more—more deaths, more blood, blurring the line between vengeance and justice until there was no line at all."

Edmund's brow raised as he listened, the sharp edges of his rage blunted by her words.

"And Cassius?" he asked, his voice low, wary. "How does he fit into your plan for 'justice'?"

Lucien's expression darkened, shadows flitting across her

face.

"Cassius was different. He wasn't drawn to the vial by accident but by choice. He embraced what it offered, without restraint or purpose—just hunger. I tried to stop him before the blood had pulled him too far, but by then, he was lost. He took what he wanted, reveled in it, leaving devastation in his wake."

The room seemed to hold its breath as Lucien continued.

"I stayed with him for years, hoping to change him. But each foul deed only proved that the vial's influence was more cunning than either of us could imagine. It fed on ambition, on rage, shaping him into something monstrous. And when I finally confronted him, I was already too late." Her voice broke, just a fraction, as the ache of failure pressed down on her.

Edmund sat motionless, absorbing the reality she painted. The truth she spoke was laced with dread, but there was something else there, too—a shared pain that resonated with the hollowness inside him.

"And now?" he asked, the question slipping out before he could stop it. "Now, you want it all to end, don't you?"

Lucien nodded, eyes cast down.

"I've carried the curse long enough, held onto this twisted existence thinking I could use it for something greater. But it consumes everything. It turns us into shadows of who we once were." She looked up, her gaze locking onto his, fierce and determined. "If you've seen enough to believe me, then you know that this cannot go on. I want it to end. I need it to end."

Edmund absorbed her confession, the anger and disbelief unraveling into something more complex—a cautious understanding, a kinship rooted in loss. The room's silence deepened as both of them sat, bound by the heavy truth that, for now, refused to let them go.

"And I need *your* help."

* * *

She reached for the vial on the table, the crimson liquid glowing in the shifting lantern light, casting red across their faces once she had blown off the dust of the aristocrat.

"You need to take this," Lucien said, calm determination in her voice.

Edmund's gaze narrowed, his instincts recoiling.

"Are you serious? No. I won't touch that thing. Not after everything you've said."

Lucien's eyes darkened with urgency, her fingers turning the vial in her grasp. An icy draft slipped through the floorboards, curling at her ankles, and for a brief moment, she hesitated. Could she tell him the truth about the beings hunting the vial—the forces her mother had warned of with such conviction?

Her gaze flicked to Edmund's face. Exhaustion and pain were etched into every line, yet his eyes held a fierce resolve. But would he believe her? Or worse, would the truth about the dangers it drew drive him away? If she told him, he might refuse it entirely, leaving her trapped with the burden once again.

And deep down, a darker question gnawed at her: did she even believe it anymore?

Cassius's scornful words echoed in her mind. She had never seen these so-called evil beings—no proof they existed beyond the shadows her mother had woven into her tales. Was the danger real, or was it a story to bind her to this curse, to convince her to carry on a responsibility she had never chosen? The thought slithered through her, unsettling and poisonous.

But the doubt cut both ways.

If they were real, and she gave the vial to Edmund without warning him, he would be defenseless. Yet, the thought of that possibility—her being freed of the vial forever—overpowered her hesitation. If he refused, then she would never find peace. She had made her decision. She couldn't bear to keep this existence any longer.

Lucien straightened, the conflict buried deep within. Her voice steadied.

"You must. If it stays here, it will call to others, just as it called to me and Cassius. It will start all over again. Please. You're a good man, Edmund."

She leaned closer, her voice dropping to a plea that carried centuries of warning.

"Keep it hidden. Guard it with your life, but never—" her eyes bored into his with a rawness that stilled the room— "never drink from it."

Lucien grabbed his wrist and pulled him closer still. Pain shot through his ribs as she placed the vial in his hand. The glass was cool against his palm, deceptively delicate as it thrummed—a dark and subtle pulse beneath his fingers.

The hairs on his neck stood at attention as Lucien exhaled, a brief hint of relief softening her features. Every instinct screamed at him to refuse, to deny this bizarre fate, but he found no words.

She stood, moving to the heavy drapes that had shielded the

room from the moon's gaze. With a swift motion, she grabbed the lantern and threw it against the ground, shattering the glass and covering the edges of the drapes in burning oil. Her actions were swift and deliberate, a final act to erase the dark legacy tied to this place. Fire roared to life, devouring the velvet in an instant, the light bathing the room in an urgent blaze that pushed back the shadows.

"Get up," she said, her voice now steel.

She looped an arm under Edmund's, hauling him from the bed despite the pain evident on his face. The heat of the fire seared across the room, sweat trickling down his temple as he leaned heavily on her, each step a battle against pain and gravity.

"What are you doing?" he rasped, eyes wide as the fire spread, licking hungrily at the walls.

"I'm making sure this ends here," Lucien replied, her tone final.

The room behind them was a maelstrom of fire, the flames consuming their way through the wooden beams, breathing out ghastly ribbons and heat.

She turned to him, eyes softer now, a rare tenderness in their depths.

"Listen to me, Edmund. You go through this door, you push that armoire against it, and you don't look back. No matter what you hear, no matter what happens, you leave this place and don't open that door."

Confusion and dread lined his face as he stared at her.

"Lucien, what are you—"

"No questions." Her voice faltered for a heartbeat. "Promise me you'll take it."

A lump formed in his throat as he nodded, the wordless

agreement pulled from a place deep and primal. He glanced back at the flickering inferno, then at her, memorizing the outline of the woman who had shifted from foe to something achingly close to an ally.

"Go, Edmund. Make sure this ends with me," she urged, and with a final push, she stepped back into the room, the flames roaring in their dance around her as she slammed the door shut. Edmund heard the thud of the door being barred over the sound of the inferno.

* * *

Edmund staggered into the hallway. Flickers of light seeped through the cracks around the door, casting restless, wavering shadows that danced along the walls and ceiling. Raising his hand toward his face and opening his fist, he found intricate patterns of deep pink pressed into his pale palm. Smoke began to curl into the space, stinging his eyes.

He placed the vial into his trousers and did as he was instructed, throwing himself against the armoire that stood against the opposite wall. The ancient wood groaned as he pushed, muscles straining, pain flaring from his wounds. His breath came in short, desperate gasps, sweat trickling down his brow as he heaved again. The heavy piece of furniture finally tipped, crashing down in front of the door with a resounding thud. The impact sent splinters flying, and items tumbled out—a cracked porcelain bowl, a dusty book, forgotten relics of another life.

The muffled roar of the fire grew louder, punctuated by the crackling of timber as flames devoured the room beyond. A crash within signaled the collapse of a beam, and Edmund

232

flinched, pressing his hands against the armoire as if he could somehow hold back the chaos.

A scream cut through the noise, sharp and anguished—unmistakably Lucien's voice. Edmund's blood ran cold, every instinct screaming at him to help her. Her fierce command, *"Don't look back,"* replayed in his mind, colliding with the raw urge to save her. The scream tapered off, swallowed by the roar of the fire reclaiming its dominance.

He clenched his jaw, eyes shut tight, and took a shuddering breath. The rising smoke stung his throat and eyes, adding to the burn of helplessness coursing through him. Edmund forced himself to step away, stumbling down the hall as the light behind him grew stronger, casting jagged, fiery shadows that stretched down the walls like grasping hands.

The stairs seemed endless, each step rattling through his bones. At last, he reached the entrance and shoved the heavy doors open, stumbling into the night.

Cool air surged over him, sharp and bracing, biting into his sweat-soaked skin—a jarring contrast to the inferno roaring behind. He gasped, drawing in the air as if it could cleanse the ash and fire from his chest. Turning, his eyes met the flames that surged higher, pouring through shattered windows and cracks, painting the sky in an angry crimson hue. The estate groaned under the fire's assault, beams splintering and walls buckling, sending sparks arcing into the night like fireflies fleeing the blaze.

For a moment, time slowed, the crackling of the fire mingling with the pounding of his heart. He reached into his pocket and felt the cool glass—a reminder that his nightmare was far from over. His chest heaved, each breath torn between exhaustion and the realization of what he now carried. Edmund's gaze locked on the flames as if searching for some trace of Lucien, some movement, anything to break the finality pressing down on him. But the fire swallowed all, reducing every hope, every sound, to nothing. The night settled into silence, punctuated by the roar of the blaze and the steady thrum of the vial in his grasp, as though it acknowledged its own indomitable presence—a burden that no flame could cleanse or erase.

IV

Part Four

26

The Offer

The world around me seemed to blur, and for a moment, I was entirely consumed by the pull of the vial. The marketplace sounds faded, leaving only a quiet stirring in the distance as my focus tightened on the small glass object in my hand, its murky red liquid catching glints of the late afternoon sun. I shook myself, grounding back into the present, forcing myself to set the vial back on the counter in front of Hassan.

I cleared my throat, trying to keep my voice steady.

"So, um, how exactly did it end up with you, Hassan?" I asked, glancing around at the bustling, thinning crowd as if to remind myself that I wasn't alone here. "I mean, what happened next? That was, what—" I paused, estimating. "Years ago?"

Hassan tilted his head, a hint of amusement curling at the corners of his mouth.

"Ah, yes. How did it end up here?" He turned his gaze out to the thinning crowd, as though trying to draw the answer from beyond the shadows. "I suppose you could say it found me. Or perhaps I found it... Who's to say which is which?"

I narrowed my eyes, not willing to let him off that easily.

"So, what happened to it? What did this Edmund character actually do with it? He didn't drink from it, right?" I paused, trying to keep the skepticism out of my voice. "Or did he... is he still out there?" I glanced over my shoulder mockingly.

Hassan chuckled softly, resting his fingers on the vial, caressing it as if it were some precious relic.

"Ah, the tale of Edmund is for another time," he murmured. "Some say Edmund triumphed; others say he vanished without a trace." His fingers stilled, and he glanced up at me, eyes dark and unreadable. "Perhaps the vial did not want him as its keeper after all."

A chill slid down my spine.

"And then what?" I asked, hoping to ground myself with practicality. "How'd you end up with it?"

Hassan sighed, as if he'd been waiting for that question.

"The vial travels with a purpose, Mr. Armstrong. It finds its way into the hands of those who are... curious." He lifted the vial and held it in the light, studying it with reverence. "It has crossed oceans and continents. It has seen wars, empires rise and fall... and now, it's here. With you."

I blinked, momentarily thrown off.

"With me?" My laugh was half-hearted, an instinctive attempt to push back the unease crawling up my spine. "You think it's just... fate? That this little glass bottle has some grand cosmic plan?"

Hassan set the vial back on the table with deliberate care, his hands folding over one another.

"Not fate, necessarily," he said, his voice measured. "But perhaps it seeks those who might understand it. Those who are not afraid to look beyond what is seen."

I scoffed, though unease lingered.

"That doesn't explain why you'd hand it over to me. You've had it this long—why don't you just keep it?"

Hassan's smile faded, replaced by something heavier, more solemn.

"Because I cannot carry it any longer. My time grows short, Mr. Armstrong. And this vial…" His gaze darkened as he tapped the counter beside it. "It requires a new keeper. Someone it chooses."

"Chooses," I repeated flatly, my lips curling into a wry smirk. "And it just so happens to choose me? You don't think that's a little *con-ve-ni-ent*?"

Hassan tilted his head, his eyes sharp with an unsettling clarity. "Not convenient. Necessary. A man like you— brilliant, curious—doesn't come along often. Your work on XN-34 alone makes you uniquely suited for this."

I blinked, the air shifting around me.

"What did you say?" My voice faltered as I processed the words.

"XN-34," Hassan repeated calmly, as if this were a casual conversation. "The protein you've been studying. Regeneration, yes? Quite fascinating. A discovery that could redefine what we know about life itself."

My pulse quickened. I was here in Jerusalem for that very reason—to deliver a keynote on XN-34. But hearing those words from a merchant in a dimly lit stall made the familiar sound foreign, ominous even.

"How do you know about that?" I asked, my voice sharpened with suspicion.

Hassan didn't flinch.

"I may not seem the academic type, Mr. Armstrong, but even I can appreciate the impact of your research. A keynote address, was it? One that has stirred no small amount of attention."

His words sent a flicker of relief through me, but only briefly.

"So you read the program?" I said, narrowing my eyes. "What does XN-34 have to do with… any of this?"

Hassan regarded me in silence for a moment, as if weighing how much to reveal.

"Because your work seeks to unravel the mysteries of re-generation," he said finally. "And this"—his fingers tapped the vial—"is a mystery of regeneration that has defied explanation for millennia. Perhaps it has been waiting for someone like you."

The connection felt tenuous, almost laughable. But his tone carried a conviction that gnawed at me.

"You're saying this… *thing* is alive?" I asked, my voice dripping with skepticism.

"Not alive," Hassan replied, his gaze steady. "But it holds power. A power that regenerates endlessly, defying all attempts to destroy it. Surely, Mr. Armstrong, a scientist of your caliber would be intrigued by such a phenomenon.

You are curious, are you not? A man of science. You have heard its story, its legacy, and yet you still linger here, questioning instead of walking away." He paused, letting the words settle. "That is why it chose *you*."

The absurdity of his statement rattled me.

"I'm not walking away because I'm trying to make sense of this, not because I want it," I snapped. "And what if I don't take it? What if I leave it here and let someone else deal with this… mess?"

Hassan's gaze didn't waver.

"Then it will find its way back to you. Or to someone else, someone less prepared. The vial does not rest, Mr. Armstrong. It moves with purpose."

My frustration boiled over. I rose from the bench and pointed at the vial.

"You keep saying it has purpose, that it chooses people, that it can't be destroyed. But what if it's just a damn bottle, *huh*? What if this is all just a story?"

Hassan regarded me silently for a long moment, his expression unreadable. Then he reached into the shadows of his stall, producing a heavy brass weight, its edges worn smooth. He placed it on the counter with a deliberate thud.

"Prove me wrong," he said simply, his tone even. "If it is just a story, then this will end it."

I stared at him, my breath caught in my throat. Then, without thinking, I grabbed the weight and slammed it down onto the vial. The impact reverberated through my hand, but as the weight broke into jagged pieces, the vial remained untouched.

I stepped back, my hands trembling.

"What the hell…"

Hassan's voice was calm, almost sympathetic.

"Now you begin to see."

I stared at the shattered brass weight, its jagged edges scattered in front of me. My pulse roared in my ears, drowning out the hum of the marketplace around us. The vial sat there, unmarked, undisturbed, as though it had swallowed the impact whole.

"This isn't…" My voice faltered as the rational part of my

mind clawed for an explanation. "There has to be something. A trick. Reinforced glass, or… or…" I trailed off, the words dissolving under Hassan's unwavering gaze.

"It does not break," he said, his voice soft but firm, each word cutting through my doubts. "It does not yield. And you cannot ignore that."

I wanted to argue, to push back, but my own words betrayed me. The impossible lay bare before me, leaving no room for my usual defenses. Slowly, my hand curled into a fist at my side, a futile effort to anchor myself.

"What do you expect me to do with it?" I asked finally, my voice strained. "If it can't be destroyed, then what's the point? Just… hold onto it forever?"

Hassan shook his head, his expression grave.

"Not forever. But perhaps long enough to understand it. To uncover the truth behind its power, its curse. And, if you are fortunate, to end it."

"You make it sound so simple," I said bitterly. "But even if I wanted to do what you're asking, how do I stop myself from becoming just another story of ruin? You said it's cursed. Wouldn't it destroy me too?"

"It might," Hassan admitted, his voice dropping to a somber note. "It has undone many before you. But the curse does not act alone—it is fed by desire. By ambition, hunger, greed." He leaned forward, his eyes narrowing. "You must resist its promises, its whispers. Keep it close, but do not let it consume you. That is the only way."

His words sent a chill down my spine, but they also lit a spark of defiance.

"You make it sound like this thing wants to kill me."

"Kill *you*?" Hassan chuckled dryly, though there was no

humor in it. "No. But it is patient, and it knows how to wait for weakness."

I stared at him, the sincerity of his words settling uncomfortably over me. The vial, impossibly unbroken from earlier, rested on the counter as if taunting me. My rational mind grappled with the scene, trying to reduce it to a trick, a clever deception. But the logical threads unraveled in the moment. No trick could explain what I had just witnessed.

The thought prickled at the back of my mind: *What if he's right?* The vial was dangerous—Hassan's warnings made that much clear. The temptation to leave it behind, to walk away and let someone else deal with it, clawed at me. But even as the thought surfaced, another voice pushed through, louder, more insistent: *If it really is what he says it is... then it's too important to ignore.*

I thought of the lab, of XN-34, and the years I'd spent trying to make sense of something few dared to study. That protein had consumed so much of my life—pushing me into endless cycles of research, travel, speaking engagements. I'd already told myself I was ready to step back, to let others take up the mantle, to find some semblance of peace.

But this... this vial was something else entirely. If it truly held the power Hassan claimed, if it could not only ruin lives but also heal... then I couldn't just leave it here. I'd take it back, study it, understand the fluid's properties. And then I'd destroy it—find a way, no matter what it took. This could be the work that defined everything, the final piece of the puzzle I didn't know I'd been searching for. Yet, deep down, I couldn't ignore the nagging thought: *What if it consumes me too?*

I exhaled slowly, steadying myself. The unease coiled tightly in my stomach didn't loosen, but a grim resolve settled over me. I couldn't walk away from this. Not now.

I reached for the vial, my fingers hovering over its smooth surface before closing around it. The glass felt cool in my hand, but beneath the chill, I swore I felt a faint hum, like a heartbeat just out of sync with my own. I pulled my hand back sharply, staring at the thing as if it might lunge at me.

"I don't even know where to start," I muttered.

"You start," Hassan said, his voice steady, "by taking it away from here. By keeping it hidden. Study it if you must, but never let it out of your sight." His eyes bore into mine with intensity. "And above all, Mr. Armstrong, do not drink from it. No matter how desperate, no matter how tempting. Promise me that."

I nodded slowly, the motion jerky and unsure.

"Fine," I said, tucking the vial into the inner pocket of my coat, its form pressing against my ribs like a cold brand. "But I'm only taking this to figure out what it is. Don't expect me to believe all this about curses and whispers."

Hassan inclined his head, the faintest smile tugging at his lips. "Of course, Mr. Armstrong. I would expect no less from a man of science."

I turned to leave, the sounds of the marketplace rushing back into focus as I stepped away from the stall. But before I had taken more than a few steps, Hassan's voice cut through the din, low and clear.

"Good luck, Mr. Armstrong. You will need it."

27

Going Home

The moment I settled into my seat for the flight back to Raleigh-Durham International Airport, a wave of exhaustion washed over me. I leaned back, closing my eyes as the engines roared to life, filling the cabin with a dull, comforting drone. My thoughts drifted to Sara, and a pang of guilt crept in.

She'd tried to be understanding—through every trip, every delayed return, every rushed phone call with promises of *"I'll be back soon."* And Ethan, always growing, changing, slipping further into adulthood with each passing year. It killed me to miss moving him into his dorm room. Luckily, through the miracle of technology, I was still able to get the grand tour—which took all of three seconds.

My eyes fluttered open with a sudden need to check that the vial was safe. I unbuckled my seatbelt and stood, unlatching the overhead compartment to retrieve my carry-on. My fingers found the sterile package tucked securely inside. Bagged and officially labeled as a research sample, it had passed through security in my carry-on without question, yet its presence felt heavier than its modest weight. *It was just a trinket,* I told myself again. Settling back into the worn cushion, I peeled open the packaging, the crisp crinkle of plastic startlingly loud against the quiet hum of the cabin.

The glass was cool and smooth in my hand. For a moment, I tilted it slightly, watching the liquid catch the reading light, shifting in a way that felt unnervingly alive.

I pulled my laptop from the crap-catcher in front of me and slipped the vial into the inside breast pocket of my jacket. I began writing every word Hassan had told me. No detail would be left out, from the precise location of *Hassan's Things* to the approximate location of the estate, and each twisting turn of events in between. Perhaps within them, some clue might be found as to what this thing really was. Though more likely, capturing the story would allow me to retell it more vividly to colleagues who questioned my motives.

My seat neighbors had fallen asleep before I boarded the plane, the woman's head cocked uncomfortably at ninety degrees, resting on the man's shoulder, and his head resting atop hers. Their necks were going to be a wreck once we landed. Across the cabin, passengers dozed or stared into the glow of their screens, heads dipping forward only to jolt upright again—a slow, unconscious rhythm of exhaustion.

I looked up from the screen to my neighbor across the aisle and found him looking at me. Not at my screen, but at me. We made eye contact for a second longer than I'd have liked before he turned away. A few minutes later, the same thing. I gave him the old *what-the-hell?*-empty-hands shrug, and he gave me the raised-eyebrows *I-don't-know-what-you-mean* look in return. I angled my laptop away and brushed it off—a coincidence, nothing more. But as the hours dragged on, his stare ate at me.

The flight attendant, a young woman with a bright smile, paused by my seat to offer a drink. I closed the laptop, satisfied with my documentation, and looked up at her. She wasn't looking at my eyes, though. Her gaze lingered at my chest, the way a creeper might at a voluptuous woman. I nodded my chin upward to break her stare and forced a polite smile, trying to ignore the unease in my stomach.

"Ginger ale, please," I murmured, crossing my arms tightly, as though that would muffle whatever strange signal the vial seemed to be broadcasting. She nodded and moved on, but her look lingered a moment too long, her brow furrowing before she finally turned.

Did she know something? Did she sense the power contained in this small, unassuming object? I shook my head, willing the thoughts away. My stomach tonic never came. I just needed to get home, get some sleep, and let the madness of the past few days fade into memory.

As the flight continued, I tried to rest, letting the steady sound of the cabin lull me into a quiet reverie. I found myself again thinking of Sara—the subtle way she'd smile when she thought I wasn't looking, the way her fingers would lightly brush mine as she passed a coffee cup across the table in the mornings. It had been too long since I'd seen her smile like that.

We'd had countless quiet moments together over the years, but somehow, I'd let them slip further and further apart. I'd become so caught up in my work—the endless travel, the bright lights of one conference hall after another—that I'd almost forgotten the warmth of home.

For the first time in years, I felt a pang of longing. The way she looked at me when I walked through the door, the sound of her voice saying *"Welcome home"*—it had all started to feel like a memory. But now, with just hours left until I could see her, the image of Sara waiting for me at the door felt as vivid as it had in the early years when every homecoming felt like an event.

And Ethan. I smiled inside, thinking of him—my son, my pride, off at college and doing better than I could have imagined. He'd inherited Sara's sharp wit and her persistence, always pushing himself, always dreaming big. The house had felt emptier since he'd left, a reminder of how quickly time slipped by. But Sara told me he'd be home when I got back.

We'd all be together, the three of us, if only for a short while.

It was a rare chance, a rare moment where work would take a back seat. I could imagine it clearly: the three of us around the dinner table, laughing, talking, catching up on all the things I'd missed.

My fingers brushed the edge of my jacket pocket, feeling the vial's hard outline beneath the fabric, but I reluctantly pulled my hand away. I wanted nothing to interrupt that moment—not even the strange object, a prop from an even stranger story.

I took a deep breath, watching the clouds drift by outside the window, and allowed myself to imagine my son's smile, my wife's laugh. Soon, I'd be home, and for once, nothing else would matter.

28

Welcome Home

The thin layer of snow crunched under my tires as I steered into the driveway. Our home looked warm. The familiar golden glow peeked through the cracks in the white shutters into the frigid dusk air. Sara had left the porch light on for me, like always. I slow-slid to a stop on the icy driveway. Traffic was a mess due to the inch of snow on the ground and people suddenly forgetting how to drive in the weather, but I was home now, and that was enough for me to begin releasing the tension in my neck.

I turned off the ignition and leaned my head against the headrest, savoring the silence after hours of planes, customs lines, and idiot drivers. The light tapping of branches swaying in the breeze on the hood reminded me it was time to get inside.

The trip had been everything I expected—hectic, enlightening, exhausting—and more. And as much as I loved explaining the importance of my work, the pats on the back, and exploring a new city, I was ready for a break. No more flights, no more conferences. Just time with Sara and Ethan.

Reaching over to the passenger seat, I grabbed my leather computer bag and carry-on, careful with the souvenirs inside. I was so excited to see what Ethan thought of the tonic. Would he roll his eyes at me for falling for a ridiculous sales pitch? Probably. I smiled at the thought, already picturing his reaction.

The porch light flickered when I began my ascent up the slippery steps.

I've been meaning to fix that, but it can wait, I thought to myself—winning a small battle against perfectionism.

The chimney, exhaling a steady stream of warmth, brought a smile to my face. Sara knew I loved a fire.

My body ached from the travel, but I made it to the top of the five steps successfully, my carry-on awkwardly catching on the last one.

I reached for the doorknob, but before my hand made contact, the door creaked open.

* * *

There she was—Sara, her curved hips the first thing I saw. She leaned casually against the frame, her arms crossed but her eyes bright.

"You're early," she said, a teasing lilt in her voice.

"Yeah, we caught a nice tailwind at about 33,000 feet."

I stepped inside, setting my bags down near the door. The house enveloped me in its familiar warmth, the soft light spilling from the living room feeling like an embrace all its own.

Sara let out a small laugh, shaking her head as she moved closer.

"Glad to hear it, Mr. Pilot." She reached for me, her arms brushing lightly against mine as she closed the distance.

I cupped her face gently with both hands, letting my thumbs graze her cheekbones as I leaned down to kiss her. It wasn't rushed or overly eager, just a moment filled with relief, comfort, and love—a way to ground myself after weeks of absence.

When I pulled back, her eyes softened, and she smiled up at me.

"I missed you too," she said, her hands resting lightly on my forearms. She gave a small squeeze before threading her fingers through mine, guiding me into the house. "It's been way too quiet around here without you."

I chuckled, glancing toward the living room. "Quiet? With Ethan home? Hard to believe."

"Oh, don't worry," Sara said, rolling her eyes playfully. "He's excited you're home. Probably already plotting how to drag you into one of his marathon conversations about fitness or nonlinear equations."

"Good. I've got a few stories to tell him too."

Sara gestured toward the kitchen as she stepped aside, giving me room to take in the familiar comforts of home.

"Come on, then. Close that door before you catch a cold."

"I know you know that's not how it works," I laughed, grabbing my bags, hitting the door closed with my hip, and following the view I had missed so desperately.

The warm light from the overhead fixture highlighted the cluttered table—a mix of the everyday life I was glad to return to. Mail sat in a pile next to a metal water bottle, and Sara's open laptop whirred, reminding me it was beyond time for a replacement.

I hefted my computer bag onto one of the kitchen chairs before dropping my carry-on onto the table.

"Ethan!" Sara called toward the stairs, her voice carrying with that gentle authority only she could pull off. "Your dad's home!"

Heavy footsteps immediately thundered down the staircase, and I couldn't help but grin. Moments later, Ethan burst into the kitchen, his energy filling the room like a gust of fresh air.

"Dad!" Ethan said, grinning wide as he crossed the space and pulled me into a quick hug.

"Good to see you, buddy," I said, clapping him on the back.

"You too, Dad," Ethan replied. But as he stepped back slightly, his brow furrowed. "Hey, what's that?"

The hug had been too tight. He must have felt the hard outline of the vial pressing between us. A quick wave of nausea rolled through me, panic flaring before I forced out a laugh, patting his shoulder to steer the moment away.

"Oh, it's nothing. Just... a work thing," I said casually, adjusting my coat to obscure the outline. "You've been working on those new muscles, huh? Let's see if they're the real deal."

Ethan's grin widened, his curiosity momentarily sidelined.

"Oh, are you jealous, old man?" he said, flexing exaggeratedly.

"Old man?" I raised an eyebrow, laughing as I reached out and ruffled his hair, earning a half-hearted swat in return. "Let's see what you've got."

Ethan lunged, grabbing my arm, and we tussled like we had when he was younger. I let him push me back a step before wriggling free and holding up my hands in mock surrender.

"Alright, alright. You win this one."

"Of course I do," Ethan said triumphantly, shaking out his arms like a prizefighter. Then, his expression shifted to one of mock seriousness. "Time to pay up. And I hope it's something good—not another airport sweatshirt."

"But you are *Too Sugoi to Handle*," I laughed, grateful for the shift in focus.

The confused expression on his face when he held up the sweatshirt and saw the illustration of a cat wearing sunglasses with *Too Sugoi to Handle* was worth the 6,000 yen I spent on it. But I haven't seen him wear it once.

"Don't worry. I think you'll like what I brought back this time."

Ethan leaned back against the counter, arms crossed, his grin curious.

"So, what was Jerusalem like? Did you get to explore, or was it all work?"

I sank into a chair, stretching my legs.

"A little of both. The city's incredible—modern in parts, ancient in others. It's like walking through layers of history. The streets are packed with people, it was a bit chaotic, but there's so much to see."

Sara turned from the sink, drying her hands with a towel.

"What about the conference?" she asked. "How'd the keynote go?"

I scratched the back of my neck, shrugging modestly.

"It went well, I think. A lot of questions afterward, which is always a good sign. They seemed interested."

Her lips quirked into a smile. "Of course they were. You've been working on this for ages. I'm sure they were impressed."

Ethan gave a small, teasing laugh. "Yeah, Dad. No one's going to top you talking about the role of XN-34 in cellular signaling pathways."

"Nor its implications for regenerative medicine," I corrected, putting on my best mock-serious tone and shooting him a pointed look.

"How could I forget?" Ethan said, grinning. "But you're back now, and we've got real priorities—like the souvenirs."

"Patience, Iago," I said, toying with his enthusiasm. "I'll get to it, I promise."

"So, did anything… weird happen?" Ethan asked. "Jerusalem seems like the kind of place where you'd run into something unexpected."

I paused for just a fraction of a second, the memory surfacing briefly in my mind before I waved the thought away.

"The markets were definitely… colorful," I said, choosing my words carefully. "Met some interesting people, saw some things I hadn't expected. But mostly, it was work."

Sara raised a brow at that but didn't press. Ethan, on the other hand, leaned forward, undeterred.

"Come on, Dad. You can't just say 'interesting people' and leave it at that."

I leaned toward my carry-on with a quiet laugh. "Don't I owe you a souvenir?" Pulling the bag closer, I couldn't help but smile at the anticipation lighting up Ethan's face.

"Let's start with this," I said, reaching into the carry-on and pulling out a small, neatly wrapped package. I set it on the table in front of Sara.

She raised a brow, clearly amused.

"For me?"

"Of course," I said with a smirk. "Go ahead, open it."

Sara carefully unwrapped the package, her fingers pausing as the gold necklace slipped into view, the emerald stone at its center even more magnificent in the warm light of the kitchen.

"Oh, James," she said softly, lifting the necklace to get a better look. "It's beautiful."

Ethan leaned over for a better view. "Wow. Looks expensive."

"The woman who sold it to me assured me it's 'most definitely real gold,'" I said jokingly. "Green always looks good on you."

"It's perfect," Sara said, her voice sincere as she smiled at me. She leaned over and pressed a quick kiss to my cheek. "Thank you."

Ethan straightened, his grin widening. "Okay, my turn. What'd you get me?"

I laughed and reached into the bag again, pulling out a dark glass bottle with an ornate label.

"This," I said, setting it on the table in front of him, "is a miracle brew—or so the guy selling it claimed. Supposedly boosts strength, endurance, and vitality."

Ethan picked up the bottle, examining it with a mix of curiosity and skepticism. "Miracle brew, huh? You're saying if I drink this, I'll be able to bench like twice my max?"

I chuckled. "That's what the vendor promised. I figured you could use all the help you can get."

"You're such a schmuck," Ethan laughed. "Well, I'll give it a shot. Who knows? Maybe it'll turn me into Superman. *L'chaim!*"

In a swift movement, he unscrewed the sealed cap and swallowed the entire tonic in one large gulp.

"Gah! That's awful," he stammered through stifled choking. "Hey, is it working?"

"Let's have a look," I teased.

Ethan pushed up his sleeves, leaned forward, and flexed into his best Arnold-the-bodybuilder impersonation.

Sara smiled coyly. "Wow, Ethan! How could the ladies possibly resist you?"

"Yeah, whatever, Mom," he said, standing and brushing his sleeves back down. "So how about that thing in your jacket? Can I see it?"

I froze, trepidation clearly visible on my face. "Well, I said it's a work thing."

Sara folded her arms. She hated secrets.

I grinned, reaching into my jacket pocket as though searching. "I mean, let me check…"

Why didn't I put it in my office as soon as I got home? What they didn't know couldn't hurt them.

Hesitating for just a moment, I pulled it out and set it on the table. Through the plastic bag, the dark liquid shifted almost imperceptibly.

Ethan's gaze locked on immediately, curiosity flaring in his eyes.

"What's that?"

Sara tilted her head, her eyes narrowing.

"James?"

I hesitated, then gave a dismissive shrug.

"It's just something I picked up in the market. The guy who sold it to me had this whole wild story about it. I thought it looked interesting and figured I'd bring it back to test in the lab. Kinda cool, right?"

Ethan reached out. "It looks like—"

"Don't!" I urged him, a bit too loudly. He pulled his arm back like a reprimanded child.

"Blood?" Sara finished, her tone skeptical.

I forced a grin, plucking the vial from the table and slipping it into my computer bag.

"It's not," I said, raising my eyebrows slightly. "It's just some kind of dye or pigment—you know, an illusion to take advantage of traveling schmucks like me. But best not to leave it lying around here," I said, winking at Sara.

She shook her head, clearly unconvinced but not interested enough to press. Ethan, though, still looked intrigued.

"Tomorrow," I said, steering the conversation away. "I'll test it tomorrow and figure out what it actually is. But I'm hungry, and I smell roasted chicken."

* * *

I carried my bags down the hallway, the warm glow of the kitchen fading behind me as I entered my office, its shadows stretching long across the room. The space was quiet, the air faintly scented with old books and the musk of wood polish. It had always been my sanctuary, a place where the noise of the world faded away, replaced by the steady rhythm of thought and focus.

Setting my computer bag down on my desk, I hesitated. The magnetic clasp released with a slight tug. Pulling out the bag labeled "Research Sample," I studied it under the soft glow of the desk lamp.

Why couldn't I just walk away? I thought.

For a fleeting moment, I wondered why Hassan insisted that I'd need luck—was that his weird way of wishing me safe travels, or was I a fool for taking this thing with me? Yet here it was, as inescapable as the questions it brought with it.

My chest tightened as I thought back to the moment Hassan had pressed it into my hands, his quiet, knowing gaze lingering long after I'd left the stall.

I shook my head, pushing the thoughts aside. No. Whatever Hassan believed, I wasn't about to let his stories dictate my reality. This was an artifact, nothing more—an object to study, analyze, and demystify. Still, the unease lingered, a quiet hum at the back of my mind.

I opened the drawer of my desk and placed the bag inside. Sliding the drawer shut with a decisive motion, I exhaled, my fingers gripping the handle for a moment longer than necessary.

Out of sight, out of mind.

The sound of laughter from the kitchen pulled me from my thoughts—Sara's voice, warm and steady, with Ethan's a brighter tone. I allowed myself a small smile, the burden on my shoulders easing slightly. This was what mattered—this moment, this life.

Shutting the office door behind me, I walked back toward the light and the laughter, leaving the shadows to linger where they belonged.

* * *

The scent of roasted chicken and rosemary mingled with the crackle of the fireplace as the three of us settled into our seats. Plates clinked softly as Sara passed around a basket of bread, her expression warm but still carrying a thread of curiosity.

"Alright," Ethan said, tearing into a roll with the enthusiasm of someone who'd been waiting for this moment. "So, about these 'interesting people' you mentioned…"

"Oh my God, Ethan. You would have loved the brute that sold me that tonic. So I'm walking down the crowded streets, minding my own business, and he shouts, 'Strength and honor!'"

"Oh dang, Dad, you got that tonic from Maximus Meridius?" Ethan replied with a laugh. "That's so cool. You think it really was him?"

His words were thick with sarcasm, and I couldn't help but feel proud.

"How about the guy who gave you that 'research sample,' Dad? What was he like?"

I smiled, gently setting down my fork. "Hassan. Easily the most eccentric person I've ever met. He had a stall at the market—it was full of bizarre things: amulets, charms, talismans, bottles, coins. Should I have gotten you some coins, son?" I asked sarcastically.

"It's okay, Dad," he nodded, pretending to accept the disappointment.

I continued, "Everything looked ancient, but probably half of it was just for show. What stood out was his... intensity, like he believed every word he said about his stuff."

Ethan tilted his head, grinning. "Did he, like, chant over the vial or something?"

"Not quite," I said with a scoff. "But he did have a flair for the dramatic. He spun this whole story about how the vial came from an ancient bloodline, passed down for centuries, supposedly holding some... essence of immortality or power."

"Immortality?" Sara's eyebrows shot up. She leaned forward, her tone teasing but with an edge of concern. "And you just... brought that into our home?"

I waved her off, keeping my tone light. "It's just a story. The kind of pitch you expect in a place like that. The vial itself is well-made, and I thought it might be interesting to analyze."

Ethan glanced over at Sara, then back at me.

"So you're saying it's not cursed, but it *might* be cursed?"

I barked a laugh, and a piece of chicken landed on my plate.

"It's not cursed. Just a curious souvenir. It'll go to the lab tomorrow, and I'll figure out exactly what's in it."

Sara wasn't letting it go so easily. She set her fork down and gave me that familiar look—the one that said she was trying to decide if she should trust me or not.

"You're absolutely sure it's safe?"

"Completely," I said, injecting as much confidence into my voice as I could muster. "Whatever's in it is probably centuries old and degraded into nothing. It's just a decorative piece at this point."

Sara exhaled slowly, her expression softening.

"Alright. But no experimenting with mysterious liquids at home, got it?"

"Got it. It's tucked away in my office, and it'll be gone tomorrow," I said, smiling at her.

Ethan leaned back in his chair, shaking his head with mock seriousness.

"This is how it always starts in the movies, you know. You bring back the weird artifact, someone opens it, and boom—*cursed family.*"

The rest of the night passed with easier conversation and the blissfully ordinary rhythms of life. We sat by the fire and talked about Ethan's classes and Sara's latest book club debate, the small, comfortable pieces of life that made home feel like home.

We made good use of our bed, and I drifted to sleep easily

with Sara's smooth skin touching mine.

29

Tragedy, at the Armstrong Residence

"James? James, what was that?"

"Huh?" I groaned.

"James, I heard something."

"It's just the house settling."

Sara gave a quick, tight shake of her head. "I don't think so. Listen."

I listened—and I nearly fell asleep listening. But then I heard something too. A cabinet closing, or the refrigerator condenser turning on, I thought.

"There it is again."

I held my breath, ears pinned back, straining to decipher the noise coming from downstairs.

It was definitely downstairs. Probably.

I raised myself to a seated position in bed and tried shaking some feeling back into my arm.

"Go," Sara urged, pushing me out of bed.

"I'm checking it out. Just give me a sec," I whispered, already swinging my legs over the side of the bed.

The cold floor met my feet, and I regretted leaving my

262

slippers in the bathroom. I reached for my phone on the nightstand, its harsh light illuminating Sara's worried face.

"James, wait." She sat up, pulling the blanket around her shoulders. "I think you're right—it's probably just the house. Or Ethan getting a snack."

That felt good to hear, but then there was a sound that neither of us could rationalize.

"What the hell was that?" Sara whispered, looking at me with concern.

"I don't know. But stay here," I said, fully alert. But before I could stand, she was already reaching for her robe.

"I'm coming with you," she insisted, slipping her arms into the sleeves. "If it's nothing, then it's nothing. But you might need backup."

I smiled at her through the phone light and nodded toward the door. The hallway greeted us with a biting chill, the kind that didn't belong inside. Shadows stretched and danced on the walls, shifting across the family portraits and Ethan's graduation photo that lined the hall.

"Ethan?" Sara called, hoping for a reassuring response.

"Buddy, is that you?" I said, stepping toward his door. I pushed it open and leaned in, lighting the space with my phone.

Empty. No sound. No movement.

Then, the sound of glass breaking, and a thud against the floor.

I locked eyes with Sara, her face pale in the phone's light. Side by side, we stumbled down the stairs. Sara made it to the bottom first and stopped abruptly. I caught myself on her shoulders, nearly toppling both of us.

Then I saw what she saw.

* * *

The fire bathed the living room in warmth, but the scene before us chilled my blood. Ethan lay crumpled on the rug in front of the fireplace, his body curled in on itself, his face pale and still.

"Ethan!" Sara's voice cracked, and before I could stop her, she rushed forward, dropping to her knees beside him. Blood dripped from the corner of his mouth.

"Call 9-1-1!" Sara shouted at me, her voice sharp with panic. She reached out, brushing his hair back to search for injuries. "Ethan, can you hear me? It's Mom, sweetie, wake up." Her hands moved to his shoulders, shaking him gently, then more firmly.

I stayed rooted to the threshold, my eyes fixed on him. There wasn't much blood—just a small trickle from the corner of his lips, barely noticeable against his skin.

My eyes swept the room, landing on the broken picture frame—the photo inside capturing the three of us on the Ferris wheel at the Ocean City Boardwalk when Ethan was five—and the empty vial lying near the hearth, its delicate glass reflecting the firelight.

Shit.

"James!" Sara snapped, pulling me from my thoughts. "Call someone! He's not waking up!"

I dropped to a crouch beside her, my fingers pressing against Ethan's neck. His skin was warm—not as warm as it should have been—and there it was: the steady pulse beneath my touch. Relief washed through me, but it carried an undercurrent of dread.

"He's alive," I said, my voice low. "He's just… unconscious."

"Why is that out here?" Sara questioned, her eyes having found the vial as well.

I didn't know what to say in response.

"James, why is your *'work thingy'* out here?"

"I put it in my desk. He didn't know I put it there—"

"And you didn't lock it?"

"No, I just—"

Sara let out a shaky breath as she cupped Ethan's face in her hands. "What happened to him? Is he sick?" Her voice cracked, worry overpowering her composure.

I wanted to reassure her, but the words stuck in my throat. My gaze fell back to Ethan's mouth, to the thin trail of blood running from the corner of his lips down his cheek. It wasn't much, but it was enough. Enough to make me think of the stories I had dismissed as fantasy just hours ago.

I opened my mouth, but no answer came. My thoughts churned—flashes of Hassan's voice, the cathedral, the stories, the warnings. My pulse pounded as I whispered, "Move away from him, Sara. We need to be careful."

Sara shot me a sharp look, her expression a mixture of anger, confusion, and fear.

"What are you talking about? He's hurt, James! We need to help him."

I nodded, swallowing the rising tide of panic. I didn't have the words to explain—not yet. But my instincts screamed at me that something was deeply wrong. I leaned forward and placed a firm hand on Sara's shoulder, pulling her back gently, but she stayed fixed at his side. I stood and watched her put her ear to his mouth.

And then, Ethan's fingers twitched.

Sara flinched at the movement—a gentle rub of his fingers

on the rug. Her breath hitched, and she cupped his face in her hands again.

"Ethan? Honey, can you hear me?"

His eyelids fluttered.

"Good, Ethan. Wake up."

His head moved, subtly at first, then it turned ninety degrees to the right. A feeble groan escaped his lips, like the sound of someone trying to wake from a deep, oppressive dream.

"It's okay, sweetie," Sara murmured, her voice trembling with relief. "You're going to be fine. Just open your eyes. We're right here."

I leaned down, a prickling tension creeping up my spine as I watched him stir. The blood at the corner of his mouth dripped from his cheek to the rug, and my stomach curdled. I wanted to believe Ethan was just waking up groggy, disoriented—but something about his movements put me on alert.

Ethan's bloodshot eyes flicked open, and Sara gasped, pulling back slightly. His gaze was unfocused, wild, darting across the floor as though he couldn't make sense of where he was. He blinked rapidly, his pupils wide and dark, swallowing the light of the fire.

"Ethan," Sara said gently, turning his face back toward hers. "It's Mom. You're safe, sweetheart. Just breathe."

He let out a sharp, shaky exhale, as his focus locked on her. His lips parted, but no words came—just a sound, low and raw. His hand moved again, this time with more purpose, his fingers curling against the floor as though testing their strength.

"James," Sara whispered. "I think he's having a night terror."

I knelt beside her, my hand hovering over Ethan's shoulder,

unsure whether to touch him.

"Ethan," I said, my voice firm but careful. "It's Dad. You're okay. Just take a deep breath."

For the briefest of moments, he locked eyes with me. There was something distant and unfamiliar in his expression. Then, just as quickly, his attention turned back to Sara. His muscles tensed, his chest rising and falling in quick, shallow breaths.

"Ethan," Sara said, more forcefully. "Just keep looking at me. It's okay. We're here with you."

"Sara, get back!" I shouted, but before she could move, it happened—so fast I almost didn't process it. Ethan's hand shot up, gripping Sara's wrist with a force that made her cry out over the sound of cracking bone. His eyes widened, and for an instant, his face contorted with something I could only describe as hunger—an unbearable, consuming need.

"Ethan, no!" I shouted, my voice tearing through the ungodly sounds coming from my son.

Ethan moved with a ferocity I couldn't comprehend, his body no longer sluggish but precise and overwhelming. He flipped her over and landed on top of her in one swift move. His grip on her shoulders held her fast to the ground. He leaned down toward his mother, and a guttural sound tore through his throat. Her left hand clawed at his arm, nails dragging for purchase, while the other flailed uselessly—bent at the wrong angle, smacking the floor like a wind-up toy with no rhythm and no hope. Her scream cracked the air like glass.

"James, help me!" Sara cried out, her voice raw with desperation.

I lunged forward, my hands gripping Ethan's shoulders, but he pulled away with an unnatural strength that sent me stumbling into the couch.

His head snapped back to Sara, his gaze wild and unrecognizable.

"Ethan, stop!" I pleaded, my voice breaking.

Sara kicked and writhed beneath him, but his strength was terrifying. In one savage, animal motion, he clamped his mouth down on her neck. The sound—wet, tearing, wrong— ripped through the room. Her scream cut off instantly, replaced by a choking gasp as blood sprayed across the hardwood floor.

"No!" The word tore from my throat. I launched myself at him, fists slamming into his back. He didn't flinch. Didn't move.

He was latched onto her neck—face buried deep—*feeding*. I could hear it. The sick, rhythmic *gulping*, punctuated by wet gasps as he swallowed mouthfuls of her blood. It spilled past his lips, down her skin, pooling beneath her. Her legs kicked once, twice—then went still.

I clawed at his shoulders, yanked at his arms, but he wouldn't let go. His jaw was locked, muscles trembling with effort, throat working like a machine. He sucked greedily, audibly, as if he were dying of thirst and she was the only thing that could save him.

He was lost in it. Consumed by it. It was hunger. Pure and bottomless.

And I couldn't stop him.

When I brought the floor lamp down on him with both hands, the impact cracked across his skull with a jolt that ran up through my arms—but he didn't even react. Didn't even lift his head.

The base of the lamp, still in my grip, swung wide with the

follow-through—and smashed straight through the window. A low gust pushed through the opening, scattering the curtains like startled birds.

Sara's body went limp in Ethan's grasp, her eyes wide with pain and disbelief as her life drained away. Blood pooled beneath her, seeping into the floorboards, gleaming in the firelight.

I grabbed at Ethan's arms, trying desperately to pull him away.

"Ethan, stop! That's your mother! Stop this!" My voice was hoarse, breaking under the reality of the unimaginable.

For a moment, it felt like time itself had fractured, each second stretching into an eternity. The fire continued burning in the hearth, oblivious to the gruesome truth unfolding before it. My vision blurred with tears, the edges of the room darkening as I strained against the impossibility of what was happening.

And then, as suddenly as it began, Ethan's body relaxed, his breathing ragged and uneven. Slowly, he pulled back, his mouth and chin stained crimson, his eyes wide with confusion and horror. He looked down at his mother, her lifeless body crumpled beneath him, and a choked gasp escaped his lips.

"No..." Ethan whispered, his voice intensifying. "No, no, no..."

He released her, his hands shaking as he backed away on his knees, staring at his bloodied fingers as though they belonged to someone else.

Ethan fell forward, catching himself with his hands, flat against the ground, anchoring himself against the tide of his unraveling reality. His breath came in a short, even tempo, and his wide eyes darted between his bloodied hands and his mother's still form.

Blood dripped from his chin with each breath, and he wiped at it absently, smearing it across his cheek.

"Mom?"

The word was a fragile whisper, barely making it past his lips and into the room.

He crawled forward a few inches before freezing, his hands hovering over her as though afraid to touch her, to confirm the truth he already knew. A tremor ran through him, and a low, throaty sound escaped him—something between a sob and a scream.

I couldn't move. My body refused to obey, stuck in the gravitational pull of the sight before me. I could only watch as anguish consumed my son. He reached out hesitantly, his fingers brushing against her blood-matted hair before recoiling as though burned.

"This isn't real," Ethan muttered, his voice cracking. His hands shot to his head, gripping his hair as his breathing quickened.

"It's not real. It can't be real." He rocked back on his knees, his movements jerky and panicked, as if trying to shake himself awake from a nightmare.

The room felt impossibly small, the walls closing in as the sound of his broken sobs filled the silence. I took a step forward, my legs weak beneath me, and knelt beside him. He didn't flinch, didn't even seem to register my presence. His gaze was locked on Sara, unblinking, as though looking away would somehow make her vanish.

"Ethan…" I managed, my voice barely audible, thick with emotion. My hand hovered just over his shoulder, hesitant to make contact. "Ethan, look at me."

Slowly, he turned his head, his tear-streaked face contorted with anguish.

"Dad…" His voice broke on the word, raw and childlike. His lips trembled as he spoke again, his words tumbling out in a desperate rush. "I didn't mean to. I don't— I don't even remember—" He choked on a sob, his hands gripping his shirt as if holding himself together might stop the pain tearing through him. "What's happening to me?"

My heart shattered at the sight of him—my son, who had been so full of life, now hollowed out by something neither of us could understand. I wanted to tell him it wasn't his fault, that it was going to be okay, but the truth wedged itself in my throat, too large to swallow.

He reached for me, his bloodied hands shaking, flicking red droplets around the room.

"Please, Dad," he pleaded, his voice a broken whisper. "Tell me this isn't real. Tell me I didn't—" His words faltered as he glanced back at Sara, his body convulsing with the effort to hold back another wave of sobs. "I can't— I didn't mean to hurt her…"

I gripped his shoulder, the strength of my hold meant to steady us both.

I badly wanted to hold my wife one last time, to somehow bring her back to life, turn back the clock and refuse Hassan's offer—or at least to reach over and close her eyes—but I worried what might happen if I lost Ethan's attention.

"Ethan, listen to me," I said, forcing my voice to stay even despite the shake I couldn't quite suppress. "This wasn't you. You didn't do this."

But my words felt hollow, and I knew he felt it too. His gaze dropped to the bloodstains on his hands, and he stared at them as though they were alien to him, unrecognizable.

"Then who did, Dad?" he whispered, his tone haunted. "Because it looks like it was me."

Ethan's words were like splinters in my heart, embedding themselves deep. The blood smeared on his face and hands, the lifeless body of Sara beside him—it all painted a picture neither of us could deny.

The blood in the vial. Hassan's story. The flashes Ethan must have seen when he drank it, vivid and haunting, like fragments of a life he'd never lived. It couldn't be true. It shouldn't be true. But here it was, staring me down.

I staggered back to my feet, my eyes darting to the empty vial discarded on the floor by the hearth. The polished glass gleaming like a taunt. My breath came in shallow, uneven gasps as the enormity of it all crashed down on me.

Hassan's voice echoed in my mind: *"The blood carries more than life—it carries memory, power, and hunger."*

The hunger. I had seen it in Ethan's eyes when he opened them, the way they glowed with something feral. I had seen it in the flashes of his movements—too fast, too strong, too unnatural. I had seen it in the aftermath—Sara, crumpled and cold.

What have I done?

The question pulsed through me, over and over, each time leaving a deeper mark. My choice to check fact from fiction, to dismiss Hassan's warning as nonsense, had brought this into our home, into our lives.

I thought of the story Hassan told me, the dark legacy stretching through centuries. The pain, the violence, the endless cycle. And now, it was here, tangled in my family, tearing us apart. My legs felt weak, my body heavy, as if gravity itself had turned against me.

Ethan's broken voice pulled me from my spiraling thoughts.

"Dad…" His tone was soft, pleading, like the little boy who used to beg me to make the monsters under his bed go away. But this time, the monster was real—and I was looking at him.

I knelt down, staring into his wide, tear-filled eyes.

"I didn't mean for this to happen," I whispered, my voice faltering. "I didn't know… I didn't believe… I'm sorry. I'm so sorry."

What good was denial now? The evidence was splattered on the floor, soaked into the rug, and written in the anguish etched into my son's face.

The fire popped in the hearth, the sound startlingly loud in the suffocating silence. My gaze shifted back to Sara—to the woman who had built this life with me, who had trusted me. I had failed her. Failed them both. My throat tightened, the grief and guilt so overwhelming I thought I might choke on it.

Ethan's hand reached out, grabbing at my sleeve.

"Dad, how did this happen?" His voice was small, his lips quivering as though he was holding back more sobs.

I covered his hand with mine, the warmth of his skin a bitter reminder that he was alive, but not in the way he had been just hours ago.

"I don't know how to fix this," I admitted, my voice breaking. My throat burned with the weight of the truth I couldn't speak aloud: *This can't be fixed.*

The realization hit like a blow, leaving me gasping for air. There was no going back. Hassan's warnings weren't just stories. The curse had come home, and the cost of undoing it… The thought stuck in my gut, a knife I couldn't pull free.

I turned my gaze back to Ethan. He was looking at me now, his eyes searching mine for answers I didn't have. For the first time, I saw the full extent of his fear. He wasn't just afraid of what he'd done—he was afraid of himself, of what he was becoming.

30

Fate

Ethan's gaze shifted to the floor, his body uneasy with a mixture of exhaustion and terror. When he finally spoke, his voice was a whisper.

"Dad… when I was out, I saw things."

I froze, the words sinking into the silence.

"What things?" I asked, concentrating on keeping my voice steady.

Ethan shook his head, his hand dragging across the blood-stained rug.

"I don't know. Faces, places, people doing horrible things… and I was doing horrible things too. It all felt so real, but it had to be a dream, right?"

A chill ran through me.

"A dream?" I repeated, my voice tight.

He nodded, his eyes unfocused as if the images still played in his mind.

"There was a cathedral. Fire everywhere. I was holding… something." His brow furrowed, and he pressed his fingers to his temple as if trying to pull the memories into focus. "It was so bright, so loud. And the blood—there was so much blood."

I swallowed hard, forcing the bile in my throat back down.

"What else?" My voice cracked despite my efforts to sound calm.

Ethan looked at me, his eyes brimming with confusion and fear.

"People were screaming, falling around me. I had a sword, and for some reason, I cut this guy's head off. It landed on my foot—I could feel it—but it wasn't me. It was like I was watching through someone else's eyes. And then..." He paused, his voice faltering. "And then I woke up, and she was—"

His voice broke, fresh sobs shaking his body. "Dad, why do I feel like this? What's inside of me?"

I stared at him, my mind a whirl of fragmented thoughts. Everything Hassan had said slammed into me with brutal clarity. The flashes Ethan described—they were memories. The memories carried by the blood.

But how could I explain that to him? How could I make him understand something I barely comprehended myself?

"Ethan," I began carefully, "what do you remember before... before you went out?"

He blinked, his brow furrowing.

"I don't..." His voice trailed off, his expression distant as he searched his thoughts. "I was playing RDR2," he said slowly, his tone uncertain at first, then sharpening with recollection. "Yeah, I was on the couch, and everything felt... off. Like my skin was crawling. I couldn't sit still."

"Go on," I urged gently, dreading where this was going.

He dragged a hand through his hair, leaving a streak of blood in its wake.

"It was like something was pulling me, like a magnet or—or a rope I couldn't see. I don't know why, but I got up and followed it into your office. It led me to your desk. I opened the drawer, and that's when I saw it."

"The vial?"

Ethan nodded, his face contorted with a mixture of shame and confusion.

"I know you didn't want me messing with it, but I couldn't stop myself. I just... I had to. It was like it was calling to me."

His voice dropped to a whisper, barely audible over the crackling fire.

"I opened it. I don't even remember deciding to do it—it just happened. And then... nothing. Just black."

The knot in my stomach constricted tighter. His words confirmed everything I feared. The pull of the blood wasn't just a myth or a story—it was real, insidious. It had drawn him in, compelled him, and now it was too late to take it back.

"I don't understand, Dad," he said, his voice cracking. "Why would I do that? Why couldn't I stop?"

My hands clenched into fists at my sides, the anger and helplessness boiling together into a toxic brew.

"It wasn't your fault," I said firmly, though my voice wavered. "Whatever's in that vial... it's not normal. It's something ancient. Something... terrible."

Ethan recoiled, his face pale.

"What does that mean? What's happening to me?"

I didn't have an answer—not one that would make sense to either of us. All I could do was stare at him, my son, my boy, now bound to something I couldn't even begin to understand.

And in that silence, the possibility of what was to come pressed down on me like a crushing tide.

Ethan's fingers curled into fists, his knuckles whitening as if holding on to his last shred of composure.

"I didn't want this," he whispered, his voice fragile but heavy with anguish. "I swear, Dad. I didn't mean for any of this to happen."

"I know," I said quietly, my throat tight with the truth I couldn't fully reveal.

But that doesn't change what's happened.

He glanced down at his bloodstained hands, his eyes puffy and red.

"I killed her," he choked out, his voice cracking under the enormity of the words. "I killed Mom."

The sentence hung in the air, unbearable and final. My own breath faltered as I searched for words that could soothe the irreparable. But there was nothing. No explanation, no excuse, could undo what had been done.

Ethan's sobs broke free, raw and jagged. He buried his face in his hands, his shoulders shaking violently.

"I don't even remember… I don't remember doing it." His voice was muffled, desperate. "How could I do that? How could I hurt her?"

I sank to my knees across from him, my body aching with a grief that felt insurmountable.

"It wasn't you, Ethan," I said, my voice shaking. "It was the blood. It… it does something. It changes you."

His hands fell to his sides, his red-rimmed eyes locking onto mine.

"What are you talking about?" he asked, his tone a mix of confusion and terror. "Things like that don't actually happen."

"But they did."

I didn't mean to say that out loud.

"They did," he repeated. His face tightened with realization. "But you brought it here. You kept it in the house." His voice rose, and Ethan got to his feet, now looming over me. "How could you, Dad? How could you keep something like that near us?"

He had every right to be angry, to demand answers I couldn't fully give.

"I didn't know," I admitted, my voice breaking. "I didn't know what it really was until now."

Ethan let out a hollow laugh, the sound bitter and broken.

"Boom—cursed family, huh?" His eyes fell to Sara's lifeless form, his face crumpling with fresh waves of anguish. "I didn't even get to say goodbye."

I didn't either. The thought echoed in my mind, but I kept my mouth sealed. Thankfully, my prefrontal cortex did its job in preventing me from saying something that would break Ethan's spirit even further.

"I know, buddy. I'm so sorry about that. But I think we need to leave."

"What?" Ethan whispered. I knew he had heard me. "Dad, we need to call an ambulance, or—or the cops or whatever."

I shook my head, my mind racing.

"Yeah, but if the police come, and they find Mom like this, what are we supposed to say happened?"

"We just tell them about the *definitely cursed* vial, Dad." Sarcasm dripped from his mouth, but his eyes betrayed the fear beneath.

"If we call the police, we'll have to tell them why Mom is... *why Mom is dead,*" I paused, considering whether he understood. "If we tell them that a cursed vial is why she's dead, they'll be having me dry-swallow pills from a paper cup, and you'll be behind bars for the rest of your life."

I watched as reason began to break free in Ethan's mind, wrestling with the impossible truth. To anyone who didn't know Hassan's story, what he had just done was unforgivable.

Ethan looked around the room, his gaze lingering on the broken vase, the overturned chair, the lamp that I'd brought down on him, and then pointed toward the large glass sliding door.

"So are we supposed to just bury her in the yard?"

"Fuck." I put my forehead in my hand and squeezed my temples. "Sorry, shoot."

"Dad, I'm not your little boy anymore. And you're right, this is completely *fucked*."

"Okay, okay. We'll leave her here, just for now. We'll go together to my lab, and come back tomorrow for her. Ethan, we need to figure out exactly what's in that vial. If I can determine what's actually happening at a cellular level, then maybe we can find a cure."

"*A cure*? I thought this was some sort of horrible bath salts incident, where shit happens, but the person goes back to being normal when it's out of their system. But you think this is *permanent*? Am I going to eat you next?"

"*Drink my blood*." The words felt harsh the moment they sprang from my lips.

Ethan recoiled, his shoulders hunching and his chin drawing toward his sternum, eyes darting around the room.

"*What the hell, Dad?*"

"No, no. You didn't *eat* Mom, you *drank her blood*." I needed him to understand the distinction.

"You're thinking about semantics right now? *Seriously?*"

"Hang on a sec." I left Ethan standing in the firelight and

kept talking while I ran to the kitchen, returning with a garbage bag in hand.

"But no, I don't think you're going to drink my blood. We're going to find a way to fix this. Go shower and change your clothes. Put everything you're wearing in here."

He took the bag—reluctantly. The soft plastic whooshed as his arm fell back to his side.

"Meet me out front when you're done."

Ethan stood silently for a moment, looking at anything but Sara's body. The fire crackled softly, casting dancing shadows that seemed to mock their stillness. The house felt different now, the silence amplifying the absence of her voice. Then, without another word, he walked upstairs.

I looked down at the floor, closed my eyes, and drew a long inhale through my nose. The scent hit me like a wave. It was intensely ferrous, that sharp metallic note magnified, almost rusted. But underneath, a touch of sweetness, like the sickly odor of iron oxide blooming in the air. I opened my eyes and scanned the room.

Blood was everywhere: sprayed on the walls, splotched on the end of the lamp that I had used to strike my son, red footprints leaving chaotic dance steps, and a thick pool of it beneath Sara's body.

Sara's body. Her *body.*

She told me I had a kind smile only moments after we sat in the booth next to the friends who had introduced us. I kissed her for the first time later that night, and approximately 19,000 times since. She smiled with her eyes—at least when she meant it. Sara believed I could change the world, but never let that get to my head. She was content to just be— regardless of what was happening around her—something I could never seem to manage.

I pulled a sheet from the hallway cupboard. When I placed it gently over her body, the white fabric clung to the pooled blood on the floor, the shroud settling to entomb her delicate features, scarcely masking the tragedy lying beneath.

"I love you, Sara," I uttered, but heard no reply.

To my right, the fire dwindled, but the vial held its glow, warmed by the embers' last light. I bent over and plucked the empty vessel from the ground. The glass felt cool to the touch, a stark contrast to the sudden warmth that flared within as I straightened.

I nearly dropped it—the damn thing was replenishing itself. As the blood reached the rim, I poured it out, a useless act, for the crimson liquid simply rose again.

Conceding to the impossible, I sealed the cap and wiped the glass clean with the edge of the sheet, leaving a bright streak of blood. I placed it inside a Ziploc bag and felt the need to label it a "research sample," but couldn't find a Sharpie.

Red lines flowed down the drain, my hands shaking under the faucet. Seeing Sara's blood disappear through the black rubber guard broke me. My chest heaved with an intensity I hadn't felt in years. She was gone. The love of my life. My reason for being. Just gone.

Snot dripped from my nose, and salty tears crossed my lips, hitting my taste buds. I wasn't sure how I would miss her, but I would—perhaps I'd see her in dreams, or maybe in the corner of my eye while awake.

Is there a right way to miss someone? I was sure I'd find out. I cleared my throat and wiped myself dry with a dishtowel, tossing it into the sink when I was done.

I found my office in complete darkness, and upon flipping

the light switch, saw the open drawer of my desk, with the labeled bag resting atop.

My jaw tightened. *Why didn't I lock the drawer?* I thought, angry at my own carelessness. But dwelling on it wouldn't change anything. The past was unchangeable.

* * *

We were in the backyard on a summer evening, the golden light of dusk filtering through the trees. Sara had just spread out a checkered blanket on the grass, her laughter carrying on the breeze as Ethan, no older than eight, darted between us with a water gun in each hand.

"You'll never catch me!" he shouted, his grin wide and triumphant.

"You better run, kiddo!" I called, grabbing one of the backup water guns from the grass.

Sara shook her head, rolling her eyes playfully.

"Oh, come on, James. You're supposed to be the responsible adult."

"Not today, Sara!" I shot back, already giving chase.

Ethan squealed with delight, weaving around the oak tree as I fired, the cold spray of water catching him on his arm.

"No fair! Mom, help!" he cried, running toward Sara, who threw her hands up, absolving herself of responsibility.

"Don't bring me into this!" she laughed, but Ethan tackled her anyway, pulling her into the game. In seconds, we were all on the ground, tangled in laughter and soaked through, the grass cool against our skin.

Later that night, as the sky deepened into twilight, we lay on the blanket, staring up at the stars. Ethan curled between us, his head resting on Sara's shoulder, his small hand clutching mine.

"Do you think stars live forever?" he asked, his voice soft with wonder.

I squeezed his hand gently.

"Not forever, buddy. But some of them are so far away and burn bright enough that we can see their light long after they're gone."

Sara had smiled at me then, her eyes full of warmth. "That's a comforting thought, isn't it?"

"How long?"

* * *

The memory dissolved like vapor, leaving me standing in the dim room once more. I had to focus on what came next: a change of clothes, my laptop, the vial, and me and Ethan heading to the lab.

The night air was crisp and carried the scent of coming snow—unusual for this area, but not impossible. I leaned against the Bronco, head tilted back toward the sky as I practiced box-breathing. Four in. Hold. Four out. Hold. Again. And again.

Somewhere nearby, a dog started barking—sharp, frantic, insistent. Another joined in, their yapping ricocheting off the quiet street.

I opened my eyes.

Across the road, a second-story window was lit. A soft, yellow glow behind gauzy curtains.

Andrea Something-or-Other was a woman to whom "family" meant her two dogs. Aside from seeing her peer through the window anytime anything happened on the street, I can't recall a time I ever saw her outside her house. Kind Sara would often deliver a plate of food, chatting in the doorway while Andrea held back her yapping Pomeranians. Sara had once told me the reason she was so utterly alone was because her husband left her after they had been married only three months, and she hadn't found love since—or hadn't found anyone because she never leaves her house.

The light turned off within a second of me turning my head her way.

Nothing to see here, Andrea, I thought, willing her back to bed. The last thing we needed right now was a nosy neighbor's eyes.

"I'm here. What do we do now?" Ethan mumbled.

* * *

The roads were empty, and the car was quiet, save for the rumble of tires on asphalt. For the first few miles, I ran through research scenarios in my mind. I glanced over at Ethan. Considering what he'd been through, I thought he would have nodded off, but he was looking at the moon through the windshield. His eyebrows were curved upward, and his eyes were glassy.

"How's school going?"

The question was entirely out of place, and we both felt its awkwardness. Ethan shifted, placing his elbow on the door and his chin in his hand.

"How are you feeling?"

"Fine. Sad, I guess."

"Me too. But do you feel alright? How's your head? I hit

you pretty hard."

"Fine, I think. I feel a little weird, like everything is too real to be real."

"Yeah?"

"I'm fine."

He said it so flatly, so automatically, that I almost believed him.

Sure you are. Because nothing says "fine" like tearing out your mother's throat and drinking her blood. I bit down on the thought, hard.

I gripped the wheel a little tighter, trying not to look at him too long.

"When we get there, we're just going to run a few tests and—"

"What's in that vial, Dad?"

"Well, that's what I'm hoping to find out."

"You said that market vendor guy told you it gave you immortality."

"I did." I hesitated. "But that isn't possible."

"Mom thought it was cursed."

"She did."

"I think she was right," Ethan whispered, barely audible over the sound of the road. After a long silence, he asked, "Is Mom going to… re… animate?"

"What?" I responded.

"Is she going to, you know, wake up?"

"No." *I don't think so.* "She's gone, son."

"Okay."

* * *

We pulled into the empty parking lot at 2:17 AM. The lab was located on the southeastern edge of Durham, a squat triangular structure flanked by trees, with a fake-brick façade lining the cylindrical entrance. I parked in the spot with my name on it, which happened to be just a few paces from the entrance. The light spilling out from the lobby was dim but flickered to full brightness as we approached the door. The card reader beeped, and the automatic lock retracted. The elevator purred as we descended to B3. When the doors pulled open, the line of overhead lights came on in sequence, illuminating the lab.

"Holy shit." The first words Ethan had said in the past hour.

"Nice, right? Hang on a sec."

We walked out through the air shower, and I held my badge against a reader. The air inside the lab was cool and sterile, with the low hum of equipment filling the space. Rows of workstations came to life, each one illuminating in the blue glow of the wake screens. To our right, a series of glass-walled clean rooms housed the most sensitive equipment. Laminar flow hoods belted out their startup sequences, and each of the flow cytometers gave off occasional beeps. The far wall was dominated by a massive biosafety cabinet, complete with drawers of PPE, eye-washing stations, and laminated posters containing our emergency response protocols.

Ethan stared, his eyes wide. "This is…"

"My sanctuary," I finished, a smile tugging at my lips. "Welcome to the NCBC Laboratory for Regenerative Medicine."

"Very nice."

"Come over here," I said, leading him to the first workstation in the middle row—my usual spot. I set down my bag, pulled the laptop out, and plugged it into the docking station. While it booted up, I flipped the toggle switch on the digital microscope, which let out a soft beep to let me know it was starting up. "Grab a seat."

Ethan rolled a chair over from the adjacent station and sat beside me.

"This is what we're here for. This will allow us to take a closer look at that blood so we can try to see what it's made of. And rather than an eyepiece, it has a camera, which lets—"

"You can spare me the Bill Nye the Science Guy explanation, Dad," Ethan cut in.

"Okay, *son*. Since you know how it all works, let's get started."

I pulled open a drawer on my left, retrieving two slides and pipettes, and placed them on the sample tray. Ethan watched quietly as I retrieved the Ziploc from my satchel and set it on the desk. After pulling on a pair of latex gloves, I carefully opened the plastic and removed the vial.

"It's full?" Ethan questioned.

"Seems so," I replied. This didn't seem the time to try and explain further.

After releasing the cap, I sucked up a small sample of the crimson fluid with the pipette and resealed the vial with my right hand. I let out three drops onto the slide, which quickly coalesced beneath the coverslip. The metallic retainer clips screeched faintly against the glass as I moved the slide into place—easily the worst part of my job.

VizPro 12.7 was already open on the screen. I clicked the rectangular blue monitor icon, and the screen lit up in a wash of pulsing red.

"Hmm."

I looked over and checked that the backlight was consistently illuminated, which it was, and looked back at the screen.

"What's wrong?"

"Nothing, it's just that it normally doesn't do that."

"Do what?"

I stared at the screen, watching the color undulate rhythmically.

"Well, typically blood samples don't pulse like that," I responded. "Let's see what's going on."

I clicked the magnifying glass icon and selected '1000x' from the dropdown. The lens shifted with a mechanical zipping sound and brought the image into focus on the screen. What I found was curious, but not entirely alarming.

"These are new," I said with a touch of surprise in my voice.

"What do you mean?"

"Well, all the ones that look kind of like jelly donuts are the erythrocytes—red blood cells. And those solid circles are the white blood cells, probably lymphocytes—they fight off infections and such."

"And..." Ethan urged me along.

"And... these... *aren't supposed to be there*." I traced a moving object on the screen with my finger, then another, and another—each shifting from shadow to light, as if giving off its own source of luminescence. "I've never seen anything like that before."

"What do you think they are?"

"I'm not sure, but they're not nothing." I pulled the sample off the plate and set it back on the tray. The device sensed the absence of a sample, and the window on the monitor went black. "Roll up your sleeve for me," I said over my shoulder as I pulled a kit from a drawer on the row of cabinets against the clean rooms.

When I returned, Ethan had the right sleeve of his flannel shirt neatly folded up above his elbow. I did my best to distract him while I prepped his arm.

"How ya doing? Still feeling a bit weird?"

"Um, yeah I guess. A little dizzy and my throat is a bit dry."

"Make a fist, please. That's probably just from the dehumidifiers. We have to keep the humidity low in here." I looked up at him after inserting the needle and the blood began to flow into the sample tube. He had been through so much in the last few hours that he was understandably exhausted, but his skin was beginning to lose its color, and that worried me.

"Want to get some breakfast after we're done here?"

"Dad, it's like four in the morning."

I glanced at my watch. "Two fifty-seven. Pancake House is just up the street. They're open twenty-four hours."

"Sure. Sounds good."

As I moved the slide into position, the retainer clips screeched again, and Ethan and I both winced at the sound.

"Okay, let's see how it looks."

Again, I clicked the monitor icon. The window lit up, and the focus ring automatically spun into place.

"What in the world?" I muttered, unable to believe what I saw.

A loud ding rang out to our right. Ethan and I swiveled our heads in unison toward the elevator. In the silent moment, I heard our hearts creating a mirroring rhythm, thumping and pulsing together in a strange, organic wave.

The doors slid open revealing a cleaning cart, and a man named Joe, who looked confused.

"Hey, Joe," I said, a bit too loud.

Joe rolled the cart forward between the doors but stayed in the elevator while he checked his watch.

"Mr. Armstrong. What are you doing here so early?" Joe questioned, looking around the room, his dark hair bobbing with each shift of his head.

"Yeah, I wanted Ethan to see where I work," I said, hoping he didn't press further.

"How's NYU treating you, buddy? You declare a major yet?"

Ethan looked back at me, clearly confused at how Joe knew him. The whites of his eyes had become pink since the last time I looked.

"He's still considering his options," I said, keeping my response short, hoping that Joe would get the hint that now wasn't a good time. "You think you could come back in thirty minutes or so? We're almost done."

The elevator doors gave a half-hearted attempt at closing, rebounding off the sides of the cart.

"Sure, sure. Hey, you know Shantell is graduating this spring. Once she's done, I'm out—retiring. T and I are going to head down to Florida and rent a bungalow— Is he alright?" Joe questioned, tilting his head to the right.

I looked back and saw Ethan with his eyes closed, chin dropped down to his chest. I have to get rid of him.

"Yeah, just tired. Give us a few minutes and come back, okay?"

"Sure, sure. I'll leave you to it. Have a good even—or morning, or whatever it is," Joe stammered as he pulled the cart back into the elevator and pressed a button.

Ethan still appeared to be resting, but as the doors began sliding closed, a deep sound reverberated in his chest, followed by a crackle in his throat. The moment the doors came together, his eyes shot open—fully bloodshot—and he lunged toward me.

V

Epilogue

31

Epilogue

A thick fog clung low to the ground, veiling the street in a spectral haze. Red and blue flashes reached through the windows of neighboring homes. The winter sky had only just begun to blush with the light of dawn when the first officer arrived on scene, passing Andrea Porter—wrapped in a knit cardigan and haloed by the dim glow of a streetlight. She pressed her ear to her shoulder as the siren approached and stood motionless, mouth half-open, clutching Itsy tightly to her chest as a second, and then a third, cruiser skidded to a stop at the curb across the street.

Officers shouted at the front door. Another disappeared momentarily along the left side of the house. When he returned, something he said to his counterparts resulted in the door being kicked in. The shouting intensified as officers disappeared into the dark mouth of the Armstrong residence.

Yellow tape now fluttered in the light breeze, anchored to the porch post and a painted mailbox, cordoning off the house like a wound that had yet to scab over. The number of onlookers grew, so that Andrea was no longer alone in her amazement. Each huddled group wondered what had caused the commotion—and whether their neighbors would be okay. And the first officers on scene had retreated outside, having found no threat within.

Sergeant Clara Hartwell and her unit parked across the street. The cooling engine ticked and pinged beneath the hush of whispers in the early morning.

"Simmons, get in there and start processing," Clara ordered, nodding toward the porch.

Detective Frederick Simmons, their forensic specialist, was already pulling his camera and evidence kit from the back of the Explorer.

Detective Isabel Vargas came around the front of the vehicle and stopped beside Clara, both of them taking a moment to pull on department-issued leather gloves—much appreciated on days as cold as this.

"Witnesses?" Isabel asked.

Clara exhaled, scanning the faces of overly curious neighbors still watching the first responders work.

"You take *Track Suit*, I'll take *Pomeranian*."

"You always get the dog," Isabel protested.

"Really? I hadn't noticed," Clara replied.

Detective Vargas pulled out her notepad and pen, giving them a quick wave as she made her way toward a middle-aged man in a red and blue tracksuit.

The fur ball spotted Clara heading its way and started yapping at the woman in uniform. Clara's outstretched hand seemed to have a calming effect on the dog. When Clara was just a step away from making contact, the dog's frenzy dissolved into gentle air-licks.

"Good afternoon, ma'am," Clara said, greeting the dog's

owner.

The woman didn't acknowledge her—just stared across the street toward the house.

"Ma'am," Clara repeated, letting the dog sniff and lick her gloved hand.

"Hmm?" The woman startled, shifting off balance. "Oh, shoot. Sorry, officer. Hi. Hello. How are you?"

A little early to be three sheets to the wind, Clara thought.

"I'm good, thank you. Did you know the family that lived there?"

"Oh, yes. Very well… considering."

"Well, I'm very sorry for your loss," Clara said, with a gentle bow of her head. "And you live—"

"Oh, right here. That's my house." She waved behind her without looking, still fixated on the crime scene. "It's just so sad. A sweet family like the…"

"Armstrongs."

"Right, the Armstrongs. I just can't believe they're gone."

The dog whimpered for more affection, but Clara's hands had already retreated to her jacket pockets. Andrea responded with a few distracted pats to its head.

"I hear you're the one who made the call, Miss…?"

"Andrea. Andrea Porter," she replied, still watching the activity across the street.

Clara followed her gaze and saw Simmons crouched in the doorway, camera raised to his eye, focused on something in the lower corner of the splintered casing.

"Miss Porter," Clara said, her tone soft but firm, "why don't we talk inside? Warm up a bit."

Andrea didn't move.

Clara pressed gently. "I'd like to ask you a few questions,

ma'am. Let's step into your house."

"Sure, sure," Andrea said, finally blinking out of the moment.

They walked up the short path to the porch, stepping around slick patches of ice. As they neared the door, another dog erupted in a shrill bark from inside. The one in her arms answered in kind, the two creating a discordant canine duet.

"Coffee?" Andrea asked over the noise, pushing the second Pomeranian aside with a gentle nudge of her foot.

"That would be great."

"Cream and sugar?"

"Please."

Clara lingered in the doorway, offering a quick greeting to her new fuzzy companions as Andrea disappeared into the kitchen. The sounds of ceramic mugs clinking and the vibrating hum of the Keurig offered a warm contrast to the chaos outside. Clara wandered slowly toward the noise, her eyes scanning the home with casual focus.

A console table stood in the entryway, cluttered with mismatched frames. In one, the two Pomeranians sat in a stroller, their tongues lolling in opposite directions, eyes glazed with unbothered bliss. Behind them, Andrea leaned in with her arm outstretched, lips pursed like she was trying to remember how duck-face worked, her head tilted to find the right angle. No one else in frame. Just her and the dogs, parked in front of a jungle gym, forever caught mid-pout. Clara smirked and set the frame back in place. Next to it was a stock photo of a catamaran slicing through a sunlit sea—still in its store-bought frame.

"Anyone live with you?" Clara asked over the constant barking. The dogs' nails clicked on the tile as they circled by the door. "A husband? Roommates?"

Andrea didn't answer. She stood at the counter with her back to Clara, her shoulders rising and falling with a tired breath.

"I don't have any cream. Sorry," she said without turning, a resigned tone in her voice. "No sugar either. I have Splenda."

"Black is fine," Clara replied. "Thank you."

Andrea finally looked over her shoulder and gave a nod, then slid a mug forward across the granite surface.

Clara pulled off her gloves and set them neatly on the counter. She took one of the stools at the island and sat down, placing her notebook beside the mug. Andrea joined her a moment later, settling stiffly on the adjacent stool. Her hands curled around the mug like she needed it to stay upright. The dogs whined and shuffled on the tile. No one spoke. Then, gradually, silence pressed in.

Andrea was the one to break it.

"I just can't believe it. Sara was so—" Her voice wavered, and she blinked hard. "So kind. I know everyone says that when someone dies, but she really was. And she didn't deserve to—"

Clara waited.

"She'd bring me food—you know?" Andrea continued, glancing down into her mug. "I live alone, to answer your question. Just me and the girls. Not leftovers, either. A proper plate. Just showed up with it, smiling, like it was the most normal thing in the world. She talked to me like… like I was someone."

The words hung in the air longer than Clara expected.

"I'm sorry," Andrea murmured, shaking her head. "This probably doesn't matter."

"It's okay," Clara said simply. "It's good to hear what she was like."

Another bark split the moment, followed by a second in reply. The dogs had resumed their duet.

Clara sipped her coffee. It was a little burnt, but hot. Her eyes stayed on Andrea.

"Do you know if they had a good relationship? Mr. and Mrs. Armstrong?"

"Sara was lovely. She seemed to really care for him. He was gone a lot, though. That seemed to bother her," Andrea said, then paused. "But I think they got along fine."

Clara looked up from her notepad. Andrea gulped from her mug.

"What was Mr. Armstrong like?" Clara asked.

Andrea's jaw tensed.

"James? He was a pretentious ass. I could tell he thought he was better than me. Never said hello. Didn't even wave whenever he saw me." She inhaled sharply, then let it out slowly.

Clara gave a neutral nod.

"You're doing fine. Can we talk about what you saw last night?"

Andrea gave the faintest nod—more of a twitch than an answer.

"Where do you want me to start?" she asked.

Clara picked up her pen.

"What was the first thing you noticed?"

"Okay…" Andrea said slowly. "We woke up to something that sounded like breaking glass. The window, I think. That was at eleven fifty-seven."

"That's awfully specific."

"I have a clock," Andrea replied flatly.

Clara gave a small nod.

"Go on."

Andrea glanced at the dogs, still barking, then back at Clara.

"Bitsy was going nuts. She was jumping up at the blinds, making this awful sound—like screaming. Or crying."

"Bitsy?" Clara asked, pointing toward the dogs.

Andrea nodded.

"Her. And Itsy started in too."

Clara noted it, her pen moving steadily.

"What did you do?"

"I tried to get them to settle, but they wouldn't. They were both jumping, rattling the blinds, whining like crazy. So I turned on the lamp and went over to get them away from the window." She paused and leaned over to look at the notepad. "That's when I heard the shouting."

Clara pulled it closer to her as she looked up. "Who was shouting? Was it a male or female voice?"

"Both," Andrea said. "Definitely both. It was definitely coming from Sara's house, but I couldn't see anything."

Clara put her hand up as a wall while she continued to write on the notepad.

"The girls calmed down eventually—"

"Itsy and Bitsy, you mean?"

"Yes," Andrea replied, glaring into Detective Hartwell's eyes. "I knew I wasn't getting back to sleep, so I picked up a book. Figured I'd read for a while."

Clara sipped her coffee. "And then?"

"After a bit, they both jumped off the bed and started barking at the window again. So I got up and looked out—and that's when I saw James."

Clara looked up. "Doing what?"

"Standing by his car. Just… standing there."

"And what time was this?"

"I don't know. Maybe twelve fifteen?"

"I thought you had a clock."

"I do—should I continue, or are you going to keep inter—"

"Details matter, Ms. Porter," Clara said, keeping her tone level. "Was he getting into the car?"

"No. Just leaning against it."

"Did he have anything in his hands?"

"Maybe. I'm not sure. It was pretty dark."

"That's okay. Continue, please," Clara said.

Andrea folded her arms. "He saw my light. Looked up right at me. Didn't wave, of course."

"Did you?" Clara asked.

Andrea blinked. "What?"

"Did you wave?"

"Of course not," Andrea scoffed. "I turned off the lamp and stepped back so he couldn't see me." She glanced at Clara. "His son came out of the house."

Clara paused mid-note. "Son? You didn't mention he had a son."

"You didn't ask," Andrea replied. "Edwin?" She looked up—into her brain—then blinked. "*Ethan.* He left for NYU last fall, but he's been home for a few days. The two of them got into the car and drove off."

"At?"

"Twelve-thirty-ish."

Clara raised an eyebrow. "Is that when you called 9-1-1?"

"Of course not," Andrea said, incredulous. "I'm not going to call the police because some people argued. I called after I went over to check if Sara was okay. But she wasn't."

Clara let the silence stretch.

"I knocked on the door. No answer. So I went around to try the back—figured maybe she didn't hear me. That's when I saw the broken window. The curtain was hanging out through the window, so I peeked in and—" Andrea's voice cracked. "She was on the floor. Someone had covered her with a sheet, but I—I knew it was her. It had to be. I could see her hair… and the way her hand was sticking out—" she swallowed, "—like it was reaching for something. There was blood… all around her."

Clara gave a quiet "Mm-hmm" and jotted something in her notebook.

"So that's when I called," Andrea said. "Right then."

"You didn't try to get inside? Check on her?"

"I didn't need to." Andrea's voice was barely above a whisper now. A tear slid down her cheek.

Clara watched her for a beat. "I see," she said at last. She pulled a card from her pocket and placed it gently on the counter.

"Thank you for your time, Ms. Porter. If anything else comes to mind, give me a call."

Clara stood and pushed the stool back. She offered Andrea a parting nod and gave Itsy and Bitsy a brief pat as she went out the door.

Outside, the morning had brightened. Peach hues had given way to blue skies. Sunlight filtered through the trees, drawing dappled patterns across the lawns. What little snow had fallen was already vanishing in the light—only thin patches remained in the shadows.

Clara pulled her coat tighter, donned her gloves, and

stepped off the porch, the crisp scent of wet asphalt rising from the street. Detective Vargas stood near the curb, notebook in hand, talking to a woman in a fleece jacket and fuzzy boots who seemed eager to tell more than she knew.

Clara waited for a natural pause.

"Anything useful?" she asked, quietly enough not to interrupt.

Vargas gave a subtle shake of her head. "Shock and sadness."

Clara nodded. "I'm heading inside."

Vargas glanced toward the Armstrong house, its broken front door hanging half-ajar. "Simmons is still processing. No one's touched anything."

"Good." Clara took a slow breath. "Have a look around the perimeter when you're done here."

She turned and walked up the steps, boots clunking softly against the concrete. At the top, she paused.

The door hung slightly crooked in its frame, the splintered jamb a visible reminder of the morning's urgency. Inside, shadows still clung to the hallway, cool and unmoved, as though the light outside hadn't been invited in. Clara stepped over the broken threshold and into the Armstrong house. She paused just inside the entryway, letting the door settle behind her with a soft creak.

To her left, at the base of a small console table, sat a white garbage bag—twisted, not tied. Inside, blood-smeared fabric pressed against the translucent plastic. A green shirt, maybe. Something darker beneath it. The shape of a pant leg, soaked through.

An orange evidence marker stood next to it like a warning cone.

Clara crouched beside the bag, tilting her head, studying it without touching.

"Why is it bagged?" she asked aloud, her voice steady but sharp. "Simmons, did you touch anything?"

From deeper in the house came his reply, clear but distant: "Not a thing."

She rose and continued through the entryway, boots silent against the hardwood. She caught a glimpse of the top of Simmons' head, crouched low behind the couch, photographing the body. He didn't look up, and Clara didn't speak.

She took another step into the hall, gaze drifting downward.

Bloody footprints trailed through the entryway—faint, incomplete, beginning to dry. Not shoe prints. Bare. The arch of a heel. The round press of toes. Uneven spacing. Whoever left them had been moving fast—maybe limping.

She followed the trail as it veered off to the right, opposite the console table.

The office door stood open.

She stepped inside.

The room was as it should be. A bay window looked out onto the front yard, sunlight spilling through the slats in the blinds and striping the floor in pale gold. A desk sat against the far wall—neat, minimal. Monitor, keyboard, cords, a few scattered pens, a single open drawer.

And an empty plastic bag.

It lay half-flattened near the mousepad, its zip-top crinkled open. One side was printed with customs documentation and small red text: RESEARCH SAMPLE – NON-HAZARDOUS.

Clara stared at it for a moment, then stepped closer. She didn't touch it—just studied the slight residue left behind where the label had peeled back from the surface. The pouch was small. Maybe five inches tall. Clear on one side, frosted on the other. The kind used for medical samples or specialty reagents.

She straightened.

"Simmons," she called, not loudly. "I want this room documented next."

There was a short pause, then his voice, carrying from the living room: "Right. Be there in two ticks."

Clara lingered just long enough to take one more look at the window—the perfect view of the street, the neighbors, Andrea's porch.

Then she stepped out and turned toward the kitchen.

The floor told part of the story first: an erratic dance of bloody bare footprints. Men's size ten, maybe eleven. They trailed from the living room and looped awkwardly toward the sink before doubling back.

She stepped closer.

Inside the basin sat a balled-up rag, soaked through with deep red. Smears lined the interior of the sink, like someone had scrubbed in a hurry—but not well. The faucet handle bore a single, dried fingerprint—rusty in color, crusted at the edge.

Clara stood still, letting the kitchen settle around her. The hum of the refrigerator. Nice cabinets. Black ceramic jars labeled in cursive—flour, coffee, tea—lined up neatly against the white backsplash. An otherwise ordinary scene, if not for the sink—and the floor.

She didn't take notes. Not yet.

A flash from Simmons' camera in the other room froze the kitchen in her mind. She stood still, trying to feel her way backward through someone else's panic.

No shoes. No time to get dressed. He rinsed his hands, maybe tried to clean the rag—then stopped. Changed his mind. Or ran out of time.

Too messy to be planned. Too fast to be in control.

Her eyes followed the bloody footprints as they curved back toward the living room.

Whatever happened, it didn't start or end here.

Another flash caught her eye.

Clara turned toward the living room. A breeze had pushed through the broken window, pulling one of the sheer curtains inward like a reaching hand. It drifted lazily in the morning light before collapsing back against the sill.

She stepped closer.

As she passed the couch, she noted a broken picture frame lying face-up on the floor. The Armstrongs in front of a Ferris wheel. Ethan had his arm around both parents. The broken glass had torn the photo straight through Sara's face.

"There's blood going up the stairs," Clara said, wondering what horror might be above.

"I checked. No second victim. No one hiding in a closet, either," Simmons said with a thin, humorless smile. "Come have a look at this."

As she turned, the scene revealed itself in full. Her breath caught—just slightly—and her stomach tightened.

Sara lay on her back, partially covered by a white, blood-stained sheet, one arm pinned awkwardly beneath her. Blood had pooled beneath her neck, a deep red shadow soaking into the rug and staining the legs of the coffee table. Spray marked the lower half of a bookshelf, fanned across a row of hardcovers.

Clara moved slowly, careful not to step where blood had dried or still glistened. But it was impossible not to cross some trace of it.

Simmons crouched beside the body, gloved hands adjusting the dials on his camera. He didn't look up.

Sara's torso had been uncovered. The sheet—thin, cotton, pale blue—had been pulled back, exposing her upper body. Her neck, torn open. Her arms limp. But the sheet still covered her legs, as if someone had tried—had wanted—to shield her modesty, then gave up halfway.

Clara frowned. "Did you move the sheet?"

Simmons looked up at her then, his face a shade paler than usual. "I did. Just enough to ID her. I shouldn't have, not without clearing it with you first. My apologies."

His voice stayed even, but there was something behind it— an edge of discomfort, maybe guilt.

Clara didn't answer. She knelt beside Sara's body, eyeing the bloodstained collar of her pajama top. Soft flannel, button-down, trimmed in blue.

Simmons nodded for her to come closer. "Look here."

Clara leaned closer as Simmons gestured to the wound.

Sara's neck had been torn open. Not cut—torn. The tissue was ragged, uneven. No sign of a clean edge. A small chunk of flesh rested on the floor a few feet away, curled like a dropped fig, an evidence marker at its side.

"Neck's the only potentially fatal wound," Simmons said, his voice calm but tight.

"*Potentially?*" Clara asked, incredulous.

He pulled his lips to the side. "Right. Well, she's got a broken wrist and quite a bit of bruising—likely restraint. But no stab wounds, no defensive cuts."

Clara's eyes narrowed. "Any indication she was moved?"

"Doesn't look like it. Blood pool says she dropped here."

Clara nodded once, still scanning the body. "Who would do that?"

"Mr. Armstrong, it seems."

"Yeah," she said quietly. "Maybe."

Simmons shifted position and pointed with a pen. "But here's the odd part. Get in closer."

Clara leaned in carefully, hands on her knees.

There was something within the torn flesh. Faint. Organic. Not thread or cloth. Pale and wet—almost translucent. Like a root or a vein, but distinct. Not part of her.

Simmons exhaled through his nose. "I've never seen anything like that before."

Clara didn't respond.

What the hell happened here?

* * *

The cold hit her face first—sharp, clean, welcome. She took a long breath and held it. The scent of thawing snow, exhaust, and distant pine replaced the humanity still clinging to her throat.

Across the street, the sunlight had fully broken through, warming the squad cars and peeling frost from the rooftops. The neighbors had all retreated to the warmth of their homes, probably still watching through the shutters, wondering when the news would reveal the fate of their neighbors.

Clara spotted Vargas near the perimeter tape, talking to a uniform. Her jacket was unzipped now, shoulders relaxed, hands in her pockets.

Clara crossed the lawn toward her.

Vargas patted the officer on the shoulder and turned as

Clara approached. Around them, the scene was winding down. The remaining uniforms had started loading gear into trunks and heading back to the station.

Vargas gave Clara a quick once-over. "Neighborhood's a wash," she said. "Most of them didn't hear anything, didn't see anything. Couple thought they heard shouting but figured it was a movie or a domestic." She shrugged. "Nobody seems to know their neighbors anymore."

Clara didn't answer.

Vargas paused, narrowing her eyes slightly. "You good?"

Clara looked up but didn't meet her gaze. "She was torn open."

That stopped Vargas cold.

Clara kept her voice flat. "No murder weapon. Just a chunk—torn from her neck."

Vargas blinked. "Jesus."

Clara nodded slowly, like she was still trying to convince herself of the reality. "There was something in the wound. Organic. Not hers. Simmons doesn't know what to make of it."

Now Vargas was staring. "Like what?"

Clara finally looked at her. "I don't know."

The two stood in silence for a moment, watching the melting snow drip from the branches above.

Then a vehicle rolled around the corner—a dark blue Bronco, slow enough to be watching, but not enough to look obvious.

Clara clocked it instantly.

James Armstrong.

Alone.

The SUV rolled past, his face unreadable behind the windshield. But his eyes—raw, hollow—gave him away. Not guilt. Not even panic.

Fear.

The kind that doesn't fade.

Clara turned to Vargas, calm and clipped.

"You got that plate?"

Vargas tapped her pen to her pad. "Got it."

Clara's voice was low, steady.

"Let's go."

Acknowledgments

This book would not have been possible without the support, encouragement, and inspiration of several incredible people.

First and foremost, to my wonderful wife, Jess. This story would not be what it is without you. Thank you for your patience and willingness to provide critical feedback, and for encouraging me to keep going.

To my children, thank you for your vivid imaginations that constantly inspire me and remind me of the mysteries of the world.

I owe a significant debt of gratitude to my editor, Angela. Your keen eye, insightful feedback, and unwavering support helped shape *Vial Darkness* into the book it is today.

To my early readers, who bravely ventured into this world while it was still in its roughest form, thank you. Dad, Mom, Uncle Mike, Carolina, Jesse, and Cameron, your feedback, enthusiasm, and willingness to offer constructive criticism were instrumental in refining the narrative. Your insights were a guiding light.

I would also like to extend thanks to my circle of friends and family for their encouragement and belief in my writing.

To Christopher Buehlman, your novel *Between Two Fires* was at my side while I wrote this book. Thank you for guiding me down weird paths.

To Hermanos Gutiérrez, your album *El Bueno Y El Malo*

was the soundtrack to the creation of this story.

Finally, to you, the reader, thank you for embarking on this journey into *Vial Darkness*. I hope this story inspires you to let your mind wander onto weird and unexpected paths.

Book Club Time

1. General Discussion Questions

1. What were your initial thoughts upon finishing the book?
   Did it end the way you expected?
2. How would you describe the tone and atmosphere of the
   novel? How did it contribute to the overall experience?
3. Which character did you relate to the most? Why?
4. The book blends elements of historical fiction, horror,
   and supernatural thriller. How did these genres comple-
   ment each other in the storytelling?
5. What were some of the key themes you noticed in the
   book? How did they evolve as the story progressed?

2. Character-Specific Questions

1. Asher's actions kicked off the tragic events in the novel.
   Do you believe he was justified in what he did?
2. Lucien's journey is central to the novel. How does she
   evolve over the course of the book? Do you think her
   transformation was inevitable?
3. Cassius plays a complex role in the story. Do you believe
   he was a villain, a victim, or something in between?
4. James, as a scientist, struggles with logic versus belief.

How does his character challenge or reinforce the novel's themes of faith and doubt?

5. What did you think of the relationship between Lucien and Edmund? Did you anticipate their dynamic shifting over time?

6. How do the mother-daughter relationships in the book shape the story? Could Lucien's fate have been different if her mother had made different choices?

3. Themes and Symbolism

1. The vial itself is both a physical object and a metaphor. What do you think it represents?

2. How does the novel explore the concept of immortality? Does it present it as a gift, a curse, or something more ambiguous?

3. Discuss the idea of fate versus free will in the novel. Were Lucien and Edmund truly in control of their own choices?

4. What role does guilt play in the story? How does it manifest in different characters?

5. Did the novel's depiction of supernatural elements feel grounded or unsettling? How did the horror elements enhance the narrative?

4. Historical and Cultural Influences

1. The novel spans different historical periods and locations. How did the setting influence the characters'

choices and conflicts?

2. How does *Vial Darkness* use historical events or settings to blur the line between myth and reality?
3. How does the book handle religious or mythological themes? Did you find any of the lore particularly compelling?

5. Speculative & Hypothetical Questions

1. If you had possession of the vial, what would you do with it? Would you be tempted to use it?
2. Do you think Lucien had a choice, or was her fate sealed from the moment she inherited the vial's curse?
3. If you could ask the author one question about the book, what would it be?
4. Imagine this book was being adapted into a film or TV series. Who would you cast in the major roles?

6. Closing Thoughts

1. What was your favorite moment in the book? What was the most shocking?
2. Did you find the ending satisfying? If not, how would you have ended it differently?
3. Would you recommend this book to others? Why or why not?

About the Author

Beck Browning has designed apps for exoskeletons to help people relearn to walk, scientists working to cure cancer, and religious organizations. In his "day job," Beck designs solutions for life's biggest challenges, aiming to improve quality of life through technology.

Prior to his career in user experience design, Beck studied Design and Media Arts at UCLA and has written creatively, primarily through songs, since childhood. A lifelong fan of horror and science fiction with a compelling story to tell, Beck blended his understanding of application design with a deep love for crafting unexpected narratives into his debut novel, Vial Darkness.

You can connect with me on:
- http://www.beckbrowning.com
- https://www.instagram.com/beckbrowning